*Praise for Alexander McCall Smith's*

# 44 SCOTLAND STREET SERIES

"McCall Smith's assessments of fellow humans are piercing and profound. . . . [His] depictions of Edinburgh are vivid and seamless."
—*San Francisco Chronicle*

"Alexander McCall Smith once again proves himself a wry but gentle chronicler of humanity and its foibles."
—*The Miami Herald*

"McCall Smith [shows] an Austen-like sensitivity to the interactions of daily life."
—*Montreal Gazette*

"Packed with charming characters, piercing perceptions, and shrewd yet gentle humor."
—*Chicago Sun-Times*

"Long live the folks on Scotland Street."
—New Orleans *Times-Picayune*

"Delightfully charming. . . . McCall Smith's plots offer wit, charm, and intrigue in equal doses."
—*Richmond Times-Dispatch*

ALEXANDER McCALL SMITH

# THE STELLAR DEBUT
# OF GALACTICA MacFEE

Alexander McCall Smith is the author of the No. 1 Ladies' Detective Agency novels and a number of other series and stand-alone books. His works have been translated into more than forty languages and have been bestsellers throughout the world. He lives in Scotland.

alexandermccallsmith.com

# BOOKS BY ALEXANDER McCALL SMITH

## In the 44 Scotland Street Series

*44 Scotland Street*

*Espresso Tales*

*Love Over Scotland*

*The World According to Bertie*

*The Unbearable Lightness of Scones*

*The Importance of Being Seven*

*Bertie Plays the Blues*

*Sunshine on Scotland Street*

*Bertie's Guide to Life and Mothers*

*The Revolving Door of Life*

*The Bertie Project*

*A Time of Love and Tartan*

*The Peppermint Tea Chronicles*

*A Promise of Ankles*

*Love in the Time of Bertie*

*The Enigma of Garlic*

## In the No. 1 Ladies' Detective Agency Series

*The No. 1 Ladies' Detective Agency*

*Tears of the Giraffe*

*Morality for Beautiful Girls*

*The Kalahari Typing School for Men*

*The Full Cupboard of Life*

*In the Company of Cheerful Ladies*

*Blue Shoes and Happiness*

*The Good Husband of Zebra Drive*

*The Miracle at Speedy Motors*

*Tea Time for the Traditionally Built*

*The Double Comfort Safari Club*

*The Saturday Big Tent Wedding Party*

*The Limpopo Academy of Private Detection*

*The Minor Adjustment Beauty Salon*

*The Handsome Man's De Luxe Café*

*The Woman Who Walked in Sunshine*

Precious and Grace
The House of
  Unexpected Sisters
The Colors of All
  the Cattle
To the Land of Long
  Lost Friends
How to Raise an Elephant
The Joy and Light
  Bus Company
A Song of Comfortable Chairs
From a Far and Lovely
  Country

## In the Isabel Dalhousie Series

The Sunday Philosophy Club
Friends, Lovers, Chocolate
The Right Attitude to Rain
The Careful Use of
  Compliments
The Comforts of a Muddy
  Saturday
The Lost Art of Gratitude
The Charming Quirks of
  Others
The Forgotten Affairs of
  Youth
The Perils of Morning Coffee
  (eBook only)
The Uncommon Appeal of
  Clouds
The Novel Habits of
  Happiness
At the Reunion Buffet
  (eBook only)
Sweet, Thoughtful Valentine
  (eBook only)
A Distant View of Everything
The Quiet Side of Passion
The Geometry of Holding
  Hands
The Sweet Remnants of
  Summer

## In the Paul Stuart Series

My Italian Bulldozer
The Second-Worst Restaurant
  in France

## In the Detective Varg Series

The Department of Sensitive
  Crimes
The Talented Mr. Varg
The Man with the Silver Saab
The Discreet Charm of the
  Big Bad Wolf
The Strange Case of the
  Moderate Extremists
  (eBook only)

## In the Corduroy Mansions Series

Corduroy Mansions

The Dog Who Came in from
the Cold

A Conspiracy of
Friends

## In the Portuguese Irregular Verbs Series

Portuguese Irregular
Verbs

The Finer Points of
Sausage Dogs

At the Villa of Reduced
Circumstances

Unusual Uses for Olive Oil

Your Inner Hedgehog

## Other Works

La's Orchestra Saves
the World

The Girl Who Married a Lion
and Other Tales
from Africa

Trains and Lovers

The Forever Girl

Fatty O'Leary's Dinner Party
(eBook only)

Emma: A Modern Retelling

Chance Developments

The Good Pilot Peter
Woodhouse

Pianos and Flowers

Tiny Tales

The Pavilion in the Clouds
(eBook only)

In a Time of Distance

The Private Life of Spies
and The Exquisite Art of
Getting Even

The Perfect Passion Company

## For Young Readers

The Great Cake Mystery

The Mystery of Meerkat Hill

The Mystery of the
Missing Lion

*The*
# STELLAR DEBUT
*of*
# GALACTICA MacFEE

ALEXANDER McCALL SMITH

# The
# STELLAR DEBUT
## of
# GALACTICA MacFEE

*A 44 Scotland Street Novel*

ILLUSTRATIONS BY
*Iain McIntosh*

VINTAGE BOOKS
*A Division of Penguin Random House LLC*
*New York*

A VINTAGE BOOKS ORIGINAL 2024

*Copyright © 2023 by Alexander McCall Smith*

All rights reserved. Published in the United States by Vintage Books,
a division of Penguin Random House LLC, New York. Originally published
in hardcover in Great Britain by Polygon Books, an imprint of
Birlinn Ltd., Edinburgh, in 2023.

This is a work of fiction. Names, characters, places,
and incidents either are the product of the author's imagination
or are used fictitiously. Any resemblance to actual persons,
living or dead, events, or locales is entirely coincidental.

This book is excerpted from a series
that originally appeared in *The Scotsman* newspaper.

Cataloging-in-Publication Data is available at the Library of Congress.

**Vintage Books Trade Paperback ISBN: 978-0-593-68829-8**
**eBook ISBN: 978-0-593-68830-4**

*Author illustration by © Iain McIntosh*

vintagebooks.com

Printed in the United States of America
10 9 8 7 6 5 4 3 2 1

*The*
STELLAR DEBUT
*of*
GALACTICA MacFEE

# 1

## *Life's Narrative Arc*

Do you have an arc in your life? An arc takes you from A to B, ascending and descending like a wave. It takes you from childhood, by way of what happens to you and what you do, to a point that occurs much later, to an ending, a resolution. That is what arcs are meant to do. They are contours, lines on the map of our lives – they are our narratives.

Not all lives, though, proceed quite like that. Some of us have no narrative arc at all, because our lives, much as we may enjoy them, meander along in an unremarkable way. And then there are those whose lives are not linear at all. They start in one place, go to another, change their mind and then end up back where they started from. An example of this progression is that of those who meet somebody, fall in love, marry that person, fall out of love, separate, but then return to their original partner at the end of the day. That is not much of an arc, it would seem; it is more of a circle.

But the point of such circularity is that it happens, and rather more often than one might imagine. And so it is not beyond the bounds of possibility that Irene Pollock, wife of Stuart Pollock, and mother of Bertie and the unfortunate Ulysses, should have left her husband, gone to Aberdeen to pursue PhD studies under the supervision of her lover, the celebrated psychotherapist Hugo Fairbairn, but should now be thinking of returning to Edinburgh, at least for several days a week, spending the remaining days in Aberdeen.

Nor should we be surprised that Stuart, who had been encouraged in the most persistent and persuasive way by his mother, Nicola, to rid himself of his termagant wife, should now apparently be prepared to take Irene back for part of each week. What sort of arc is that? Not a very satisfactory one, Nicola would say. Her own progress through life had been far more structured. She had been married to a Portuguese wine producer, who had left her for their young housekeeper – allegedly on the direct instructions of the Virgin Mary; some men, Nicola observed, will prove extremely creative in their excuses.

Reacting to this decisively – with all the confidence of one who feels she has a satisfactory arc – Nicola had returned to Scotland and to a flat in Edinburgh's Georgian New Town. There she lived in a degree of comfort, thanks to a generous divorce settlement and falling heir to an estate that included in its assets the successful Glasgow pie factory previously known as Pies for Protestants, but now renamed – with the sensitivity of the times – Inclusive Pies.

Nicola had been generous in the arrangements she made for this factory, engineering a worker management scheme, along with a profit-sharing regime markedly in the employees' favour. The factory prospered, and was widely cited as an example of liberal and enlightened capitalism, even if the pies it so successfully made – known as Scotch pies, and built in such a way as to create a reservoir of grease on the top – could hardly be described as healthy or enlightened.

Nicola felt that her son was weak, and had told him so on a number of occasions. She knew that it was not appropriate for a mother to interfere in a son's marriage, but there were circumstances in which a failure to do so amounted, in her view, to the moral equivalent of failing to wrest somebody from the coils of an encircling python. It would be as if Laocoön's mother, on that fateful day in Troy, had simply ignored the sight of her son and two grandsons toiling to defeat the serpent in which they were entwined.

Stuart was Laocoön, and had at long last come to understand that he was being suffocated by Irene. Since then, he had had one or two dalliances from which nothing had come, and he had returned to being single. He did not particularly mind that, but had eventually decided to try to meet somebody through internet dating, the method by which he had been told virtually everybody now met those with whom they became romantically involved.

The gods of internet dating – and there must be such in any modern pantheon of deities – must have been in a playful mood. Stuart had concealed his real name – out of a certain old-fashioned embarrassment – and had made a date to meet a woman in a bistro on Queen Street. When she arrived, he – and she – experienced a moment of utter disbelief: the woman he had arranged to meet turned out to be none other than Irene.

Such was the cosmic scale of this coincidence that both of them agreed that they might try to make a go of it again. Irene had changed: she realised that she had been, perhaps, a little bit too domineering, and this humility endeared her to Stuart. At the back of his mind, of course, was a desire to do his best for his two sons, and Irene, after all, was still their mother, even if she was a somewhat unusual one. Stuart was not a selfish man, and if it was in the best interests of Bertie and Ulysses that he should try once more to live with their mother, then that was something he was prepared to do, even at the cost of his recently won freedom.

They agreed that Irene would return to Edinburgh. She had made a certain amount of progress with her PhD, but she confessed to experiencing some difficulties in her relationship with Hugo Fairbairn. These were largely of an academic nature: they had disagreed on a number of points of Freudian theory, and their interpretation of certain Lacanian texts had diverged widely. More seriously, Dr Fairbairn had announced that self-analysis on his part had revealed to him that he was beginning to think of Irene as his mother, and that this had triggered Oedipal complications that were proving difficult to resolve, given that his father was already dead and could not therefore be the subject of repressed homicidal wishes. She had contested this, and they had then drifted into an acrimonious exchange in which reference was made to anxieties relating to castration. It was at that point that he had suggested that she might consider returning to Edinburgh. "I'm not trying to get rid of you, carissima," he said. "It's just that I think you should go back to Edinburgh, where you belong."

"*Incroyable!*" Irene had blurted out in riposte. "And where do you come from yourself, Hugissimo? Edinburgh, *n'est-ce pas?*"

Dr Fairbairn had sighed, but had given no answer, and Irene had left the room. In the heat of the moment, her Italian had deserted her, and she had lapsed into French – a sign that not only was she losing the argument, she had already lost it.

# 2

## *Circe, Jason etc.*

After an initial foray back to Edinburgh, on which she had stayed with Antonia and Sister Maria-Fiore dei Fiori di Montagna, Irene had returned to Aberdeen, and to her PhD research. There was not much to do at the university there: she and Hugo Fairbairn had found that their new status as former lovers suited them rather better than had their previous, somewhat fraught relationship. Apologies were made on both sides for intemperate remarks about castration anxiety, and Dr Fairbairn was kind enough to suggest that Irene's thesis, as far as it had got, showed every sign of being publishable, and that he himself would recommend it to an academic publisher on whose editorial board he served. A new series was being proposed – 'Fresh Directions in Psychoanalytical Theory' – and Irene's work appeared to fit that rather well.

It was agreed that Irene could continue to work on her thesis even if she was from now on to divide her time between Aberdeen and Edinburgh

This proposal struck Irene as being entirely satisfactory. She was looking forward to being back in Edinburgh – at least for part of the time – although she had not been unhappy in Aberdeen. "I don't regret anything," she remarked one day. "Do you, Hugo?"

"Nothing," he said. "*Je ne regrette rien.* Regrets are the traps into which the old self lures us. We must be wary of that – every bit as much as Jason was obliged to beware of the Sirens."

"Indeed," said Irene. She was not sure about this reference to Sirens. Was he suggesting, even subtly, that she, Irene, was some sort of Siren? Or even a Medusa-like figure? That would have been deeply insulting, and she quickly discounted the possibility. However, it was certainly true that our language is littered with unintended references to our real feelings, and that we give ourselves away in overtly innocent allusions. Perhaps he felt that she was a distraction, and that her influence had somehow to be resisted. For a moment she imagined Dr Fairbairn tied to the mast while the *Argo* navigated a narrow passage, if not off the coast of Capri, as suggested by Virgil and Ovid, then perhaps in the Sound of Mull; while she, seated on a rock near Lochaline or Tobermory, lured him shoreward with her singing, possibly of the 'Mingulay Boat Song' or the 'Eriskay Love Lilt'.

Dr Fairbairn had taken to peppering his remarks with classical references, and was currently working on deep structure in the story of Circe. This gave his observations an added depth, and indeed authority, but it was difficult for Irene, who had only recently acquired any familiarity with Greek mythology. She had been particularly pained, not to say embarrassed, to discover that Ulysses, after whom she had inadvertently named her younger son, was, in fact, such a vindictive, unreconstructed man. He had behaved appallingly to his female retainers when he arrived back on Ithaca, and she could not understand why Penelope had not finished her weaving and gone off with one of the young men who frequented her palace. Now, in response to this unexpected reference to Jason, she asked, "What was he looking for, do you think? Was it really just a golden fleece hanging on a tree?"

Dr Fairbairn sighed. "More or less certainly not. Most of us who embark on a search are unaware of the thing for which we are really looking. That is hidden from us – in most cases."

"Very true," said Irene. "I sometimes feel that I have almost found what I am looking for, and then I see that it isn't there after all. Do you find that too?"

"Almost invariably," said Dr Fairbairn. "And I feel that Scotland, too, is engaged on just such a search. We are, as a nation, looking for something. We feel that we have lost something that we need to recover."

"Our sense of ourselves?" asked Irene. "Our sense of who we are?"

"Possibly. We are all Argonauts, you see – in our individual ways. Perhaps we imagine that we are looking for our sense of ourselves while at the same time we are really looking for something else."

The discussion had gone no further. Irene would have liked to continue to explore the question of what people in Scotland were looking for, but Dr Fairbairn had had another appointment and had taken a glance at his watch. Their love affair, she thought, had been a great and noble one: they had been two souls that had briefly glimpsed a sense of completeness in which alienated and separated moieties had achieved a completeness, a healing that the world did not readily give. That had been something special, something important, and she was grateful for it. But that sense of discovery had worn thin, and she felt now that it was time to *move on* . . . she almost said this to herself, but stopped just in time. That was not an expression that should be used, she thought, by somebody like herself: that was the language of pop psychology, the cheap, ersatz terminology that *lay* people used to give voice to their psychic dramas. You could never *really* move on, Irene pointed out to friends who had talked of moving on: we are what we are, which is an accumulation of experiences and attitudes, and we can never rid ourselves of our past. Nobody can abandon the baggage on which her name is written, she pointed out. It is our baggage, and it accompanies us no matter how hard we try to . . . to move on. There! She had thought it, and it had been a *necessary* thought: there were no other words for the process. We moved on, whether we liked the term or not: one may as well accept the demotic. We moved on, we reached out, we did all the things for which such clichéd expressions had been coined. Our language limited us, no matter what our aspirations to nuance and subtlety might be: perhaps the Sapir–Whorf hypothesis was correct after all: the extent of our inner lives depended on having the words to describe it.

Now, though, was not the time to reflect on the extent to which language constrained us: Irene had started to take an interest in cold-water therapy, and it was time for her to make her way to the beach, where she expected to find her Aberdonian friend, Jan Finnan, a fellow devotee of the benefits of swimming in the North Sea in every season. That required a certain hardiness, and a commitment to the curative properties of cold water. Aberdeen was a perfect place for a cold-water therapist to practise, and she and Jan had an appointment that very afternoon to accompany their therapist into the sea at the two-mile-long beach not far from the city centre. It would not do to be late for cold-water therapy, lest one find the instructor frozen to death by the time one arrives. That is particularly likely in Aberdeen, which is a cold city, at least in its externals, although at heart it is full of humour and love, similar in spirit to Naples and Sorrento. (There are some differences between Scottish cities and their Italian counterparts, of course: Irn-Bru is unknown in Italy, and head-butting as a means of settling disputes – or, indeed, creating them – is rare to non-existent in those Mediterranean latitudes. Apart from that, the similarities are striking. *In Scozia si trova un cuore Italiano,* they said – or at least some of them did.)

# 3

## Cold-water Therapy

Irene reached the beach shortly before two that afternoon. She had agreed that she and Jan would meet their cold-water therapist, Mark Carnoustie, at two fifteen, and they would then immerse themselves in the waves for approximately twenty minutes, the optimum time of exposure, he said, to the chilly temperatures of the North Sea at that latitude.

It was Jan who had introduced Irene to cold-water therapy and who had induced her to join her one day in the ice bath she had had installed in her back garden. She had given Irene a full explanation of the scientific basis for the treatment, detailing its beneficial effects on the circulation and the relief it provided for conditions ranging from muscular discomfort to depression.

"Cold water increases the blood supply to certain important parts of the body," she said. "This can reduce inflammation. It also lowers your core temperature, which invigorates you and tones up your immune system."

Irene had listened with interest. "I've heard that you sleep better if you take a cold shower before you go to bed," she said.

"You absolutely do," said Jan. "And some also say that it helps them lose weight. It's nothing new, you know. People have been practising this for centuries – it's just that we forget about these things and then we rediscover them."

Irene had enjoyed her first ice bath – at least she enjoyed it in retrospect, after she had emerged from the ice tub, blue and shivering, and had rubbed herself dry with a rough towel provided by her friend.

"Better?" asked Jan.

Irene nodded. "Much better," she said. "I feel I have a renewed focus."

Jan had introduced Irene to Mark Carnoustie, who planned a programme of what he called "guided therapy". Together they had regular sessions in pools of varying temperatures, followed by prolonged meditation sessions. Any scepticism that Irene might have entertained at the outset soon evaporated, or froze, perhaps, and she now became something of a proselyte for this new approach to well-being. With the zeal of the convert, she was looking forward to enrolling Stuart, Bertie and Ulysses in a cold-water programme once she returned to Edinburgh. She would start with the boys' regular evening bath, a time of great splashing and shouting: that could continue, but would take place in cold water rather than warm. A few ice cubes would be added from the freezer, which would take the temperature down further, and bring Bertie and Ulysses additional benefits. Stuart, she thought, could begin by taking cold showers, although she anticipated that she might need to exert some pressure on him to comply – at least at the beginning. He could be contrary at times, and she feared that his recent experience of single life might have pushed him further down the road of resistance to reason. No matter: he would be brought round, once he began to enjoy the feeling of enhanced well-being that cold showers would bring him.

Irene had travelled to the beach by bus and now stood in the car park, waiting for Jan to arrive. Jan was usually punctual, but that afternoon they had not arrived by ten minutes after the appointed time, and Irene was becoming impatient.

At two thirty she telephoned Jan to find out what could be causing the delay. The answer was simple: Irene had mistaken the date. When she had called to make the arrangement, she had, in fact, suggested the following Tuesday, exactly a week later.

Irene apologised. "I take it you're not free to come down here now," she said.

Jan was not. She was a piano teacher, and she had two pupils coming for their lessons. "I can't cancel," she said. "So sorry." Then she added, "Why don't you take a dip by youself? Careful, though . . ."

Irene accepted that it was her fault. She felt disappointed, though, that having prepared herself psychologically for an immersion, this was now not to take place. She looked out over the beach, out to the line of grey-blue sea, out towards Norway. Not far offshore, a trawler ploughed a furrow in the watery field that was the sea, a line of white wake behind it, and circling, optimistic gulls waited to swoop on scraps from the fishermen's table.

She filled her lungs with air. She thought she could smell the salt, and the iodine of the tangle. She closed her eyes and saw herself in the waves, the foam around her, buoyant in the water's embrace.

She made her decision. She would have her cold-water therapy session by herself; she did not need others to be there to hold her hand. She would stick to the shallow water and not go too far out. It was perfectly safe, even though the beach was almost entirely deserted. Off in the far distance there was somebody else – a woman walking a dog – but there was no risk if one kept close enough to shore to stand up in the water if necessary. And the waves, although slightly higher than they had been the last time she was there, were nothing to worry about. After all, she was not intending to surf; she was here to wallow, to immerse herself.

She had her swimming costume on under her clothing, and now she placed her clothes in a neat pile, along with her towel and kit bag. Then, stepping out onto the beach, she ran down towards the line of the incoming tide. Irene believed it best to throw oneself into the water straightaway, rather than venturing in slowly. In this way the shock of the cold was encountered, and mastered, more quickly.

She gasped as she felt the cold envelop her. Then, launching herself forwards, she struck out for slightly deeper water. As she did so, she glanced up at the sky, high, empty, immense above her. An aircraft vapour trail intersected the expanse of blue; a gull mewed into the wind, dipped and wheeled.

She began to turn back, but she felt the water resist her change of direction. She persisted, but the current fought back. She looked back towards the beach, now receding fast. Irene was being carried out to sea, and there was nobody to witness her plight.

She gave a cry – a sharp, curtailed cry, half-swallowed, inaudible against the sounds of the waves and the wind that had now sprung up. She wondered what it would be like to drown. Was it peaceful, as people sometimes said it was? Did oblivion come quickly after the first gulp of water reached the lungs? This is happening to *me*, she thought – not to somebody else – to *me*. Personal extinction, she thought: the dissolution of self. And then she thought: if I survive this – somehow – I will be a much better person. I really will. I'll try; I'll try.

On the deck of the *Aberdeen Belle*, a fishing trawler based in Peterhead, returning from the fishing grounds east of Shetland, a young man pointed towards the shore. "There's a wifie in the water," he shouted to the skipper. "Look."

"Aye," said the skipper. "Ging ower to port a wee bittie, Doddie. An ca canny. The peer soul looks fair founert."

# 4

## A Personal Statement

Far to the south, Bertie's teacher, Miss Campbell, was introducing the class to a new member who was joining it for the first time that morning.

"This, boys and girls," she said, "is our new member. This is . . ." She hesitated. She was used to unusual names – after all there was a Tofu in the class, as well as a Valentina and a Brexita – and so no eyebrow should have been raised by the arrival of one Galactica MacFee, a girl of seven and a half with neatly plaited blonde hair and a pert, retroussé nose.

"Galactica," Miss Campbell continued, "has come to us from Stirling. Her parents are now living in Edinburgh – that's so, isn't it, Galactica, dear?"

"That's correct," said Galactica. "We've moved to Ann Street. Do you know where that is?"

The teacher shot her a glance.

"It's the best street in Edinburgh, my mummy says. Miles better than Heriot Row. She says that Edinburgh is full of streets that are suitable for people like us."

"I see," said Miss Campbell, through clenched teeth.

"My daddy has taken a job in Edinburgh," Galactica continued. "He's a neurologist. Neurologists are very clever. They know all about nerves and brains and things." She paused. "I shall be a neurologist when I grow up. I already know quite a bit about it."

The class remained silent as they eyed Galactica.

"There are so many things we can become when we are

grown-up," said Miss Campbell, breezily. "Sometimes the choice is just too great, I fear."

Galactica lowered her voice, as if to impart a confidence. "I don't have to worry about any of that. They're keeping a place for me at Edinburgh. It's official."

"Well," said Miss Campbell, "I think you'll still have to apply for medicine in the fullness of time. That's a long way away, though."

Galactica stared at her. "We'll see," she said, enigmatically.

"Galactica can sit next to Bertie, I think," said Miss Campbell. "You can put your things in the desk, dear. We'll find you a peg later on."

"This is a bit of a dump," said Galactica.

Miss Campbell frowned. "We don't say things like that, Galactica. It's not nice to call other people's classrooms dumps."

"Even if they are?" asked Galactica.

Miss Campbell ignored the question. "I think you'll find this a very friendly school, Galactica. We are all here to support one another." She gave Galactica a warning look as she said this, and then went on, "Everyone can be what they want to be here. Everybody has a chance. Do you see what I mean?"

"Yes, I do," said Galactica. "I was in the Brownies. I would have been a Sixer if I had stayed. I played hockey for the school under-ten team. I can write my name. I can spell Edinburgh and Callander. I have started to write a book that I will finish when I am fourteen or fifteen. I have plenty of time. I can speak fourteen words of Catalan. I'm going to get a pilot's licence when I'm seventeen. That's my personal statement." She paused, and then added, "That's my truth, you see."

"Very good," said Miss Campbell. "It's so nice that you're a busy wee soul."

And she thought: *Why did I get these children – and their*

*mothers? This one's going to be an ocean-going little madam
– no two ways about it. And just think of her mother* . . .

Galactica took her place, next to Bertie, who smiled at
her encouragingly, even if with a measure of caution. For a
few minutes she busied herself unpacking her satchel, placing
an array of sharpened pencils on the desktop before her
and opening a small blue jotter at a page already headed by
the day's date, carefully lettered in red. Then she turned to
scrutinise Bertie.

"So," she began. "So, you're Bertie, then."

Bertie nodded. "My full name is Bertie Pollock. I live in
Scotland Street."

Galactica absorbed this information with a curt nod. "I
see," she said. "And have you got any brothers and sisters?"

"I've got one brother," said Bertie. "He's younger than me.
He's at nursery school. He often gets projectile vomiting."

Galactica reached for a pencil. "Do you mind if I take
notes?" she said.

Bertie frowned. "Why?" he asked.

Galactica tapped her pencil. "Because I like to keep a
record," she said. "You never know, do you, Bertie Pollock?"

Bertie said that he did not mind. His voice was wary. Olive
and Pansy were difficult enough, but this new girl seemed to
be in a wholly different league. Why were girls so demanding?
Why did they have to make it so hard for boys?

"And what is your brother's name?" asked Galactica.

Bertie hesitated. Other boys had brothers called Bill or Jim,
or Harry, even. He had Ulysses.

"He's called Ulysses," he answered, almost apologetically.

Galactica began to note that down, but gave up on the
spelling. Now she looked about her, which gave Bertie a
feeling of relief.

"Who's that girl over there?" she whispered, as Miss
Campbell had begun to address the class about something.

Bertie followed Galactica's gaze. He knew at whom she must be looking, even before his glance confirmed it. It had to be Olive. This was destined to be.

"That's Olive," he whispered back.

Galactica's verdict came quickly. "That's a stupid name. An olive is a little green thing that people eat. You may as well be called Tomato."

Bertie allowed himself a smile. That was a line that he might take with Olive, had he the courage. That would show her. But of course that would be to invite retribution on an unimaginable scale and he would never do it. Not even Tofu would dare, and Tofu was, for the most part, fearless.

"And that girl next to her?" Galactica continued. "The one with the thin arms. Who does she think she is?"

*Who does she think she is?* Bertie's eyes widened as he played with the words in his mind. This was monumental. Olive and Pansy were . . . they were the *Kremlin* – not that Galactica was to know.

"She's called Pansy," he said. "She's Olive's . . ." He searched for the right word. "She's Olive's assistant."

Galactica made a quick note, which Bertie tried to decipher before its author placed a concealing hand over the words. He transferred his gaze to the other side of the classroom, where Olive, he noticed, was staring back at Galactica. Bertie sensed trouble. It was as clear to him as if there had been an official declaration of war, complete with sounding trumpets and unfurled battleground banners. He did not welcome this. Bertie wanted only that people should be kind to one another; but they never were. That was not the way the world was, it seemed, and sometimes, as he thought about it, his small soul, composed as it as was of pure goodness, felt overwhelmed by the nature of the world in which he was obliged to live.

# 5

## Glasgist Attitudes

In Scotland Street itself, in their flat with its view up towards Drummond Place and down towards Canonmills, Domenica Macdonald, anthropologist and wry observer of Edinburgh life, sat with her husband, Angus Lordie, and contemplated the morning's post. There was a leaflet from a rug shop, advertising a forthcoming exhibition of lion rugs from Iran; a renewal notice from an insurance company; and the latest copy of *Scottish Field*, to which Angus had for years been a subscriber.

Angus picked up the rug shop leaflet. This was headed by a colourful picture of a kilim, on which a stylised lion was depicted, its head and mane strangely angular, as if constructed from children's building bricks.

"The Persian lion is extinct, I believe," Angus said. "And yet they still like them as symbols."

"Everyone likes symbolic lions," said Domenica. "Real lions are trickier. They smell, I believe, rather like tomcats. They have voracious appetites, and are quite happy to eat us if there's nothing better on the menu."

Angus agreed. "I have no particular desire to see a lion in the wild," he said. "I like the *idea* of lions, but that's as far as it goes. Lions are useful for metaphor, I suppose. Richard Coeur de Lion, the Lion of Kashmir, being lionhearted – and so on." He paused. Other animals had metaphorical work to do: pigs certainly did – and sheep, too, when it came to the analysis of voting habits.

"I was reading about lion imagery in Auden's poetry,"

Domenica remarked. "He refers to lions in various poems. And yet there's no evidence that he ever actually saw a lion."

"I loved *Born Free* when I was young," said Angus. "I thought that idea of forging a friendship with a lioness was just so exciting."

"I came across somebody who met her," Domenica remembered. "Joy Adamson – not Elsa. They said that she was a rather strong character, which was putting it mildly. Some of that Happy Valley set were somewhat colourful. What was her name – that other one? Diana Delamere? The woman who was friendly with Lord Erroll, who was so unfortunately shot in his car. The person I knew who knew Joy Adamson also knew her, apparently. She said to me that Diana Delamere did not shoot Erroll, and nor was it her husband, Jock Delves Broughton. He was very deeply in love with his wife, who nonetheless had an eye for other men, I'm afraid."

"They were a racy lot," Angus said. Then she remembered Gavin Maxwell and his otters. "Of course, there was *Ring of Bright Water?*"

"Yes," said Domenica. "It's a powerful genre. Person meets an animal. They communicate with one another and then the animal goes back to the wild. Everybody's sad. The animal doesn't forget the human friend. It's an ancient theme. Androcles and the lion, in Aesop, for example. The lion was grateful to Androcles and declined to eat him when the slave was tossed into the ring."

Angus changed the subject. He had been out for a walk that morning with his dog, Cyril, and they had seen Stuart. Cyril liked Stuart, whom he associated with Bertie, and had bounded up to the other man and licked his hands enthusiastically.

"Stuart told me that Irene's coming back to Edinburgh part-time."

Domenica put down the lion rug exhibition circular. "I see," she said.

"Yes. Apparently, they're going to try to patch it up."

Domenica sighed. "I'm not sure that will work. Poor Bertie."

"Stuart's mother won't be pleased," said Angus. "She's settled in downstairs. She still keeps her flat round the corner, but she's here most of the time."

"Nicola has never had any time for Irene," Domenica said. "And who can blame her? I know that we've all tried to look at her in a different light recently, but what worries me is that she'll simply revert to her old ways."

"What do they say?" said Angus. "You can take some people out of Glasgow, but you can't take Glasgow out of some people."

Domenica looked at him reprovingly. "I'm not sure you should say that sort of thing, Angus."

"I wasn't saying it," he protested "I was simply reporting what some people used to say. I wasn't endorsing it."

"Even so," said Domenica. "You'll be accused of *Glasgism* – of being prejudiced against Glasgow."

"But I don't think that way at all," he said. "I've never been stand-offish about Glasgow. It's a great place – for Glaswegians, that is. No, that didn't sound right. I didn't mean that. I meant to say: as Glaswegians will point out, Glasgow's a great place. That's what I meant."

Domenica did not pursue the matter. She was careful about what she said – Angus was less so. And, of course, he was being honest about his feelings for Glasgow: he liked the city and its ways, particularly when he was tired of the slightly disapproving side of Edinburgh. Glasgow was robust and direct-speaking; it did not mince its words and it knew how to enjoy itself. It was warm and welcoming, and Angus would have been happy enough to live there – had he drawn one of life's short straws. But he had not; he lived in Edinburgh, and did not feel that he had to apologise for that. There was nothing worse than somebody who lived in Edinburgh affecting Glasgow attitudes. We are what we are, thought Angus – and no amount of desire to be something different made us what we might like to be. *If you're bourgeois, get over it.* It was a question of authenticity: Jean-Paul Sartre was right about that, he thought.

He looked at Domenica. "By the way," he began.

It was a classic Glaswegian expression, he reminded himself. They were always saying "by the way" over there. "By the way, I had a very strange experience in Drummond Place Gardens yesterday. I meant to tell you yesterday, but I forgot."

"You saw something strange in Drummond Place Gardens?" asked Domenica. "How very Stella Gibbons!"

It was a moment or two before Angus took the reference to *Cold Comfort Farm* and Aunt Ada Doom. "I didn't see something nasty in the woodshed," he said.

"I've often wondered what Ada Doom saw," said Domenica. "Freud's primal scene?"

"Let's not go there," said Angus.

# 6

## *We Must Love One Another*

"I was taking Cyril for his evening walk," Angus began to tell Domenica. "It was rather later than usual. About half past ten. You'd gone to bed already, but Cyril was a bit unsettled and I decided that he might benefit from a circuit or two of the gardens. You know how he whines if he feels the day hasn't been brought to a satisfactory conclusion."

Domenica nodded. Cyril was Angus's responsibility and although she had become fond of the dog, she had never developed her husband's ability to read Cyril's moods and respond to his needs. There were dog people, she thought, and there were cat people – and she was, she suspected, more comfortable in the latter group than in the former. Cats, she felt, were more subtle than dogs. It was true that their alliance with humanity was shakier than the contract that dogs long ago entered into with man, but cats still appreciated our company even if mostly on their own terms. Certainly, cats were less demanding, not requiring the constant affirmation by which dogs seemed to set such store. People were always telling dogs that they were good: "good dog" was the most common compliment paid to dogs, while nobody ever said "good cat". Indeed, uttering "good cat" would result in a cold stare from whatever cat to whom the remark was addressed. *Good cat? Moi?*

"Anyway," Angus continued, "I took Cyril and we headed up the street towards Drummond Place. It was a lovely evening. It was just getting dark, but there was still a very faint glow in the sky over in the west. And the air was still

– there was no movement at all in the branches of the trees. Nothing.

"The streets were deserted. We reached the top of Scotland Street before we saw anybody, and you know who that was? Sister Maria-Fiore dei Fiori di Montagna, no less. Scurrying along from the direction of Northumberland Street."

Domenica raised an eyebrow. "Coming back from the pub?"

Angus laughed. "She likes to drop into the Wally Dug. She holds court there – I've seen it. Sister Maria-Fiore dei Fiori di Montagna perches on a bar stool and various acolytes gather round. She delivers opinions on a wide range of subjects – always to nods of agreement. She has an air of sagacity about her, you see."

"And, of course, there are her aphorisms," Domenica said. "She has an observation for every occasion. People love it. Antonia Collie, I believe, is working on a collection of her *aperçus*. Creative Scotland has already approved a publication grant."

Angus shook his head in wonderment. "Remarkable."

"Yes," agreed Domenica. "Antonia was telling me about it. She says that she envisages something along the lines of Kahlil Gibran's *The Prophet*. She thinks that Sister Maria-Fiore dei Fiori di Montagna may end up being in the same league."

Angus shook his head again. "But how many copies of *The Prophet* have been sold? Countless millions?"

"I happen to know a little bit about that," said Domenica. "I became interested after Antonia made her claim – which I thought highly unlikely, by the way. I read that the original American edition had a print run of two thousand copies, but went on to sell nine million. Frankly, I would have expected even more, given that there was a time when every college student had one in his or her bedroom. Do you remember when you first read it?"

Angus thought for a moment. "Well, yes, I do, as it happens. I was at the art college. I went into James Thin's to get a book about post-impressionism and I came out with a copy of *The Prophet*. I'd picked it up by chance – I'd never heard of it before then – and I started to read one of the poems and I thought it the most moving thing I'd ever read. I was at that age, you see – the age when one is ready for a dose of Lebanese mysticism. It's the same stage in life at which one reads Jack Kerouac. I thought *On the Road* was so liberating."

Domenica smiled. "Jack Kerouac is more for young men than for young women, I think. I tried to read Kerouac, but found he did nothing for me."

Angus looked thoughtful. "Do you think there's a distinction between men's books and women's books?"

"Of course there is," said Domenica. "It may not be fashionable in androgynous times to make that distinction, but it's there. Do more men than women read Patrick O'Brian, for example? I suspect they do. Naval history is, I think, more of a masculine interest than a feminine one."

"And what would be a quintessentially feminine book?" asked Angus.

"Something non-naval," said Domenica. "Perhaps romantic fiction. That must be read by many more women than men. I've never looked at any figures, but they must be there. There's a whole genre of fiction that's churned out for that market. And it's becoming increasingly steamy."

"Are women themselves becoming steamier?" said Angus, adding, quickly, "Just asking, of course."

Domenica said that she thought they were. They now openly enjoyed erotic fiction, whereas previously any interest on their part in such books would have been concealed, or perhaps suppressed by men who felt threatened by it.

Angus sighed. "We live in an age of exhibitionism," he said. "And exhibitionism goes hand in hand with the weakening of the concept of the private. That inevitably leads, some argue, to a coarsening of sensibilities. "

Domenica did not disagree, but before she could say anything to that effect, Angus continued, "Have you noticed how discourtesy and aggression are infecting our public life? What happened to gentleness? What happened to *agape*, to non-erotic love? "

Domenica stared out of the window. "Do you think Scotland has changed?" she asked suddenly. "Do you think we've become more dismissive of one another? "

Angus did not answer immediately. He had set out to tell her about his experience last night in Drummond Place, but they had ended up talking about these broader issues. Now another memory came to him – of Hamish Henderson, who reminded us not to disfigure ourselves with hatred. How right he was, that tall, benign figure, with his tweedy hat, who sang 'Freedom Come-All-Ye' in Sandy Bell's, and who could so easily bring forth tears for the values of a vanishing Scotland. He thought: who is there today to speak out for love? Who is there today to say that we must love one another – that we simply have to?

# 7

## The Man in the Rhododendrons

"Did she have anything to say?" asked Domenica. "Sister Maria-Fiore dei Fiori di Montagna?"

"Yes."

Angus replied, "Well, she did, actually. There was a little bit of small talk to begin with – nothing consequential – something about Antonia having had a bad cold and dosing herself with vitamin C – and then she drew me aside – she gripped my elbow – and said that she had just seen something suspicious."

Domenica waited. If you see something suspicious, she thought, tell somebody . . . In an age of mutual distrust, that was the message the authorities seemed keen to promote.

"She said that she had been overtaken as she was walking down Nelson Street," Angus continued, "by a man who seemed in a hurry."

"Everyone is in a hurry these days," observed Domenica. "Nothing unusual there."

"That's true. We do rush around a bit. But this man, Sister Maria-Fiore dei Fiori di Montagna said, looked furtive."

Domenica thought about this. How does one look furtive? she wondered. By looking over one's shoulder to see who's watching? By anxious sideways glances?

"She said that he had slipped into the Drummond Place Gardens and disappeared."

Domenica raised an eyebrow. "Do you think she'd been drinking? It all sounds a bit fanciful. After all, people do nip into the gardens for an evening walk – neighbours, I mean

– ordinary people." She paused. "And some neighbours, I suppose, might look furtive because that's just the way they are. Appearances can be deceptive."

Angus nodded. "I wasn't sure what she expected me to do. I told her, though, that I was taking Cyril into the gardens for a walk, and that I'd keep an eye open for anything untoward."

"For any suspicious characters," Domenica prompted, with a smile.

"Yes."

Domenica shook her head. "She has a vivid imagination, that woman. She makes things sound like a Five Find-Outers story."

Angus smiled. "Oh, I was a great fan of those stories when I was a boy. Enid Blyton. I preferred them to the Famous Five. I so admired the gang – Larry, Pip, Daisy . . ."

"Not to mention Fatty and Bets."

"Yes," said Angus. "Is Fatty still in the books, I wonder? Or have they been all been bowdlerised?"

"I suspect there are those who would like to ban them outright. The censors are still with us. The Mrs Grundys and so on. Or perhaps they would just be satisfied with a sensitivity warning – the sort of warning that goes with Shakespeare and Jane Austen nowadays."

"Possibly," said Angus. "But the point is this: I don't think we should dismiss our Italian friend's warning too lightly."

"You mean you actually found this furtive character? You found him lurking in the bushes?"

Angus nodded. "Strange to relate, I did. There was somebody lurking in the bushes, as I was soon to discover."

Domenica began to laugh, but then she saw that Angus was serious, and she stopped herself. "Tell me what happened," she said.

"I went into the gardens," Angus continued. "Cyril always wants to walk widdershins round the gardens, but I prefer deasil. So there was a brief tugging match once I had closed the gate behind me, and of course I got my way, because Cyril ultimately accepts his subservient position in the pack. He tries it on, of course, as all dogs do, but ultimately he accepts my authority and he doesn't argue the point.

"So, we started our walk. Cyril was picking up evidence of squirrels, I think, and was keen to go and sniff at the tree trunks they had scampered up. But I made it clear to him that the point of this walk was exercise, and I think he got the message.

"We had gone halfway round the outer path when it happened. You know those rhododendron bushes near the Dublin Street corner? The vegetation there is quite thick and provides perfectly adequate cover for anybody trying to conceal himself. And it was from those rhododendrons that he stepped out – or partly stepped out."

"Who?" interjected Domenica. "This furtive character of Sister Maria-Fiore dei Fiori di Montagna's?"

Angus confirmed this with an inclination of his head. "Yes. I assume it was him. Anyway, Cyril started to growl. I can always tell when he growls for good reason. He really means it – and he meant it then. And a moment or two later, a figure half-stepped out of the rhododendron bush. Not entirely out – but half. He remained to all intents and purposes hidden by the vegetation."

Domenica smiled. "One doesn't exactly expect people to emerge from rhododendrons – at least not in Edinburgh. There may be places, of course, where . . ." That was a joke, and Angus took it as such.

"Our rhododendrons are, as a general rule, uninhabited," he said.

"Although this one was not . . ."

"Exactly. I was frozen to the spot. And even Cyril had a fright. He had sensed something, of course – he had uttered that growl – but he was not prepared for this actual appearance. Anyway, he bristled, and growled a bit more *sotto voce*, or *sotto abbaio* in his case. Then he stopped, and the man in the rhododendrons spoke to me."

Domenica leaned forward in her eagerness to hear what came next. "And what did he say?"

Angus waited. He was enjoying the drama of his account, and now he lowered his voice accordingly. "He said: 'Good evening, Mr Linklater.'"

Domenica's eyes widened. "He thought you were Magnus?" Magnus Linklater, a well-known editor and journalist, had once lived nearby.

Angus nodded. "I started to deny that I was Magnus, but I don't think he heard me. He went on to say: 'I've got some very important material for you. I can't give it to you right now, but I'll get it to you next week.'"

Domenica sat back. "This is extraordinary, Angus. Deep Throat all over again."

"That's what I thought. It took me right back to Watergate. Deep Throat met Woodward and Bernstein in the car park, remember? In the shadows."

Domenica remembered it well. "They never really saw his face. He stuck to the shadows. And he told them all about the cover-up in the White House."

"Exactly."

Domenica shook her head. "Did you try again to let him know that you weren't Magnus?"

"I did," said Angus. "But he wasn't really listening to me. He was the one who wanted to do the talking. He finished by saying, 'Be here next week – same time.' And then he disappeared. He just seemed to vanish – I think he went back into the rhododendrons and then out by another gate."

Domenica did not know what to say. Was this man about to pass on information about the *government*? She looked at

Angus, who seemed to have nothing further to say. From the floor, Cyril looked up at them. He found silences difficult to interpret – as most dogs do.

# 8

## *At The Nutcracker*

Big Lou did not expect nor ask for much from life. Having been born and raised on a farm near Arbroath – Snell Mains – she had been brought up in a simple and cautious tradition, one in which nothing was ever wasted, in which pleasures were simple – and always earned – and in which people were accustomed not to complain nor engage in self-pity. She subscribed to these values willingly and without reservation. She had never complained very much; life, she thought, had never been fair, and although you might combat unfairness when you encountered it, your efforts would never be enough. You made the most of what you had; you did your best, and, as far as you could, you helped others along the way. In many respects, then, Big Lou was markedly unfashionable.

She was never plagued by doubts. There was right and there was wrong, and she could not understand why some people found it difficult to distinguish between them. Nor should anybody have too much difficulty, she thought, in distinguishing between people who were solid and trustworthy (often, as it happened, people from the rural parts of North East Scotland, especially the area around Arbroath) and people who could not be relied upon to quite the same extent. If this suggested a somewhat old-fashioned world view, then that was indeed what it was, but that in itself was, for many who met Big Lou, something positive. The world was full of modern, up-to-the-minute people who reflected the mores of their times. That was unsurprising, but what if the zeitgeist was selfish, intolerant, and punitive (as in some respects it now seemed to be)? Then somebody like Big Lou, with her constancy, respect for others and disinclination to demonise those with whom she happened to disagree, might seem a refreshing exception.

As Angus once put it to Domenica, talking to Big Lou was rather like talking to somebody for whom it was still 1955, a time when men still wore hats, gave up their seats on buses to those in greater need of them and still used their surnames when introducing themselves; a time when women rarely swore, turned the collars of shirts when they frayed, and called one another *hen* in a spirit of solidarity and sympathy. "Not that I'm saying everything was perfect then," Angus added quickly. "I'm just saying it was different."

"Life was far from perfect then," Domenica had replied. "There was a great deal of injustice."

"I know, I know," insisted Angus. "I didn't suggest other wise. You should listen to what I say, Domenica – not that I'm criticising you, my dear." He left it at that, although he thought he might have gone further, and pointed out that in 1955 people were still allowed to express views that diverged from the consensus. Domenica understood that, of course, and shared his concern over contemporary intolerance, with its Orwellian whiff, but Angus had other things to think about and the conversation had drifted off in another direction altogether.

In marrying Fat Bob, a Highland Games strongman, Big Lou felt that she had found somebody with whom she had common ground. She had never been a particular devotee of Highland Games, but she understood the world that they served. In particular, she appreciated the simple pleasure to be derived from watching men throwing hammers and tottering about under the weight of telegraph poles. She understood why the tug-of-war should give rise to such excitement, and why people should thrill to the sight of young women in tartan skirts dancing to the recorded strains of Jimmy Shand

and his band, or of their contemporary musical heirs. All that, she understood because it had been part of her upbringing at Snell Mains.

Fat Bob had gone out of his way to be kind to Finlay, Big Lou's foster child, and the boy had reciprocated his affection. They had gone off together to the museum on Chambers Street, where Fat Bob had explained to Finlay all about Charles Edward Stuart and the Jacobites, and had also spent hours examining fossils, dinosaur bones, and models of Scottish engineering achievements. They had visited the *Britannia* in its dock in Leith, and there Bob, who had a feeling for machinery, had been at pains to explain the working of the ship's great engines and the bridge telegraph that controlled them.

Finlay had responded well to this attention, and had been particularly relieved that Bob had encouraged his interest in ballet. Ballet was not something that Bob had much experience of – in fact, he had never seen a ballet performance – but when he went with Finlay to a production of *The Nutcracker Suite* at the Festival Theatre, he was smitten by the spectacle. It was a matinee show, on a rather dreich Saturday afternoon, but a large crowd had turned out in support of Scottish Ballet, and the theatre was packed. Bob noticed that it was a different audience from the one that might attend the Pitlochry Highland Games, but when the first strains of Tchaikovsky rose from the orchestra pit, Bob caught his breath, and more or less held it until the final bars some two hours later.

Finlay saw the effect, and was pleased.

"You enjoyed that, Bob?" he asked.

Bob sighed. "Aye, Finlay – that was pure dead brilliant."

They went out onto the crowded pavements of the early evening, and joined the queue for a bus to take them back to Canonmills.

"Miss Eliot says that one day I might be able to audition for a role in that," said Finlay.

Miss Eliot was Finlay's ballet teacher at the ballet school he now attended, as a weekly boarder, in Glasgow.

Bob smiled. "I reckon you'd get it easily enough, Finlay. Big Lou says that you're pretty good."

Finlay smiled modestly. "It's hard, you know. Ballet involves a lot of work. You have to keep yourself fit."

"I'm sure you do," said Bob.

"And you can't let yourself put on weight," Finlay continued. "Did you see the principal dancers, Bob? Did you see them? Those guys had really strong muscles. No fat."

Bob nodded. "I noticed that."

Finlay looked up at him. "Do you think you could lose some weight, Bob?"

Bob did not answer immediately. He looked away. He was a big man – he had always been a big man – and it was his size that made him successful as a Highland Games strongman. At the same time, he would never have pretended that all his weight was muscle: he knew that a great deal of it was not. And that was why he had been called Fat Bob, rather than Bob. He had been given the soubriquet years ago, when people were perhaps less sensitive to these things, and where, in strongman circles, it had been a positive advantage. He had not minded. There were fat people and there were thin people – that was just the way it was.

But now, this innocent question from Finlay brought a moment of self-consciousness – and regret – and he found it difficult to respond.

"Are you all right, Bob?" asked Finlay, tugging at his sleeve.

"Aye, I'm fine, Finlay," Bob answered.

But that was not, strictly speaking, true.

# 9

## Wee Feartie

*The Nutcracker* having been a matinée performance, Bob and Finlay stepped off the 23 bus at Canonmills shortly before six that evening.

Finlay looked up at Bob as they made their way towards their front door. "You're really kind, Bob," the small boy said. "I think you're the kindest man in Scotland."

The words touched Bob's heart. "Oh, that can't be true, Finlay," he said, trying to keep his voice even. "There are lots of people who are much kinder."

"Name one," said Finlay.

Bob smiled. "Well, there's one name comes to mind straight away. Big Lou. I don't know anybody kinder than her, come to think of it."

Finlay frowned. "I said *man*. Big Lou's a woman. There are loads of kind women. Loads."

"Are you saying that women are kinder than men?" Bob asked.

Finlay did not hesitate. "Yes. Girls are nicer than boys – everybody knows that."

Bob reached out to put a hand on Finlay's shoulder. He tried to remember what it was like to be nine. Had he thought, when he was nine, that girls were nicer than boys? Did he think *now*, for that matter, that women were nicer than men? It all depended, surely, on what one meant by nice.

He decided to find out more about what Finlay felt.

"Do you prefer to be with girls or with boys?" he asked. "I mean, would you rather spend time with girls than with boys?"

Finlay looked thoughtful. "It all depends," he said. "I like some boys, and I like some girls. It depends on what's going on at the time."

Bob thought about that. *It depends on what's going on at the time.* That was a factor that played a part in any judgement about anything.

"I like to play football with boys," Finlay went on. "But I don't like it when other boys fight."

"Don't girls fight?" asked Bob.

Finlay shook his head. "No. Girls aren't as violent as boys. Everybody knows that."

Bob felt that he had to agree. Women were not as interested in war and destruction as men were. Everybody knew that.

"I like talking to girls," Finlay went on, "because they ask you what you feel about things."

"And boys don't?"

Finlay shook his head. "No. Boys want you to feel the same way as they do – about everything."

Bob smiled. "I see." He paused. "Do some boys laugh at you because you like ballet? Does that happen?"

Finlay shrugged. "Some do. But not many."

Bob thought back to his childhood. Boys had become more civilised, it seemed.

"And the ones that do are usually just trying to look strong," Finlay continued, "when they really aren't – not inside."

"That's true," reflected Bob. "Really strong people don't laugh at things like ballet."

"And you should know," said Finlay. "You're a strongman, aren't you?"

"It's one of the things I do," said Bob. "Only at Highland Games, though."

Then Finlay said, "Those boys down on Bonnington Road were laughing at you, you know. They said you called yourself a strongman when you should really call yourself a fat man."

Bob winced. "You heard them?"

Finlay nodded. "They were laughing at you. Particularly that boy called Jimmy Purves. You know him. He's in P5, but he tells people he's in P7. He's a big fibber. He's the one who said it."

"I hope you ignored him," said Bob, through clenched teeth.

"Yes," said Finlay. "I ignored him – but only after I'd hit him."

Bob stifled a laugh. "You shouldn't hit people, Finlay. You know that. Hitting people solves nothing." That was the official position, of course. In reality, Bob took great pleasure in the thought that Finlay had hit Jimmy Purves. It was so well-deserved. He knew the father – Wally Purves – and had never had much time for him.

"I know," said Finlay. "I know I shouldn't. Sorry, Bob."

Bob winked. "But I bet he didn't like it. I bet he ran away."

"Yes," said Finlay. "Wee feartie."

They had reached the front door. In the kitchen, Big Lou had prepared sausages and chips for their tea, and the three of then sat round the table and discussed *The Nutcracker*.

"The Russians are very musical people," Big Lou said. "Strange, isn't it? They're always upset about something. All their songs are so soulful."

"They never got to the moon," Finlay said.

"Neither did we," said Bob, and laughed.

Big Lou gave Finlay a second helping of chips. Then she offered the pan to Bob, who looked into it, eyeing the crispy slices of fried potatoes. He saw the salt glisten on their surface; he noted the way the gold faded into brown. It was difficult, if not impossible, to imagine anything more delicious.

"These sausages are from Saunderson's," said Big Lou cheerfully. "You won't find a better sausage."

"I like them a lot," said Finlay. "I like sausages and pizza and . . ."

"Anything unhealthy," said Big Lou. "They're all right, but you must remember to eat your broccoli and carrots and so on. We don't want you to turn into a great lump like . . ."

She did not finish.

*Like me?* thought Bob.

"Like Lard O'Connor," Big Lou finished.

"Who's Lard O'Connor?" asked Finlay.

"Was," said Big Lou. "He's deid now. He was a man from Glasgow. Some folk said he was a bit of a rascal."

"Big time," said Bob. "I never met him, but people used to talk about him down in Leith. He went there from time to time when he wasn't in Barlinnie."

Bob pushed the chip pan away. "No thanks, Lou," he said. "I've had enough."

Big Lou looked at him with astonishment. "Are you feeling all right, Bob? I've never known you to turn away a second helping of my French fries."

"Well, I have now," said Bob.

Finlay yawned. "I'm feeling really tired," he said. "Can I go and read in my room?"

"Of course you can," said Big Lou. "Have a bath first, and then straight off to bed."

Now they were alone at the table, and Big Lou turned to Bob. "You sure you're feeling okay, Bob?"

Bob took a deep breath. "I have to lose weight," he said. "I have to."

Big Lou looked at him suspiciously. "Why now? Has somebody said something? Have you been to see the doctor?"

Bob sighed. "Finlay made a remark. And passed on another one."

"Oh dear. He's only a wee boy. I'm sure he doesn't understand what he's saying."

"Oh, he kens fine," said Bob. "And he's right, Lou. I have to. Now. Not tomorrow. Not the day after that. Now."

# 10

*Diet, Height, Statistics*

It was the first time they had discussed the issue of Bob's size, and its implications for his health. As they sat together in the kitchen of the Canonmills flat, Big Lou remembered that they had once talked about the low male life expectancy in parts of Scotland, but that had been a general discussion, and although lifestyle issues had been at its heart, it had not been in any way personal.

The conversation had started with Bob's observation that if you lived in Orkney, and were male, then your life expectancy was eighty.

Big Lou had not been surprised. "Aye, and I think that tells us something, doesn't it? Live on an island, keep calm, look at seabirds, and you'll carry on for a long time."

Bob laughed. "Whereas, live in a city . . ." He paused. "But they drink in Orkney, I imagine. They like a whisky, don't they?"

"Yes," said Lou. "But I suspect they don't drink quite as much as they do in Glasgow."

She looked apologetic. "I'm not picking on Glasgow," she said. "It's a great place. And I know that people are always going on about the statistics there, but they don't, I'm afraid, make very good reading."

Bob nodded. "My pal, Tommy Maguire – he's on the weightlifting circuit – he came from Maryhill. He left us aged forty-eight."

Big Lou shook her head. "So sad. Diet. Smoking. Drinking. Bad housing. Poverty. It all adds up."

Bob corrected her. "No, Lou, in his case it happened in the gym. He was trying to beat his personal record, and the weights crushed him. That was it."

Big Lou sighed. "Poor fellow. If only we could do something about the Scottish diet. We need to get vegetables back into the mainstream. We need to get cigarettes out of the equation. And fizzy orange-coloured drinks."

"They call that *ginger* over there," said Bob. "*Ginger* or *juice*."

"Pure sugar," Lou said. "Before sugar and fats came into it, our diet was healthy enough. We got our protein from fish if we lived near the coast and from rabbits and so on if we lived in the country. We weren't doing badly. Then came sugar . . ."

"And juice."

"Yes, and juice."

"Of course, you do your bacon rolls in the café," Bob pointed out. "Perhaps you should take those off the menu, Lou, and put broccoli burgers in their place. On wholewheat."

Big Lou thought about this. "You may be right, Bob. After all, what is it about bacon that people like so much? It's the smell. We could have some bacon frying in the background – permanently – but never serve any of it. People would be able to appreciate the smell, but not undergo any of the risks."

The conversation might have gone on to Bob's weight, but it did not, as something else had cropped up. But now, after Bob's sudden resolution to embark on a weight-loss programme, the subject could hardly be avoided.

"So, what will you do?" Big Lou asked.

"I'm going to go on a low-carb diet," he answered. "That's the way forward, Lou." He paused. "And I'm going to get help. I'm going to get a personal trainer."

Big Lou looked sceptical. She did not think that people really needed assistance to do the things they needed to do

– all that was required was willpower. Personal trainers, she felt, were no substitute for that.

"Will that be necessary, Bob?" she asked. "All you have to do is get on an exercise bike or one of those running machines. Then it's up to you. Personal trainers don't do the actual exercise for you."

She smiled as she thought of how very wealthy people might perhaps have personal trainers who did their exercise for them. That would be the ultimate in luxury.

"They make up a programme for you," said Bob. "They say: ten minutes on this machine, and then ten minutes on that one. That sort of thing. They're very scientific."

"But I could tell you that," said Lou. "I could come with you to the gym and say, 'Do ten minutes on the rowing machine, Bob.' And I wouldn't charge for my advice."

Bob laughed. "Maybe it's motivation, Lou. Maybe they provide the encouragement that we need."

Big Lou conceded that this was possible. But then she asked, "Are you serious about this, Bob?"

He confirmed that he was. "I'm going to change, Lou. There's going to be a new me – you wait and see."

"But I like the existing you," Big Lou said. "I married a man called Fat Bob, and I'm happy with him. If I'd wanted a thin man, I would have found one. But I didn't. I found a nice fat man, who's just perfect for me. Just perfect."

Bob looked at her with fondness. "And I married somebody called Big Lou," he said. "I married a large-boned lady, a tall lady. If I'd wanted somebody who was petite, I would have found somebody like that. I would have gone over to the west of Scotland and found a short lady there. The average height in the west of Scotland is lower than in the east. Or I would have gone to Dublin. The Irish are slightly shorter than the Scots and the English are taller than both Irish and Scots. And the Dutch, of course, are taller than everybody else."

"So, why bother, Bob?"

Bob looked at intently. "Because I care about you, Lou. And Finlay. When that wee boy said that he wanted me to lose weight, it cut very deep, Lou. It just did."

She understood. "Then I'll stand by you, Bob. No bacon rolls for you from now on. No chips. No butter – we'll use that spread they make. No cakes. No shortbread, Highland or otherwise."

He listened solemnly. "Don't think I'm going to miss any of that, Lou. My mind's made up."

"And where will you get your personal trainer?"

"I already know one," Bob said. "I met him in the pub. He's been a personal trainer for three years now, he tells me."

"What did he do before?"

Bob explained. "He was the man who oiled the Falkirk Wheel," he said.

Big Lou looked surprised. "That's an unusual job."

"Somebody has to do it," said Bob. "If they didn't oil it, it wouldn't really turn, would it?"

Big Lou nodded. "Tell me more about carbs," she said, adding, "Such an interesting subject."

Bob gave her a sideways glance. "I'm serious about this, Lou. Deadly serious."

It was the first time an atmosphere had developed between them, and Big Lou briefly entertained the thought that so many recently married people must have, even if they never confess to it, even if they suppress it the moment it occurs: *have I married the right person?* She wanted her marriage to succeed, and did not like to think that carbs would be the rocks upon which it might flounder.

# 11

## *Kitchen Talk*

While Lou and Bob were sitting in their Canonmills flat, discussing Bob's plan to shed weight, in another kitchen altogether, that of a former farmhouse near Nine Mile Burn, Matthew and Elspeth were busy preparing dinner for the guests who were expected to arrive at eight. It was to be a proper dinner party – of the sort that Elspeth had suddenly realised they had not had for a considerable period.

"Remember," she said, "how we used to have people round for dinner? Remember? And then they would have us round to their place, where we would meet some of the people who had been at our original dinner party for them . . . And so it continued, in ever-widening circles. But people seem to have stopped doing that."

Matthew did remember. In the earlier days of their marriage, that had happened every Saturday night, and sometimes on Fridays too. That was how they kept in touch with people, and how they added to the ranks of their friends and acquaintances. But not any longer, he thought, because . . . He wondered why social habits had changed – if, indeed, they had changed. He voiced his doubts.

"It's possible that there still are dinner parties being held," he said. "It's just that we may not be invited to them."

Elspeth looked up from her task of preparing a smoked trout mousse.

"Do you mean that we're missing out?" she asked.

Matthew smiled. "There's a German word for that, I think. *Ausbremsungsangst.* The fear of not being included in some event or other."

She was doubtful. "You can add *Angst* to anything, can't you, and end up with a new word. German has infinite possibilities."

"There's a Ben Schott book in which he does just that," said Matthew, sneaking a taste of the mousse and deftly missing Elspeth's defensive swat. "*Kraftfahrzeugsinnenausstattungsneugeruchsgenuss.* That's one of his. How's that for a word?"

Elspeth said that she thought such a word unlikely. "People will have lost interest by the time you get to the end of it."

"But that's the problem with German," Matthew remarked. "If you put the verb at the end, you're asking for people to lose interest and wander away before you've finished your sentence. That's what so many German people look a bit anxious. There's probably even a German noun for their condition – fear of people losing interest before you've finished what you have to say. Something-or-other-*angst.*"

"What did that other one mean?" asked Elspeth. "The one that began with *Kraft*?"

"The pleasure you get from the smell of a new car," Matthew replied. "Which does exist, you know. I love getting into a new car and taking a deep breath."

"Fear of one's husband coming into the kitchen and sticking his finger in the trout mousse before you've finished making it," muttered Elspeth.

"I shall try to resist the impulse," he assured her. "Sampling is a form of compliment, of course. With some cooks one might wish *not* to sneak a quick preview. You should be flattered."

She finished her preparation of the mousse and stood back to admire it. Now there was a carrot purée, to which cream needed to be added. After that, small slices of garlic had to be stuck into the lamb joint.

"Anna gave this to me," she said, pointing to the lamb. "She said this will be seriously delicious." Anna was Elspeth's friend from Baddinsgill Farm, her adviser on all things culinary. "I wish I could cook like her."

"You do wonderfully," said Matthew. "I love everything you make." He paused. "I love everything you do, you know. I love . . . I love your entire *Weltanschauung.*"

He stepped forward and planted a kiss on her forehead. "I'm so lucky to have you, you know. I really am."

She looked at him tenderly. "I'm the one who's lucky."

"No, I am."

She kissed him back. "Perhaps we both are."

Matthew looked thoughtful. "Are Scotsmen demonstrative enough?" he asked. "Do we kiss those we love enough, do you think?"

Elspeth shrugged. It was hard enough for women as it was – coping with children, running households, working the same hours as men worked, picking up the pieces here and there: none of that was easy. And to have to cope with being kissed by one's husband in the middle of all that could just be the straw that broke the camel's back.

"Probably not," she said. "But then we women have so many other things on our plate. It's not just that we would discourage such things, it's more a case of having the *time*, so to speak." And then she added, "And the energy."

"Do you need energy to be kissed?"

She thought that you did – and remembered the look that her mother would adopt when her husband kissed her. "My mother used to scrunch her face up," she said. "Like this. All her facial muscles went tense."

"How unromantic."

Elspeth nodded. "Dad gave up in the end. He used to give her little waves with his hand. That was how they got along."

She thought of the bungalow in Comrie, where her parents had lived. She thought of the hills, and of how, in the late summer, some of them turned from green to purple with the heather; and the winding road to St Fillans, and the deep waters of Loch Earn. She thought of her parents, and of the disappointments of their lives, and she wondered whether she had loved them enough.

"People get along," said Matthew. "Somehow."

Elspeth looked at the clock. It was almost eight o'clock. She would need to put the lamb in the oven so that it was ready by the time they sat down to dinner. The carrot purée would just need to be heated up. The peas weren't fresh, but were frozen and were ready in the pot. One should not overcook peas, or they became mushy. She did not want her life to become mushy – it could so easily, what with having triplets and a house to run and . . . Where was life *going*? she asked herself. Where?

She sighed.

"A sigh?" asked Matthew.

"Of anticipation," she said quickly. "I haven't seen Ben for ages and I hardly know his wife."

"She's called Catriona," said Matthew. "She wears glasses with blue frames."

She sighed again. Was this what life was about? Having people to dinner – people who wore blue-framed glasses – and talking about – what would they talk about at the table – German composite nouns? The local nursery school? House prices?

Then she remembered. "Bruce is coming too, of course." That merited a sigh – at the very least.

"He was at school with Ben – the same year, I think," said Matthew

"Poor Bruce," said Elspeth.

"You mean poor Ben."

"No, I don't," said Elspeth. "I meant poor Bruce. He used to be so confident, and now . . ."

". . . and now he's just normal," suggested Matthew.

"Ben was keen for us to invite him," said Elspeth. "He's trying to involve him in some sort of business project he's dreamed up."

"Are those alarm bells I hear ringing?" said Matthew. "I've never trusted Ben."

"Then why did you invite him?"

Matthew frowned. "I thought you did," he replied.

# 12

## Small Talk

One of the first improvements that Elspeth and Matthew had made to their house at Nine Mile Burn when they had purchased it was to build a raised stone patio immediately to the front, at the point at which a rolling, unruly lawn swept up to the main building. This patio could be reached – or *accessed*, as their architect put it – through the large French doors that had been added to the kitchen, opening that room to the light from the south-west. And that light, especially in the summer, had a soft blue quality to it; it was a light, as Matthew once remarked to Angus Lordie, that reminded him of an artistic Scotland of the past, because it was there in the work of Peploe and Fergusson, of Gillies and Cowie. And if light can also be present in poetry and in song it was there in the writings of Hugh MacDiarmid, George Mackay Brown and Sorley MacLean, as much as it was in the songs of Jean Redpath.

"Light," said Angus, "often reveals to us what isn't there, just as much as it shows us what is."

Matthew had wrestled with this. At first, he thought he knew what Angus meant, then he was not so sure. But then enigmatic observations are often helpful precisely because they are enigmatic, and require us to work out what we ourselves think. An illegible signpost may be every bit as useful as one which is easily read, because it makes us think about where we are. And so, after a few moments' hesitation, Matthew simply nodded and said, "Precisely," and went on to discuss something else.

Now, in the early summer evening, with the sun still on the Lammermuir Hills, they stood on that patio, each with a glass of prosecco (Elspeth had drawn the line at champagne, which she considered showy, even if Matthew loved it and argued that he could get it from a supermarket on Gorgie Road for eleven pounds a bottle – and with an easy screw-top substitute for a cork). "You still get the bubbles," he said. "There's absolutely no difference."

"No champagne has a screw top," she said. "It just doesn't. And we can't give our guests eleven-pound champagne," she said, adding, "From a screw-top bottle."

Matthew had accepted that champagne was not to be, and had then chosen a prosecco that cost sixteen pounds a bottle. As he stored two bottles of the wine in the fridge prior to the guests' arrival, he remembered a story he had heard of somebody who had been in Italy and, keen to use his Italian, had gone up to the hotel bar and asked for "three glasses of prosciutto". He mentioned this to Elspeth, who had laughed, and said it could happen to anyone.

"One has to be so careful when using a foreign language," she said. "There's that whole issue of whether President Kennedy inadvertently described himself as a doughnut when he said *Ich bin ein Berliner*. He didn't, of course, and everybody knew what he meant." She paused as she remembered a warning about the literal translation of French. She had heard of somebody warning a friend to hurry lest she be *left behind* in boarding a ferry. "You'll be *gauche derrière*" was not quite right for that.

Ben and Catriona had arrived before Bruce, which had given them the opportunity to talk about the lightning strike in Dundas Street.

"He was considered lucky to be alive," said Ben. "Normally ..."

Catriona interrupted him. "There are plenty of people

who survive a lightning strike. It's a myth that you always succumb."

"I wouldn't like to risk it," said Matthew. He gave a shudder. He had had a morbid fear of electricity all his life, and the thought of being struck by lightning did not appeal. There was also a primitive judgemental aspect to it: people who were struck by lightning were singled out, were picked out for punishment, so to speak, by the gods. That was nonsense, he told himself, as ridiculous as the belief that human illness could be some sort of retribution for bad behaviour. The emperor Justinian had believed that sexual nonconformity caused earthquakes, and there were those who held that lying caused diseases of the jaw. Such nonsense. But, on the other hand, if there was anybody whose vanity might attract the attention of Nemesis, then surely that was Bruce. Hubris was what she was on the lookout for, he thought, but she might also take objection to narcissism, and Bruce had once been described as an "ocean-going narcissist", a description which Matthew had smiled at, but which now he thought should have worried him a bit more.

"Well," said Ben, "if I were Bruce, I'd take it as a warning. And I gather that he probably has."

Elspeth was interested. "Bruce has changed?"

"Definitely," said Ben. "You know what he used to be like. That clove-scented hair gel. That obsession with grooming. He read GQ from cover to cover every month – closely. All those male models and their grooming tips."

"And gadgets," added Matthew. "They have pages of gadget reviews. Electronic gizmos. Cars. Motorbikes. All the accoutrements."

"Why are men obsessed with gadgets?" asked Catriona.

"Perhaps because . . ." began Matthew, only to be interrupted by Catriona, who said that her question was directed to Elspeth.

"I wanted Elspeth's view," she said, giving Matthew a cool glance through her blue-framed spectacles. "Men don't understand their own weaknesses."

Matthew bit his lip. Why was it that women could get away with such sexist remarks when men, if they were to say such a thing, would be immediately condemned?

Elspeth looked at Matthew. She had been struck by Catriona's blue-framed glasses. But she did not like her manner.

She thought: What if I were to say that dinner was cancelled – that I had double-booked and we had to go into town immediately? I could. I could say that.

But Catriona seemed to have moved on from her provocative question. Looking about her, she saw the two old-fashioned deckchairs that had been placed at the far end of the patio, facing the view of the hills. She stared at these for a few moments. The evening sun was upon them, brightening the faded green canvas seating.

"Those chairs," she said, pointing to them.

Elspeth followed her gaze. "They're ancient," she said. "They belonged to Matthew's father."

Catriona absorbed this information. "Do you like Edward Hopper?" she asked.

"The artist?"

"Yes. He painted a marvellous picture – it's one of my favourites. It's called *People in the Sun*, and it shows four or five people sitting in deckchairs just like that, on a patio just like this, looking at the sun. One of the women is wearing a wide-brimmed sun hat; the men are wearing jackets and ties. Men did in those days."

"And?" asked Elspeth.

"Light," said Catriona. "Hopper painted light."

# 13

## Hopper, Loneliness, Greek Revival

Matthew looked at Catriona with interest. He had met her only once before, and she had not made much of an impression on him then. That was possibly because they had exchanged no more than a few words, and he had found out nothing about her. He had not anticipated that she would talk about light and the paintings of Edward Hopper – both subjects in which Matthew had an intense interest and which he rarely had the opportunity to discuss in any depth. Most people, in his experience, thought very little about light they took it for granted, or, at best, were only dimly aware of how important it was for mood and for perception – for everything, really. And now here was Catriona, with her slightly unnerving blue spectacles, raising the subject of light, when he had imagined they might by now be emmeshed in the sort of small talk that characterised Edinburgh dinner parties and from which there was sometimes little relief or prospect of escape.

"Hopper," he said. "I take it that you like him?"

She took a sip of her prosecco. He wished that he had insisted on champagne: somebody who understood the nuances of light might well be expected to appreciate the difference between prosecco and the real thing.

On impulse he leaned forward and whispered to her, "I'm so sorry that isn't champagne. I almost served champagne."

She looked at him over the rim of her glass. "I thought it was," she said.

He smiled. "You're being polite."

She returned his smile. "Possibly. But carbon dioxide is carbon dioxide."

He steered the conversation back to Hopper. "What is it about Hopper that appeals?"

"Everything," she replied. "But the light in particular. It's a sort of yellow, buttery light that I think is rather hard for an artist to capture, but he does."

"I think of him as a painter of loneliness," said Matthew. "I went to an exhibition of Hopper at the Whitney Museum in New York. Have you been there?"

She shook her head. "We're too hard up to go to New York."

Matthew felt embarrassed. "I wasn't being boastful. I wasn't saying 'Oh, la-di-da, when I was in New York' – that sort of thing. There are people in this city who say that, you know, but not me."

"Well, we can't afford it at the moment. Ben says that we might go somewhere next year. He has a project, you see, and it's using all our money."

Matthew nodded. "Money seeps away, doesn't it?"

"Don't tell me."

"Anyway, there was this marvellous exhibition at the Whitney and I went to it. It was all about Hopper and the city. He lived in Washington Square – or thereabouts. You know, near NYU."

She shook her head. "I don't know the geography of New York."

"New York's pretty simple," said Matthew. "It goes from north to south, and from east to west. Edinburgh doesn't do that. Edinburgh's all over the place."

"That's because we've got hills," said Catriona. "There are seven of them, aren't there? New York doesn't have hills."

Matthew nodded. "Our topography is similar to what you find in Athens. In fact, that was one of the reasons why people called Edinburgh the Athens of the North. Although there were more complicated reasons than that." He paused. "There's been a fascinating treatment of this. Iain Gordon Brown's book. He goes into all the reasons why Edinburgh fancied itself as the northern Athens – part of which was the desire to find a role."

Catriona asked why Edinburgh should have been seeking a role. Surely cities, she said, just *were* – they did not have to ask themselves *who* or *what* they were.

"It was because of the Union with England," Matthew said. "Edinburgh suddenly found itself eclipsed by London. All the action, so to speak, was down there, and what was left for Edinburgh? They didn't fancy being a provincial city, and so they thought they would be the Greeks to the new Rome. Hence all those Grecian influences in the architecture of the place.'

"And the Parthenon up on Calton Hill?"

Matthew grinned. "That was meant to be the crowning glory – but it was never finished. How many pillars are there? Twelve – and the architraves – and that's it. A great, purpose-built ruin – a monument to unfinished projects everywhere."

He looked at Catriona. She had a slightly Hopperish look to her. But why? Her clothes? Was she dressed like one of Hopper's women – with their long skirts and that quintessentially 1920s feel to them? The stenographers, the women in those nowhere diners, the women in hotel rooms, looking out of windows. It was loneliness distilled, boiled down, reduced like a sauce at the bottom of the pan.

"Hopper's paintings are so empty," he said. "They have people in them – yes – but the people are all isolated. Even when there are two or three people in one of his paintings, the people are somehow detached from one another."

"Is America a lonely place?" she asked. "Is that what it's like?"

He thought about this. There was a certain loneliness in America, he thought, because it was so large and there were so many people. Did people know one another in the way in which they knew one another in a small country like Scotland? And if they did not, then how could they be anything but lonely?

He opened his mouth to answer her, but then he stopped. Her question had raised a disturbing possibility in his mind – that Scotland was becoming a much lonelier country because we were busy erecting barriers of distrust and suspicion between people. We were making people frightened of one another – frightened of offending others – frightened to express what one might think, because there could be somebody who might disagree with you and berate you for holding an opinion that differed from their own. We were finding ways in which people differed from one another, rather than ways in which they shared an identity. Yes, that was happening – it was happening with alarming speed and intensity. And in its wake, it brought isolation and loneliness and unhappiness. He muttered something, not intending to be overheard, but it was heard by Catriona. "There used to be a great wee country called Scotland," Matthew said. "And we liked one another and were happy, and then . . ."

She looked at him, but he did not finish. Rather, he said, "I find Hopper haunting."

She said, "Would you mind if I asked for more prosecco? I love that stuff. It goes down so easily."

"Not at all."

He looked over to the Lammermuir Hills, and then back at Catriona.

"We are so lucky," he said, as he started off to fetch a bottle.

"Why?"

"To be alive. Now. In this company. With those hills over

there and that sky and being alive in this great empty universe that is itself a great empty Hopper painting, when you come to think of it."

# 14

## Reintroducing Wolves

In his visits to the local library with his grandmother, Nicola, Bertie rarely spent much time in the children's section, with its bright primary colours and diminutive chairs. He was a voracious reader, and required no encouragement to engage with books that normally would not be found on the bedside table of the average, or indeed *any*, seven-year-old boy. So while such tables might be graced with the usual juvenile literature – expurgated, of course, to remove any trace of undesirable authorial attitudes, and given the *nihil obstat* of the censors – in Bertie's case, tales of talking pigs were conspicuously absent. He understood the appeal of such stories to readers younger than himself – his brother, Ulysses, for example, was beginning to show an interest in such a literary diet – but he himself preferred books of greater weight and substance.

These literary tastes had been encouraged by his mother, Irene, who had been much inspired by a book she had come across, *The Literate Baby*. The subtitle of this work had, in fact, caught her eye before the title itself. This was *How to Ensure Your Infant Has the Best Available Start*. That had been very much what Irene wished to do when she embarked upon what she called The Bertie Project. That was on the very day she returned with Bertie to the flat in Scotland Street from the maternity unit, now renamed Arrivals, of the Royal Infirmary of Edinburgh. That change of name, intended to reflect official ambitions to remove the word *mother* from hospital usage, had occasioned some debate both in the hospital and the columns of the local newspaper. Local newspapers, of course, have a tendency to reflect reactionary opinion, and it was no surprise, therefore, that the *Edinburgh Evening News* should have expressed mild surprise that the use of the word *mother* was offensive and that a neutral term, such as *individual,* should be used to refer to those who came to the hospital with the intention of giving birth there to what were previously known as *babies* and were now known in official documents as *emergent persons.* Some uninformed readers had even laughed at this – but there are always ignorant and ill-disposed people about and the health authorities took the view that they could be, and were, ignored.

*Arrivals* was an obvious choice in the sensitive bureaucratic mind, but once again, ignorant opinion had questioned whether this was not redolent of the terminology found in airports, where large signs stated *Arrivals* and, indeed, *Departures.* If people came into the hospital and saw a sign saying *Arrivals,* might they not think that this referred to them, irrespective of their mission, and that this would result in everybody coming to the hospital making their way to what was previously known as the Maternity department? The staff who worked at *Arrivals* would soon find themselves overwhelmed by those with broken arms and similar complaints, along with numerous potential out-patients, in-patients, and visitors.

That objection was considered, but quickly discounted. The average person would understand that this was a hospital, not an airport, and would, as a result, not be confused. Airports consisted largely of duty-free emporia, and these were not normally found in hospitals. At least not yet: if there was already no distinction, in terms of price, between hospital and airport car parks, then might it not be possible, the hospital management asked itself, to create large duty-free sections just inside the hospital entrance? This would have the effect of reassuring and calming people coming to the hospital, as they walked a winding path through tempting displays of expensive perfume, Swiss chocolate, and, of course, numerous obscure brands of whisky. Visitors to the hospital might be provided with small trollies into which they could load their purchases before reaching the point where they were directed to Arrivals (A), Radiology (X) and so on.

The debate had continued for some time, and some of the suggestions were less than helpful, particularly those that pointed out that if there were to be a sign for *Arrivals*, then what about that other important airport sign, *Departures*? To which hospital department would that direct the visitor or the patient? And would that not have the effect of undoing any calming effect achieved by the hospital duty-free experience?

Of course, these issues were yet to arise when Bertie was brought back, an emergent person in arms, to the flat in Scotland Street, to begin the education that would shape his reading interests. Fortunately, he proved receptive to Irene's tuition, and by the age of two he was already reading simple sentences. When he was four, Irene found him reading a copy of the *New York Review of Books* that she had left lying on the kitchen table, and by five he had started on her Penguin *The Complete Psychological Works of Sigmund Freud*. There was obviously much of this that he did not understand, but he nonetheless absorbed a great deal of what he read and was able to talk with some maturity about Freud's famous case of Little Hans and, to a lesser extent, the Wolf Man.

He had been much exercised by wolves, anyway, as he had read the Canadian author Farley Mowat, who knew a great deal about lupine affairs, as well as a number of Jack London's tales of the far north. Bertie had read, too, of the plans of those who would reintroduce the wolf into Scotland, and had discussed this at some length with his father. Where exactly would these wolves be released? According to what Bertie had read in the papers, there was some opposition in the Highlands to the release of wolves there, with more than one member of the Scottish Parliament representing a Highland community, expressing the view that people in the Highlands were fed up with proposals to land them with everything for which a place could not be found elsewhere. This included nuclear waste, satellite launching pads, and, occasionally, high-risk prisoners.

Could wolves not be released in Glasgow? Bertie asked. There had been few rewilding efforts there, and there were several large parks where wolves could perhaps make their dens unnoticed. There was the issue of food source, of course, but Bertie felt that there were always sufficient abandoned half-full fast-food boxes to provide sustenance for wild creatures, and these could be supplemented by official feeding programmes. After all, rewilding came at a cost, and if we were to have reintroduced beavers and wolves, then we should be prepared to sacrifice a few salmon, ancient trees and newborn lambs.

Bertie's father, Stuart, had smiled at this suggestion. "I'm not sure that they would want wolves in Glasgow," he said. "They have their own ideas over there, you know."

Bertie was sure they did. He admired Glasgow and its independent-minded inhabitants. To him, Glasgow represented freedom, and wolves would love that – of course they would.

# 15

## *Everything's Ruined – It's Official*

Of course he loved Glasgow, with or without any introduced wolves, but Bertie knew that the chances of his moving there were slender, and that for the foreseeable future he would be in Edinburgh, in Scotland Street, with his family. On reaching the age of eighteen he could move to Glasgow of his own accord and without his mother's permission, and he never doubted for a moment that he would do just that. He had even made enquiries about the purchase of an Edinburgh to Glasgow one-way rail ticket for eleven years in the future, but was told by the rail authorities that booking for those trains was not yet open, and it would be best to come back closer to the time. He would do that, he assured the incredulous voice on the other end of the line, and the conversation had come to an end. He felt, though, that in making this preliminary enquiry he had at least done something to advance the course of his freedom, to lay down a marker, in a sense, even if the day of liberation itself was an impossibly long way off.

His domestic circumstances, of course, were not quite as bad as they might be and were certainly an improvement on those that had prevailed in the first six years of his life. During that period, Bertie had been obliged to put up with an ambitious and somewhat demanding mother, whose programme for her young son included Italian *conversazione* sessions, saxophone lessons, yoga classes and weekly psychotherapy. But then his mother, Irene, had gone off to Aberdeen, and the intervention of his grandmother, Nicola, had brought freedom and reason to Bertie's small hearth. Life had taken an immediate turn for the better: Nicola had read to him from books that would never have been given Irene's imprimatur – books such as *Treasure Island, Kidnapped*, and, of course, *Scouting for Boys*; she had allowed him to watch television, including ancient films with titles such as *Lassie the Wonder Dog* and *Well Done, Secret Seven*; and, unlike his mother, she had not insisted he wear crushed strawberry dungarees. This gave Bertie a glimpse of how small boys might lead their lives in Glasgow, where yoga and psychotherapy were virtually unheard of, and where freedom was not an impossible dream but an everyday reality.

Now his mother had returned, but although she was intermittently back in Edinburgh, and although she and Stuart were trying to make a go of their relationship once more, Stuart had very wisely stipulated that when Irene came back from Aberdeen she should live separately. This was in a flat in nearby Gayfield Square, recently purchased as an investment by his mother, Nicola, who was now living in Scotland Street with her son and the two boys.

"Let's see if we can navigate our way back into a proper relationship," Stuart said to Irene. "Step by step. And my mother, of course, mustn't be messed about. She's given up a lot to look after the boys, and we can't ask her to move out just like that."

Irene, in her new mood of reasonableness, had acceded to this request. "I fully understand, Stuart," she said. "Let's not hurry anything. We can't get rid of your mother . . . ask her, rather, to move out later on. Everything in due course." And then had added, for emphasis, "*Davvero* and *assolutamente*."

Bertie was pleased to have his mother back in Edinburgh, but was, at the same time, relieved that she would be staying a few blocks away. "It's just round the corner, Mummy," he said to Irene. "And it's Georgian."

Irene had moved some of her possessions to the Gayfield Square flat. It was a spacious flat, and since nothing had been said about payment, she imagined that she would be living rent-free. It had the advantage, too, of being directly opposite Valvona & Crolla, the delicatessen on Elm Row where she had long been accustomed to buying her sun-dried tomatoes, San Daniele ham, and Tuscan olive oil – all of which formed part of her staple diet. It suited her very well to be back in Edinburgh, where she felt there was work for her to do. And being in Edinburgh had the additional advantage of assuaging the guilt that had been building up within her from not seeing enough of her two young sons. They were well looked-after, of course, but she was not at all sure that Stuart's mother, with her old-fashioned ideas on child-raising, was the best of influences. No, there was work for her to do, and over the coming months she would tackle it.

Not only had Bertie's existence been improved by the dilution of Irene's influence, but his social life had been transformed by the influence of Ranald Braveheart Macpherson, a boy of his own age with whom he had formed a firm friendship. Ranald, who now lived in Albert Terrace in Morningside, liked nothing more than to plan with Bertie the various adventures that they had in the garden or, occasionally, on short, unauthorised expeditions further afield. Now, on that Saturday morning, he was waiting at the door for Bertie to be delivered by Nicola for a long-arranged play-date.

"There's something I need to talk to you about," said Ranald, shortly after Nicola had dropped Bertie off. "Something really confidential."

"You can tell me whatever you like, Ranald," Bertie assured his friend.

"It's about my birthday party," said Ranald. "I've been talking to my mummy about it and she says I have to invite Olive."

Bertie groaned. "Are you sure, Ranald? Olive will spoil everything. You may as well not have a birthday at all."

"I know," said Ranald. "But it gets worse. My mummy has gone and invited her already, and also Pansy . . ."

"Oh no," said Bertie. "That's really bad, Ranald."

"And Galactica MacFee," Ranald complained. "You know her. She's that girl with the stuck-up nose. Her."

"Your party will be a disaster," said Bertie sadly. "I'm sorry, Ranald, but I think it will."

Ranald stared at his friend. Tears were welling up in his eyes. "I've been looking forward to my party, Bertie," he said. "Now everything's ruined – it's official."

"True," said Bertie.

Then Bertie had an idea. "We could write to their mummies, Ranald. We could write letters pretending to be from your mummy and telling them the party's cancelled. Then it will be just you and me and Tofu. And if Tofu forgets to come, it would be just the two of us, which would be even better."

"We could try," said Ranald. "Can you write the letter? Your handwriting's much neater than mine."

"And you can't spell," Bertie observed.

"True," said Ranald. "Just write: Dear Mrs MacFee, I regret to say that Ranald's party has been cancelled due to . . ."

"Leprosy," suggested Bertie.

"Due to leprosy," continued Ranald. "Please tell Pansy's mummy. And Olive's too. So sorry. Maybe some other day. Yours sincerely, Mrs Macpherson. How about that, Bertie?"

"Perfect," said Bertie.

# 16

## *Galactica's Debut*

While the Zinoviev letter is an example of a forged document that had a marked effect on the course of political history, the short note dictated by Ranald Braveheart Macpherson and painstakingly written out by Bertie had no impact at all, other than to cause a brief outburst of mirth on the part of Georgina MacFee, to whom the letter had been addressed. "Leprosy!" she exclaimed. "Where on earth do these children get their ideas?"

The sharp-eared Galactica, who missed very little of what went on in the MacFee household, affected surprise. "Who's said anything about leprosy, Mummy?" she asked. She had, in fact, steamed open the letter before her mother opened it – a practice she had learned about on a children's television programme and that she frequently used to open items of correspondence addressed to her mother.

"Oh, it's just some childish prank," replied her mother. "Presumably Ranald himself thinks it funny. Nothing to worry about, darling."

"Boys are so stupid," said Galactica. "And some boys are stupider than others."

Georgina remonstrated with his daughter – but only mildly. "Not all boys are stupid, darling," she said. "Some may be, admittedly, but remember that there are many who are not. Look at Daddy, for instance."

Galactica cast a quick glance at her father, and then looked away again. "I really want to go to Ranald's party, Mummy," she said. "Everyone's going to be there."

"Of course you're going," Georgina assured her. "I spoke to Ranald's mother, and she was delighted to invite you. She said that it was very important that Ranald and his friends played with some of the girls." She paused. "Who is Ranald friendly with, do you think?"

Galactica looked thoughtful. "There's a boy called Bertie Pollock," she said. "They're always playing together. Ranald looks up to him, I think. I can't see why."

"People get different things from friendship," said Georgina. "They see things in others that, well, we may not see ourselves. I'm sure that Bertie is a very nice little boy. As is Ranald." She paused. "I'm so glad that you're happy in Edinburgh. I thought that you might miss Stirling awfully, but here you are, settling in so nicely, and Daddy and I are very pleased."

"It's okay," said Galactica.

"Well, birthday parties always help, don't they?" said her mother. "But let's take a little peek in your wardrobe and see which outfit you'd like to wear to Ranald's party."

And now Galactica stood on the threshold of the Macpherson house in Albert Terrace, on the very edge of Morningside, the first of Ranald's guests to arrive. From within the house, Ranald stared out with a growing sense of dismay; the letter had not worked, he realised, for here was Galactica, and presumably Olive and Pansy would not be far behind. The situation was bleak, and for a few moments he considered running into the garden and taking refuge in the shed, which could be locked from inside. If he did that, he might be safe enough while the party went on without him. None of them – with the exception of Bertie – had come to see him, and would be kept quite happy with the ice cream and cake that was being provided for the guests. But if he hid, then Bertie would face dealing with the guests without him, and even if Tofu and Larch turned up, they would be little help. No, taking refuge in the shed would be tantamount to running away in the face of the enemy, and Ranald, whose instincts were loyal, was not prepared to do that.

Galactica duly breezed in.

"So, this is where you live, Ranald," she said, looking about her. "Sad."

Ranald frowned. "There's nothing wrong with our house, Galactica," he said.

Galactica smiled tolerantly. "Oh, I'm sure it suits you, Ranald Braveheart Macpherson, but I'm not sure that I'd care to live in a house that shared its walls with other houses."

Albert Terrace was, as the name suggested, a row of terraced houses, and as such, the walls were mutual. They were, however, constructed of stone and were of Georgian proportions, making it one of the most sought-after and attractive streets in Edinburgh. To the south, each house had a substantial walled garden, falling away to Morningside down below. From the windows to the rear, the Pentlands could be seen, with their promise of a romantic hinterland of gentle blue hills. Ranald was proud of his house, and Galactica's opening foray cut deep.

"We have nice people living next to us," he said defensively. "And George Watson's is just at the other end of the road."

"Hah!" said Galactica. "George Watson's College!"

"And they have a pipe band," said Ranald.

Galactica waved a dismissive hand. "Oh, don't talk to me about the bagpipes," she said airily.

Ranald tried to stand his ground. "Why not?" he asked.

"They make a very tiresome noise," said Galactica. "I don't mind being Scottish, Ranald, but I don't think being Scottish is an excuse to make such a loud noise, do you?"

She looked about her. "If I lived here, Ranald," she said. "I would paint this room a different colour."

Ranald bit his lip. "What's wrong with white, Galactica? Lots of people have white walls."

Galactica laughed. She had a special laugh – a high-pitched

trill – that she employed on occasion to dismiss especially trivial questions.

"White is very boring, Ranald,' she said. "I'm not saying *you're* boring. I'm not saying that. All I'm saying is that your house is painted a boring colour. That's different, you see."

The doorbell rang. "Other guests," said Galactica. "You'd better go and let them in before they change their mind and go away, Ranald."

Ranald Braveheart Macpherson made his way through the hall towards the front door. He looked at the walls about him. They were white. He had never thought about that – to him they had simply been walls. He hated Galactica. He had hated her the first time he saw her. She was utterly, completely hateful. Bertie would hate her too, he thought, because Bertie was the opposite of Galactica. Bertie was kind. Bertie had never said anything – not once – about his walls being boring, even if he secretly thought it, which Ranald thought he did not.

Ranald's mother was already at the door. "Well, well," she said. "How nice to see you, Olive. And this is your friend Pansy, I believe. Hello, Pansy. You look very pretty in that dress. And you do, too, Olive."

She turned to her son. "Isn't this nice, Ranald?" And then to the guests she said, "Galactica's already here, girls."

Olive received this information in silence. She hated Galactica. Pansy hated Galactica too. This party's toast, thought Olive. *Toast.* It was enough to make one feel sorry for Ranald Braveheart Macpherson, she told herself. Or almost sorry. She despised his spindly knees, of course. She always had. Pansy had too, and they had often discussed them. "Such a shame," said Pansy. "It's so sad to see thin knees like that on a boy. They really ruin his life chances, Olive."

And Olive had agreed.

# 17

## *Initial Exchanges*

From a discreet corner, pretending to take an interest in the contents of a bookshelf, Bertie watched Galactica enter the room in which Ranald Braveheart Macpherson's guests were now assembled. Ranald himself was the perfect host, standing at the door, solemnly receiving his birthday presents, expressing his thanks and placing them on a table behind him. On coming into the room, Galactica had glanced around to take in the guest list before deciding who might deserve her company. Bertie, keen to make himself as inconspicuous as possible, peered ever more intently at the bookshelf. Galactica, though, had already spotted him and he was obliged to acknowledge her nod in his direction. Then, to his relief, she spotted a boy standing near the window and swept across the room to engage him in conversation. Bertie recognised this boy as Moss, who, like Galactica, had recently joined his class. Bertie was unsure what to make of Moss, who had shown signs of gravitating to Tofu's camp and who therefore would have to be treated with a degree of circumspection. If he could occupy Galactica's attentions, though, then that at least would divert attention that might otherwise be focused on Bertie and Ranald – and that was something for which to be grateful.

Moss, however, proved to be no more than a temporary distraction, for now Galactica noticed Olive and Pansy standing near the table on which Ranald's mother had laid out plates of food, including one of iced biscuits in the shape of various animals – always a popular item at a birthday party. Detaching herself from Moss, she strode across the room to join the two other girls. In the safety of his corner, Bertie swallowed hard as he imagined the scene that might ensue.

Although they were in the same class at school, Galactica and Olive had yet to have a conversation. Looks had been exchanged, and strategies planned, but the opportunity of a face-to-face encounter had yet to present itself. From Galactica's point of view, this phoney war was something to be welcomed, as it gave her the time to recruit allies before battle was joined. Galactica preferred to have boys on her side: Moss was a possibility, although he was perhaps a bit insipid; more promising was Socrates Dunbar, another new arrival in the class, who seemed to her to have all the qualities expected of a useful lieutenant. Once she was flanked by such supporters, the odds would be stacked against Olive, who had Pansy alone to provide backup in her campaigns.

Now the moment had arrived when hostilities might begin between the two factions – for Galactica, even without attendants, clearly amounted to a faction. This was the moment when the *casus belli*, even if now purely hypothetical, would at last become real.

The first fusillade was to come from Galactica. "So, Olive," she said. "I see that Ranald has invited you after all."

Olive had not been expecting this and did not have time to conceal her puzzlement. "He was always going to invite me," she responded testily. "Why wouldn't he?"

Galactica assumed the expression of one who wished to protect another from an uncomfortable truth.

"Oh, of course, of course," she said. "It's just that I was under the impression that Ranald Braveheart Macpherson was moving on. I was obviously wrong – thank heavens."

Pansy stepped forward – and quite properly so, as her role was to provide deep defence, now so clearly needed.

"Moving on from what?" she challenged. "Who said that Ranald needed to move on?"

"Oh, I didn't say that anybody in particular said that," Galactica replied. "I must have heard something, though – you know how you hear people say things, and you don't remember who exactly it was." She paused. Fixing Pansy with a penetrating stare, she continued, "You must tell me your name, by the way." She knew perfectly well who Pansy was, but this was not an opportunity to be missed.

Pansy seethed.

"Don't tell her your name, Pansy," Olive instructed.

"So, you're Pansy," Galactica said brightly. "I've heard people talking about you."

As this unsettling remark sank in, Galactica changed tack. "I must introduce you to some of the boys," she said graciously. "I'm sure they'd like to meet you."

"We already know them," snapped Olive. "I've known these boys for ages."

Galactica raised an eyebrow. "Even Bertie?"

Olive nodded emphatically. "Of course I know Bertie," she said. "Bertie and I go back a long way, I can tell you."

This was the signal for Pansy to fire the artillery round that would surely silence this *parvenu*. "And I can tell you something, Galactica," she began, her voice full of triumph. "Bertie and Olive are engaged. They've been engaged for years. Everybody knows that – the whole school, in fact. You can ask anybody."

"Engaged?" asked Galactica. "My, my – that's old-fashioned. That's really quaint, Posy."

The provocation hit home. "Pansy," said Pansy, through gritted teeth.

"Of course. Pansy, then. It's such a pity that engagement doesn't count for anything these days."

Olive rose to the bait. "What do you mean by that?" she asked.

"Oh, I think that girls mean it when they say they're

engaged," Galactica explained. "But it's different for boys. They say that they're engaged purely to keep other girls from asking them to marry them. Everybody knows that – I'm surprised you didn't."

"Bertie isn't like that," said Olive, her voice rising in anger. "Bertie is the nicest boy in Scotland. He'd never pretend to be engaged if he didn't mean it."

"Olive's right," chimed Pansy. "So you just shut your face, Galactica."

"Temper, temper!" Galactica chided.

This was too much. Who was this person from Stirling to accuse Pansy of losing her temper? Pansy's response was sudden and dramatic – and a blatant escalation. Taking a step forward, she gave Galactica a push. This provoked Galactica to seize one of Pansy's plaits and pull at it sharply, causing her head to jerk to one side. Olive then kicked Galactica firmly, and painfully, in the shins.

Ranald Braveheart Macpherson's mother happened to come into the room at the time and witnessed this unseemly breakdown of order. Rushing forward, she separated the three brawling girls. "Girls," she admonished. "This is *not* the way we behave in Edinburgh,"

Bertie watched in horror. This was worse than he had anticipated, and if this was only round one, what would round two be like? Of course, he did not realise at the time that he himself would be drawn into this unseemly dispute, no matter how determined he was not to get involved. Neutrality, though, is more frequently aspired to than achieved – not that Bertie was to know this, just yet.

# 18

## *Icelandic Words*

Angus and Domenica had both been thinking of the curious incident of the man in the rhododendrons. Their initial discussion of what had happened on that evening when Angus had been approached in the Drummond Place Gardens had been sidetracked by a discussion of the appropriate plural of the noun *rhododendron*. Issues of nomenclature can derail, or at least cause deviation in, even the most important exchanges; indeed, disputes of this nature can themselves be the cause of the disagreement in the first place. A contested place name in a territorial dispute may be the spark that ignites the tinder of irredentist claims, as when one faction claims the priority of their place name while another, with an equal sense of entitlement, asserts that their preferred choice has the backing of history, common usage, the law and, in the final analysis, of God himself.

Scotland has not been immune to internecine argument. Scottish history is characterised by a great deal of bad behaviour of one sort or another, and some of this still casts a shadow. The Massacre of Glencoe – now, for reasons of tact, widely referred to as the Misunderstanding of Glencoe – is an egregious example of the sort of thing that happened in pre-Enlightenment Scotland, but it is not the only one. Bad behaviour at a dinner party was also manifested on the occasion when King James II invited the eighth Earl of Douglas to dinner in Stirling Castle. Guests do not expect to be stabbed twenty-six times by their host and his friends, and then unceremoniously thrown out of the window. That, however, is what appears to have happened.

Yet such inflammatory incidents as the Misunderstanding of Glencoe and the Defenestration of Stirling sometimes seem to pale in their effect when compared with the arguments surrounding the pronunciation of Gullane, a small coastal town outside Edinburgh.

The spelling of Gullane suggests that it should be pronounced *gull* (as in seagull) and then *an* (as in the name Anne). The correct pronunciation, though, is *gill* (as in a fish's gill), followed by the agreed *an*. This is on the basis of the origins of the word, which are generally agreed to be Welsh, since, to complicate matters, it was that form of Celtic language that was spoken in the area when the settlement first came into existence. In spite of the linguistic evidence, there are those who insist on what they see as the demotic pronunciation. This leads to significant distress on the part of the linguistic purists and, on more than one occasion, has resulted in the trading of sharp words in the bar at Muirfield, one of the local golf clubs.

Angus and Domenica were generally above such things, but nonetheless spent some time debating whether, in his narration of the encounter in Drummond Place Gardens, Angus should refer to "the man in the *rhododendrons*" or "the man in the *rhododendra*". The discussion was amicable, and showed none of the animus that surfaces when the pronunciation of Gullane is debated. Yet it did take some time. Angus took the view that even if the correct form were to be *rhododendra* – since the word is a Greek neuter noun – common usage was, in this case, to be preferred, and that favoured *rhododendrons*. Domenica listened to his argument courteously, but pointed out that if common usage were to be the deciding factor in such matters, then where did that leave us with the pronunciation of Gullane? If it were the case – and she thought it probably was – that more people said *gull* than said *gill*, then *gull* should be considered correct.

Angus saw this, and acknowledged that it raised major issues. "I suppose that language *does* change," he said. "If it didn't, we'd all still be speaking . . . well, whatever it was that we spoke a long time ago. In our case, Pictish, perhaps – not that anybody can be absolutely certain what that was."

"A Celtic language," said Domenica quickly.

"Well, we'd still be speaking that if we refused to recognise change." He paused. "Can you imagine being a linguistic purist and discovering that everybody around you has started to talk a different language – and you feel you have to stick to what you think is the correct form. Imagine that."

Domenica smiled. "One might imagine a Roman stick-in-the-mud insisting on Latin even when all his neighbours have switched to Italian. Or a Norwegian insisting on Old Norse when everybody else in Oslo or Bergen was chatting away happily in Norwegian."

Angus looked thoughtful. "Have you ever thought about Icelandic?" he asked. "That sticks to very old forms, I believe. And they make up new words to cope with the modern world. They try to keep loan words out."

Domenica said that she sympathised with the preservation of languages that were threatened by the tsunami of English. "We lose so much when words die," she said. "We lose a particular way of looking at the world. It's like losing . . ." She searched for the metaphor. "Like losing a rare flower."

Now she remembered reading about an Icelandic word that was just that – a rare flower. "There's a word in Icelandic – I can't recall exactly what it is – but it's a single word and it refers to that time before dawn each day when there is just enough light to see your sheep."

But then, to the surprise of both of them, the word came back. It had been lodged in her mind, one of her half-handful of Icelandic words, it seemed, and now it returned, in all its poetry. "*Sauðljóst,*" she said. And she repeated it, and Angus uttered it too, as one might respond in a liturgy.

"That's all the Icelandic I know," she said. "Other than *ut*, which means *out*, and sounds just like the Scottish *oot*."

"But they'll say *greet* for cry, I imagine," said Angus. "Just as in Scots – and all the other Scandinavian languages, I think."

Domenica remembered something else. "And don't they have an Icelandic Naming Committee that stops you calling your baby an un-Icelandic name? I believe they do."

Angus considered this. It seemed illiberal to prevent people calling their children what they wished to call them, but a stock of common names made for a sense of belonging, of association. And the more we split ourselves off from those around us – the more we asserted our individuality – the lonelier we became. That was what Angus thought.

"Rhododendrons," he muttered.

# 19

## *The Rhododendron Man*

"Yes," said Domenica, putting Icelandic linguistics out of her mind for the moment. "What are you going to do, Angus? That man in the gardens said he'd be back in a week, and that's today, isn't it?"

Angus nodded. "It is. I assume he meant ten o'clock tonight. That's when we met before. It'll be getting dark then."

"And I think he needs darkness," remarked Domenica. "The original Deep Throat did, didn't he? He skulked in the shadows of an underground car park."

Angus shivered. There was something about this that made him feel distinctly uncomfortable. There was the cloak-and-dagger aspect of it, of course – what sort of person thinks it necessary to hide in a rhododendron bush, of all places? And then there was the issue of mistaken identity. The Rhododendron Man, as he now thought of him, was labouring under a fundamental misapprehension. He believed that he was talking to Magnus Linklater, who had, in fact, once lived in Drummond Place and who would, in the past, have been one of those who strolled in the gardens. Presumably he had singled out Magnus as a suitable recipient of some confidence or other. It was not uncommon for people who wanted to get things into the press to pass information to a journalist informally, and sometimes even clandestinely – a tip-off, as such approaches were called. Journalistic ethics would prevent the revealing of sources in such a case – an important protection for the whistle-blower. But was it necessary to hide in rhododendrons to do that? Was that not just a bit too theatrical?

But more than that, there was the question of mistaken identity. If strangers mistook you for somebody else, then surely you had a moral duty to let them know that you were not the person they took you to be. That was basic good manners, after all. And it was not difficult: all you had to say was *I think you're mistaking me for somebody else.* That sort of thing happened all the time, and the only thing to do was to avoid further embarrassment by correcting the mistake. A failure to do that amounted to deliberate and culpable deception – it was as simple as that.

So Angus said, "I suppose I should tell him."

Domenica was silent.

"I'll go this evening," Angus continued. "I'll take Cyril. And when he appears, I'll say, *Look, I'm not Magnus Linklater – I'm Angus Lordie.* That's what I'll say."

Domenica looked out of the window. "A pity," she said.

Angus frowned. "A pity? Why?"

Domenica shrugged. "It's rather intriguing. I'd love to know what he has to tell you."

Angus hesitated. "Why?" he asked.

"Well," explained Domenica, "don't you sometimes get the impression that our lives lack drama? Intriguing things happen to other people, but not, it seems, to us."

Angus thought about this. "I think my life is eventful enough," he said. "I'm not sure that I want to spice it up."

Domenica smiled. "Do you really think it's eventful? When did anything dramatic happen in our existence, Angus?"

Angus was about to answer, but he stopped. His life had its saliences, he felt, but what exactly were they? Now that Domenica had asked the question, he found the answer dispiriting.

"Maybe not a great deal happens here," he said. "But do we mind?"

"Oh, I don't *mind*," said Domenica, "but I just wonder whether we're missing out. That's all."

Angus closed his eyes. Life was slipping through his fingers – there was no doubt about that. What did Auden say? *In headaches and in worry, vaguely life leaks away* . . . That was so true, and yes, Domenica was right: nothing really exciting happened to either of them. Now he opened his eyes, turned to her and said, "Should I just hear what he has to say? Should I hear him out, and then tell him that he's got the wrong person?"

Domenica nodded. "You could do that," she said. "And as long as you tell him, you won't have done anything wrong."

Angus was not so sure. It seemed to him that he would have obtained information – whatever it proved to be about – under false pretences. But then, on the other hand, he had not pretended anything to anybody. All he had done was to go for a walk in the Drummond Place Gardens. And if you did that and somebody happened to emerge from the rhododendron bushes to impart some confidence, then that wouldn't be the result of anything you did. You might as well blame somebody for listening to the birds singing in the trees.

A moral philosopher, of course, could have disposed of that argument. There was indeed a moral distinction between action and inaction, but it was rarely as stark as people might believe it to be, and nor did it exculpate as readily as one might imagine. But Angus was not in a mood to entertain these complexities, and Domenica's description of his life as uneventful had seemed to him to be a sort of reproach.

Now he made up his mind. "I'll go," he said. "I'll go and find out what this man wants to tell me."

Domenica looked pleased. "I must say, I think that's a good idea. It'll probably be some ridiculous piece of nonsense, and we'll all have a good laugh."

"On the other hand," Angus cautioned, "it could be something really serious."

Domenica might have admitted that it could, but now that

Angus had made his decision, she did not want him to change his mind.

He read quietly until the time came to fetch Cyril's lead and leave the flat. He had been immersed in a book about espionage, and it occurred to him it was perfectly possible that the man in the rhododendrons was somehow involved in the murky world of spies. There were spies in Scotland – there had to be – as Scotland occupied a strategically significant position in the North Atlantic, with hostile submarines always prowling around her shores. Could this man have something to do with all that – an agent who needed to . . . come in from the cold? No, that was a bit of romantic nonsense. This would never be anything as colourful as that. At the most, this might be about some issue pertaining to the Gardens Committee, or the local community council. It would be a damp squib, a storm in a teacup . . . there was language enough available to express utter insignificance, and as Angus made his way downstairs, with Cyril panting at the end of his lead, he tried to think of just the right metaphor to describe what was about to happen.

# 20

## *Eheu Fugaces*

Cyril required no encouragement. If the canonical hours divide our human day precisely – matins, prime, terce, etc. – then the canine day has its own divisions, less inflexible, perhaps, but quite as important for dogs and their owners: *food, walk, food, squirrels* . . . The last ritual of the day for Cyril was this evening outing with Angus, after which he would sleep contentedly in the kitchen until disturbed by Domenica when she made the morning tea. On this final walk of the day, not much would happen, as the squirrels who inhabited the gardens tended to be asleep in their dreys, and there was rarely any sign of the cats who were such a constant affront during the day. There were foxes, of course – one in particular, a scourie-looking vixen that padded down from the Queen Street Gardens – but she and Cyril paid little attention to one another. If anything, Cyril felt a vague sympathy for foxes: he acknowledged them as poor relatives, not as well-placed as he and his fellow dogs were in their social contract with humans. Foxes skulked; foxes lurked almost apologetically; foxes nipped at the heels of life; there was little to admire, Cyril thought, in the bearing of a fox.

Angus had a key to the gate of the Drummond Place Gardens. The possession of a key to one of the gardens was a highly-prized privilege in the New Town. While Edinburgh had generous swathes of public park, the formal gardens within the Georgian town were communally owned by the proprietors of the flats and houses surrounding them. The gardens were circumscribed by railings and access was through locked gates, keys being given to those who paid their dues to the local residents' committees. It was these committees that arranged the maintenance of the gardens and, importantly, made the rules that governed the use of the gardens. Entitlement to a key was a legal matter, dictated in the wording of documents of title. Broadly speaking, it depended on proximity. On these grounds, those who lived in the further reaches of Scotland Street would have no claim to the use of the Drummond Place Gardens, even if Scotland Street was a contiguous street. Similarly, the residents of Cumberland Street, the beginning of which was only a few yards away, could only gaze longingly over the railings at the bucolic delights on the other side. These people were keyless, and could only imagine what it might be like to be able to stroll on the well-kept paths, tantalisingly just out of their reach.

There were those who considered such a system unconscion able. Nature was to be shared, not denied to others, and these critics believed that the New Town gardens should be opened to the broader community rather than remain private preserves. Such sentiments are attractive in their communitarianism, and their generosity, but the defenders of current arrangements had their response ready: the gardens were already communal – it's just that they were communal in a very local way.

That was a broader and more remote issue: what was immediate and troublesome were specific claims of entitlement from those just outside the existing boundaries. If a flat had windows overlooking Drummond Place, even with no door onto the Place, then would its owner or tenant be entitled to a key to the gardens? Every rule of entitlement has its hard cases – those who fall just outside existing boundaries but who seem to be almost indistinguishable from those within. Angus and Domenica were a marginal case, but their flat had in the past been allocated a key, and this historical entitlement had been left undisturbed.

As he approached the gardens that night, Angus wondered whether the Rhododendron Man was *entitled* to be in the gardens at all. If he was, then he must be a local resident, and if he was a local resident, then why did he feel it necessary to hide in the bushes? If he showed his face at all – even if partly obscured by foliage – then he would be recognisable as a local and any attempt at anonymity would be futile. If, on the other hand, he was an interloper – somebody from elsewhere altogether – then the question arose as to how he got in. The railings were high enough to deter most and would require a stepladder to surmount. It would be possible, though, to reverse a vehicle – a van, perhaps – close enough to the railings, and then jump from the roof of the van into the gardens on the other side. That would be quite a jump, though, and Angus thought it unlikely.

Did he have a stolen key? That was possible, Angus supposed. There had been talk of illegal keys – copied from legitimate ones and shamelessly circulated amongst those whose application for access had been turned down. Indeed, there had been a case not all that long ago where a member of the Gardens Committee had observed a person, known to live in Heriot Row, blatantly letting himself into the gardens with a key that he could not have been entitled to possess. This had led to a challenge that had quickly deteriorated into a slanging match, with the intruder making offensive remarks about property prices being higher in Heriot Row than in Drummond Place, and suggesting that people in Drummond Place should consider themselves fortunate to be visited by people from Heriot Row, who had access, anyway, to the Queen Street Gardens, which were more extensive and in which this sort of rude interrogation was unlikely to occur.

Angus slipped his key into the gate, and it was at this point he noticed something. The gate had been wedged open – a small twig had been lodged in the locking mechanism. This

meant he found that his key was unnecessary. The conclusion
he reached was a disturbing one: the Rhododendron Man had
a collaborator on the inside – somebody with a key.

He looked about him. Cyril, at the end of his leash, uttered
a low growl. Something was amiss, and Angus felt fear brush
against him – a soft touch, but still unmistakably one of fear.
It was ridiculous, he thought. Meeting a stranger at night in
Drummond Place Gardens was something that an established
portrait painter did not do; not a former member of the
Scottish Arts Club committee, and . . . He stopped himself.
Was that how he saw himself? Was that what he had become?
Where was the bohemian artist, the natty dancer at the art
college dances, the regular at Milnes Bar? Where had all that
gone? The answer came to him immediately. The same place
that the youth of all of us goes.

# 21

## *They Must Be Stopped*

Angus glanced at his watch. If the man in the shadows was punctual, then he and Cyril had at least half an hour to kill before their appointed encounter. He did not mind this, though, as he would be able to complete several circuits of the perimeter path before positioning himself near the shrubs from which the man had previously appeared. That would give Cyril the exercise he needed and would, at the same time, allow Angus to survey any comings or goings that could throw a light on the provenance of his secretive interlocutor. And so the two of them set off, Cyril pulling at his leash and panting enthusiastically, having recovered his sense of purpose after his initial suspicious growl.

They had completed a half-circuit of the path when Angus heard a noise behind him. Although he could not be sure, the sound seemed to him to be that of footsteps – of crunching on the rough sand of the path. He slowed his pace: the sound behind him stopped, but then resumed. He was being followed.

His first reaction was to spin round and confront whoever it was who was behind him. Edinburgh was a safe city, and it was unusual for anybody to be robbed or assaulted on the streets. Yet such things did happen, every now and then, and it was just possible that somebody armed with a knife had found his way into the gardens and was preparing now to relieve Angus of his wallet or wristwatch, or both. There were also occasional mindless assaults, not prompted by a desire to steal, but carried out by people who were disturbed, or high on drugs or alcohol. People who fell victim to those simply had the misfortune to be in the wrong place at the wrong time. There was no rhyme nor reason to their victimhood – it was pure bad luck.

Suddenly the memory of Bible John came into his mind. He had recently watched a television programme about a series of murders carried out in Glasgow years earlier that had never been satisfactorily solved, even though there were credible theories as to the perpetrator. They had taken place in the Gorbals, a working-class district of Glasgow, in the shadow of the decaying tenements of the time, and had resulted in the largest manhunt in Scotland since the pursuit of Bonnie Prince Charlie.

Angus thought of them now – of the meeting that the first victim had in the Barrowlands Ballroom, where she and her sister had danced with a couple of men they had met there. One of them was a cut above the average man who frequented the public dance halls – he was neatly turned out and quoted the Bible in his conversation. He was also a murderer, and he left one of the sisters dead on the green – the common garden – behind a tenement.

They never found Bible John – even after he had struck again. What if somebody just like him were on the loose in Edinburgh? Why would such a man not find the Drummond Place Gardens at night just the sort of place to pursue his twisted agenda? Angus slowed down again. He felt his spine tingle. Slowly he turned round.

Sister Maria-Fiore dei Fiori di Montagna was only a few steps behind him, her hands tucked into the sleeves of her voluminous blue-and-white habit. She looked at Angus, and smiled.

"I hope I didn't frighten you," she said.

Angus felt his heart hammer within his chest.

"You did give me a bit of a scare," he said. "I wasn't expecting anybody to be walking behind me."

Sister Maria-Fiore dei Fiori di Montagna was not one to miss the opportunity to come up with an aphorism. "None of us," she pronounced, "expects the things that we do not expect."

Angus considered this. What the nun had said was obviously true, but so trite, he felt, as not to require to be said at all. One part of him wanted to remonstrate with her – to point out that if one was just going to give voice to the blindingly obvious, then why should one bother to say anything at all? Yet to say that, even though it may be justified, would be cruel. Sister Maria-Fiore dei Fiori di Montagna meant well, and presumably imagined that others appreciated her observations. That might indeed be the case. There were plenty of people who seemed to like statements of the obvious, and who were comforted by bland sentiments of this sort. To criticise that sort of thing was unkind, Angus thought, and so he said nothing, but nodded in agreement.

Sister Maria-Fiore dei Fiori di Montagna took a step forward and spoke to Angus in lowered tones.

"Have you read Calvino?" she asked.

Angus had not expected this. He had read Calvino, as it happened, and so he answered, in a rather surprised way, "I have, actually. I've read *The Baron in the Trees* and *If on a Winter's Night a Traveller.*"

Sister Maria-Fiore dei Fiori di Montagna clapped her hands together. "I am re-reading *Il barone rampante* at the moment," she said. "It's so entrancing."

Angus stared at her. At times it was hard to keep up with the unusual nun's train of thought. "Why did you mention it?" he asked.

She pointed to the trees about them. "The trees," she said. "I think of poor Cosimo going off to live the rest of his life in the trees. I was wondering what it might be like to live in these Drummond Place trees."

Angus did not know how to answer this. He felt a sudden surge of irritation. Really, Sister Maria-Fiore dei Fiori di Montagna was the end – the complete end! What was she doing in the gardens at this hour of night, creeping up behind people and talking about Italo Calvino?

But it was at this point that they heard movement in a rhododendron bush next to which they were standing.

"You don't need to see me," said a voice from within. "But listen carefully."

Angus and Sister Maria-Fiore dei Fiori di Montagna stood stock still. Neither took a breath.

"The Scottish Government is planning something completely unacceptable," said the voice. "I'm telling you because I want it to be widely known. I am a senior civil servant, and I am not meant to speak about any of this, but I believe in transparency, you see. I believe that people should know what governments are doing. I believe in that."

They waited.

"They have set up a working group," the voice said, "to amalgamate Edinburgh and Glasgow. That is what they intend to do."

Angus gasped.

"They have to be stopped," said the voice. "What they plan to do is beyond belief."

Angus found his voice. "Madness," he said.

"I agree," said the voice. "And now, I must go."

# 22

## A Conversation with Galactica

Bertie had predicted that Ranald Braveheart Macpherson's party would be a disaster – and he was proved right. Later, when he discussed it with a sobbing Ranald, Bertie tried his best to cast a favourable light on events, but it was difficult, and his words of comfort fell on largely inconsolable ground.

"At least your party went well until Galactica MacFee arrived," Bertie said. "The first five minutes were fun, Ranald. You can be grateful for that, I suppose."

This failed to assuage Ranald's sobs, and so Bertie tried again.

"Some people's parties are not even nice for five minutes," Bertie went on. "And nobody at all went to Tofu's party, you know. Nobody. Tofu stood there in the activity centre waiting for people to arrive, and nobody came. I'm not making this up, Ranald – I was one of those who didn't go."

Ranald wiped his cheeks. "Then how do you know that's what happened?" he asked.

Bertie had no answer, but felt justified in making one up, given how upset Ranald was. "It was in the newspapers," he said quickly. "I read about it."

"I'm surprised that Larch didn't go," said Ranald.

"He was grounded," said Bertie. "He cut down their neighbour's tree. The neighbour was jolly cross."

"You shouldn't cut down trees," said Ranald.

"No," said Bertie.

They lapsed into silence.

Bertie thought of something else. "At least you got some

nice presents, Ranald," he said. "And people who give you presents can't take them back."

Ranald looked glum. "Olive did," he said. "At the end she said that she had not enjoyed herself at all, and that she was taking her present back. She took it home with her."

Bertie was silent as he considered this. He could imagine Olive doing that, but even so, there was no excuse for such behaviour. He was not surprised, though, that Olive did not enjoy herself, as the outrage committed by Socrates Dunbar early on in proceedings would have ruined the party for anyone – and certainly did for the victim. Socrates, who had a reputation in the school playground for impulsivity, had crept up behind Olive and put ice cream in her hair. The assault was unprovoked – and unexpected – and neither Olive nor Pansy had been able to retaliate because Socrates had gone into the bathroom, locked himself in, and jeered triumphantly at Olive from within.

"Socrates shouldn't have put ice cream in Olive's hair," said Bertie. "That sort of thing never helps, Ranald."

"I know," said Ranald. "And it's a waste of ice cream, Bertie."

"That too," Bertie agreed.

That incident, though, had been no more than the warm-up for the uncomfortable scene that had played itself out some fifteen minutes later. Olive and Pansy had retreated to the kitchen, where they were busy attempting to wash the ice cream out of Olive's hair; in the Macpherson living room, under a few dispirited party balloons, Galactica MacFee had announced to Bertie that she wished to speak to him in private, in the hall.

"What I have to say to you is not for other people," Galactica said. "It's just for you and me, Bertie."

Bertie wondered why they could not stay where they were, but his objections were dismissed.

Galactica looked round. "There are some very indiscreet people in this room," she said. "People like that can't keep a secret."

"I don't want to know any more secrets, Galactica," Bertie pleaded. "Thank you, anyway, for offering to tell me."

Galactica shook a finger at him. "There are some things you have to do, Bertie Pollock," she said. "If everybody just did what they wanted to do, then where would Scotland be? Can you answer that, Bertie? I don't think you can."

Bertie sensed that nothing he said would change Galactica's mind, and so he reluctantly accompanied her into the hall. There she closed the door.

"Now we're alone, Bertie," said Galactica.

Bertie said nothing.

"I want you to feel at ease with me, Bertie," Galactica continued. "I want you to look on me as a friend."

Bertie swallowed. "That's fine, Galactica. Now, can we go back?"

"Not so fast, Bertie," said Galactica, reaching out to restrain him. "I have something really important to tell you."

Bertie looked down at the floor. He wished that he had sent his excuses for this party. It would have been so easy just to say that he was ill and that as a result he could not come. Nothing serious, of course – just a mild dose of leprosy, perhaps.

"As you know," Galactica said, "you can't get married until you're really old. That's the law in Scotland. You know that, don't you?"

Bertie nodded.

"I think you have to be at least twenty," Galactica continued. "That sounds late, and I suppose it means that some people are only married for a year or two before they die. But you can't argue with the law, Bertie."

"I didn't say you could," muttered Bertie.

"So, I think it's best to sort out who you're going to marry at an early stage," Galactica said. "That way there won't be any argument when you get to twenty."

Bertie bit his lip.

"And before you get married, you get engaged," Galactica informed him. "You know about that, I imagine, Bertie."

Bertie nodded – almost imperceptibly, but he nodded.

Galactica was staring at him. Now her eyes narrowed. "I've heard some rumours, Bertie," she said.

Bertie tried to sound confident. "Oh yes?"

"About you," said Galactica. "About you and Olive."

Bertie looked away. He wanted the ground to open up beneath him. He wanted a siren to go off and the house to be evacuated. He wanted to be anywhere but here, with Galactica MacFee.

"Yes," Galactica continued. "People say that you and Olive are engaged and that you're going to be married when you're twenty. That's what people say, Bertie."

Bertie took a deep breath. "That's not true, Galactica," he protested. "It's just not true. I was never, ever engaged to Olive. She's just making it up. She's been making that up for years."

Galactica listened with interest. Then, when Bertie finished, she said, "Well, I'm very pleased to hear that, Bertie, because it means that you and I can get engaged." She paused. "That's good news, isn't it, Bertie?"

# 23

## *The Air of Freedom*

If Bertie imagined that Ranald Braveheart Macpherson's party could get no worse, he was wrong. What happened next developed with all the inevitability of a Greek tragedy, small in scale, admittedly, and acted out among the seven-year-olds, but no less magnificent or poignant for that.

After broaching the subject of their engagement, Olive was brisk in her brushing aside of Bertie's attempts to object.

"But, Galactica," he began, his voice wavering, too small, perhaps, even to be heard, "I didn't say . . ."

"No need to speak, Bertie," Galactica interrupted. "It's very sweet of you, but there are times when it's unnecessary to say anything. And we have to let people know now."

Bertie's jaw dropped. "About what?" he asked.

"About our engagement, of course," said Galactica. "The whole point of an engagement, Bertie, is to show commitment. You have committed to me, and people need to know."

Bertie gasped. He wondered if he closed his eyes, this nightmare would end, and he did so briefly. But reality, grim and unvarnished, was there to greet him when he opened them again. There was Galactica, smiling with satisfaction, gazing at him in what was now a proprietary, almost protective manner, while from the living room beyond the hall there came the sound of Ranald's mother's voice, announcing a game to jolly the failing party along. "Chase the Dentist now, children," she was announcing. "I know how much you all love that game. Come along now, who's going to be the first dentist? What about you, Moss? Or you, Fox? What about you?"

Galactica opened the hall door. "All right, Bertie, let's go back to the party. We can tell people a little bit later on – before they leave. There's no rush in these things."

Bertie followed her, his heart a cold stone within him. In the living room, a round of Chase the Dentist had begun, with Fox as the first dentist. He, like Socrates Dunbar and Galactica, had recently joined the class, and Bertie did not know him very well, but had sensed an ally. And that instinct was now being shown to be well-founded, as Bertie saw Fox deliberately trip up Olive as she tried to catch them in what was, after all, merely a variety of that ancient game, Tig.

Olive was at a disadvantage, as she and Pansy had not succeeded in fully removing the ice cream that Socrates Dunbar had rubbed into her hair. Now, as she tripped and fell, she was helped to her feet again by Pansy's quick response, her face contorted in fury.

Pansy, though, was the chief accuser. "I saw that, Fox," she screamed. "I saw you trip Olive up. I saw it and I'm going to tell Ranald's mother."

Fox smirked. "No use, Olive. Ranald's mother's drunk. She won't take it in."

Ranald Braveheart Macpherson heard this. "My mummy isn't drunk," he protested. "You're telling fibs, Fox."

Fox was tolerant. This was, after all, Ranald's party, and he deserved some consideration as host. "I'm sorry, Ranald," he said, "but she is. I'm not saying it's a bad thing to be drunk at a party. I'm not saying that. That's what adults do at parties – we all know that."

Moss, who had not said very much since he arrived at the party, now made a contribution. "My mummy," he said helpfully, "says both of your parents like whisky, Ranald. So you shouldn't worry – if your mummy's drunk, then so will your dad be. So everything will be all right."

Galactica intervened. "Let's not argue," she said. "There's at least some good news."

They looked at her. She was smiling, and her smile was particularly directed at Olive. Pansy glowered. Ranald Braveheart Macpherson held back his tears – but only just.

"Bertie and I are engaged," announced Galactica. "It's very recent."

The effect on Olive and Pansy was instant and electric. But it was Pansy, ever the loyal lieutenant, who rose to the bait.

"That's impossible, Galactica," she shouted. "And you know it. Bertie is engaged to Olive – and has been for years. And you can't be engaged to two people at the same time – even you should know that, Galactica."

Olive recovered from the initial shock of the provocative announcement. She was dignified in adversity – that, she thought, was the more powerful response. Thus might Mary, Queen of Scots have addressed her scheming nobles and her difficult husband. "I'm so sorry, Galactica," she began. "I know that sometimes things aren't the way you want them to be. But I know that inside you're strong enough to take these disappointments. What Pansy says is correct." She paused. "If you need counselling, then I'm sure that some is available. You can get it at most parties, you know."

Galactica was not to be drawn into a slanging match. Her voice remained calm. "You're the one who's going to need counselling, Olive," she said. "I happen to know what the law is. It says that you can break off an engagement if you like. Then you can get engaged to a better person – if there's one available. And in this case, there is. So there."

Olive and Pansy conferred. Then Olive stepped forward and led Bertie to the side of the room, watched by Galactica, who seemed confident that any attempt by Olive to reverse her fate would fail.

"Bertie," hissed Olive. "Please tell me that this isn't true."

Bertie looked at Olive, and then down at the ground. It was so unfair. What had he done to deserve all this? If girls wanted to be engaged, why couldn't they choose boys like Fox, or even Tofu?

"I don't think I'm engaged to anybody," he replied. "I don't want to be engaged at all, Olive. I want to go home."

Olive was a realist. She had met her match in Galactica. Now she pursed her mouth before asking, "Did you tell Galactica that you're not engaged to her?"

Bertie sighed. "I don't remember what happened," he said.

Olive drew back. "You leave me with no alternative, Bertie. I'm going to sue you for breach of promise."

"What's that?" asked Bertie, his voice thick with misery.

"It means that you get taken to court," Olive replied. "And they take all your things away from you. They sell them and they give the money to me."

"But I haven't got many things, Olive," Bertie protested.

"They'll take your dad's things then. That stupid car of his. That Volvo. They'll take that and sell it to somebody else."

Bertie was silent. He surveyed the field of his disaster. His one true friend, Ranald Braveheart Macpherson, stood amidst the smoking ruins of his party. Ranald was beginning to cry, and Bertie felt the tears well in his own eyes. He had had enough of this. He would run away to Glasgow. He and Ranald. They would plan it carefully. They would take sandwiches. Olive could sue him for breach of promise if she liked, but he would not be there. He would be free, breathing the heady air of Glasgow, the air of freedom.

# 24

## *Early Scottish People*

Out at Nine Mile Burn, Elspeth and Matthew lay in bed, both awake, both finding it difficult to drop off to sleep after the guests at their dinner party had gone, the table cleared, the dishwasher loaded, and the lights switched off. Elspeth had checked on the boys – Tobermory, Fergus and Rognvald – who usually slept soundly and were doing exactly that when she looked into their room. There they were, their innocent heads on blue pillows that were decorated with cowboys and space rockets, and she stood for a few moments and stared at them. This was her life: these small boys, in wakefulness so full of energy, but now, briefly, making only the almost imperceptible movements of the sleeping child – the snuffling and slight stirring – these were her life. And for a moment she imagined how it might have been had she not had triplets – had that odd, zygotic moment been only slightly different, had been less fecund, and she had given birth to a single child, even to a girl, who would have no interest in cowboys and space rockets, because that was not what appealed to girls, even in androgynous times.

Much as she doted on her sons, she would have loved to have a daughter, to have female companionship, to indulge in the things of girlhood, which did not include the noise and destruction that made up the world of young boys. Girls became women, and women kept families together: remembered birthdays, wrote messages, nurtured, made homes. They did all that in a way in which boys and men simply did not. That was not to say that they could not also do the things that men might wish to do – they could, and one might even argue that they did them better, but that was another issue altogether, for another day.

She sighed now as she lay in bed, looking up at a sliver of moonlight above her. Against these light summer nights, when darkness would begin to drain from the sky not long after three, Elspeth had installed blackout curtains, but these always seemed to have a chink, no matter how carefully one closed them, and moonlight, or morning, would announce itself on the ceiling.

She glanced at Matthew, a form under a sheet, his feet sticking out at the end. How often, she thought, do married people look at one another – actually look at one another? Familiarity meant that they did that less frequently than they might; we do not look at the furniture to which we are accustomed. Not that Matthew was just part of the furniture . . . well, actually, he was, she thought, a bit guiltily.

Now she said, "Are you still awake?"

The answer *no* would have been unbelievable, of course.

"Yes, I'm awake."

"Thinking?" she asked.

He did not reply immediately, but then said, "Yes, I suppose so."

She had never liked being asked what she was thinking about. Her father used to say "A penny for your thoughts", and that had irritated her so much. What a person was thinking about was her own affair, and not something that others were entitled to know about. Was that somehow unfriendly? She thought not. People were too ready to share their every thought with others, posting their observations on social media, as if anybody really cared about what you thought. That day, Elspeth had come across such an announcement – *Saw a really big dog today* – and had wondered how anybody could imagine that others might be interested. And then a friend of hers, whose online offerings she looked at from time to time, had said, *Tried to make bread this morning, but failed. Really hard and flat. Yeast malfunction?* Of what possible interest could that be to anybody? In fact, thought, Elspeth, it was slightly exhibitionist to tell other people about one's yeast malfunctions.

But then, more charitably, she thought, no, the banal details of the lives of others *are* important, because such things are socially bonding snippets. These were the things that people talked about when they gathered round the parish pump – when there was a parish pump.

If Matthew had asked her what she was thinking about, she would probably have told him about that, but he did not, and her thoughts drifted off to what had happened earlier in the evening.

"Were you pleased to see Ben?" she asked.

"A bit," he said. "We're never going to be all that close."

She thought about this. Were men ever as close to their friends as women were? "You mean, you don't have all that much in common with him?"

"Possibly. I mean that I don't feel much *for* him. You know how it is?"

"No. You tell me."

Matthew turned in bed, his feet now disappearing under the sheet. "I don't like him as much as I like some other friends." He paused. "Liking is an odd thing, isn't it? What does it mean if you say you like somebody? That you share a way of looking at things? That you *approve* of the other person?"

Elspeth thought about this. "Is it a matter of wanting to be with the other person?'

"That doesn't answer the question, though. It doesn't say *why* you want to be with them."

"It must be something to do with satisfaction of wants," said Elspeth. "Friends answer our needs."

"Such as?"

"Our need for company. We're frightened of being alone

– or at least most people are. Friends dilute the loneliness."

Matthew thought about this. He, too, was staring at the moonlight.

"Ben and Bruce were always great friends. David and Jonathan. They were inseparable."

"Those early friendships don't always survive, do they? Life gets in the way."

"True. But now Ben is keen to get Bruce involved in a scheme of his. He told me about it at the table. You were talking to Catriona at the time."

"What did you think of those blue spectacles of hers?'

"I thought they suited her."

"Should I wear some?" asked Elspeth.

"You don't need specs."

"If I did," she said. "Should they have blue frames – like hers?"

"I don't mind," said Matthew. "Suit yourself."

She wondered whether she should be hurt by this indifference; a husband should be interested in the appearance of his wife's spectacles. She decided not to take offence, and she went on to ask him what scheme Ben had in mind.

"A Pictish centre," said Matthew. "He's bought an old house for it, up near Stirling."

Elspeth was silent for a few moments. Then she said, "As in *Picts*? Early Scottish people?"

"Yes," said Matthew. "And he wants me to put money into it as well."

Elspeth's voice showed her alarm. Matthew was not good with money. The gallery made little, and the boys were always needing new shoes and . . . "Money?"

"That's what I said. But listen, darlingest, I want to go to sleep. I don't want to talk about Picts and blue spectacle frames and . . ." His voice became indistinct in his drowsiness.

Elspeth sighed.

# 25

## *Fat Bob's Farewell to Bacon Rolls*

Bob had made a firm decision, not only to cut down on carbs, but also to stick to a regime of physical exercise. Weight was an advantage in the world of Highland Games, but for most other purposes – including longevity – it was quite the opposite. Spurred on by that innocent, though wounding, remark made by Finlay, Bob was now unshakeable in his determination to do something about the excess pounds. He had consulted a chart and had worked out his Body Mass Index. He had checked the figures, and then rechecked them, but the result remained stubbornly uncomfortable – not to say dangerous. From the BMI chart he moved to another set of tables that predicted the chance of what it called *an adverse event*. He wondered what the implications of an adverse event might be, and when that was elucidated he became even unhappier.

Blood pressure, it seemed to him, was the key to the avoiding of an adverse event. If he could get his blood pressure down, then the figures became much less forbidding. And getting blood pressure down was tied up with losing weight and getting an adequate amount of exercise. Well, he knew exactly what to do about those two goals. He would eat smaller portions, reduce his carbohydrate intake, and enrol at the council gym at Craiglockhart, where his new friend, Eddie, urged on his clients. Eddie had agreed to be his personal trainer, and now all that remained to be done was to attend the first session.

Eddie was there, lifting weights, when Fat Bob entered the gym. Bob quickly spotted him and went to stand beside the structure on which the weightlifting bar rested.

"That's impressive, Eddie," said Bob. "Two hundred kilos, I see."

Eddie grunted from beneath the bar. Then, replacing it on the rest, he stood up and greeted Bob.

"I've been working up to that," said Eddie. "It's taken some time."

"Could I have a go?" asked Bob.

Eddie shook his head. "You can't start at that level, Bob. You'll have to begin with twenty kilos, max. You can do a lot of damage, you know, if you strain your muscles."

Bob said that he understood that, but that he was not starting from scratch. "I do Highland Games," he said. "Even Braemar."

Eddie laughed – a tolerant laugh. "Boys' stuff," he said. "But have a go, if you insist. Don't overdo it."

Fat Bob fetched two more heavy round weights and slipped them onto the ends of the bar.

"Haud on!" protested Eddie. "That's too much, Bob. You'll bust something."

But Bob paid no attention, and was now laying prone on the lifting bench, taking the strain of the bar. Eddie moved forward in an attempt to stop the bar rising, but he was too late: Fat Bob had lifted it seemingly effortlessly. For a few moments he held it up, and then, in a fully controlled way, lowered it back onto its supports.

"Jeez," exclaimed Eddie. "Jeez, Bob – that's more than two hundred kilos there."

Bob got up off the bench. He met Eddie's gaze, which was one of profound admiration.

"I thought you were just some overweight guy who needed to lose a few pounds," said Eddie. "I had no idea, Bob."

Bob, like all strong men, was modest. "Ach, Eddie, I don't know," he said. "I used to be able to do far more than that."

Eddie let out a whistle of amazement. "I suppose you

pulled a train," he said, with a smile.

Bob nodded. "Once. For charity. I pulled a train carriage along the platform at Waverley Station. It's not all that hard, you know. You just need an initial surge and then they move easily enough."

Eddie shook his head in disbelief. "Do you mind if I examine your biceps?" he asked.

"Nae bother," said Bob, rolling back his sleeves.

"Jeez," whispered Eddie, reaching out to touch the rippling muscles.

"I've got to lose a lot of this bulk," Bob said. "I know it'll weaken me but I have to get my blood pressure down. And I'm fed up with being so large."

Eddie nodded. "We'll cut down your bulk by twenty per cent," he said. "If you're up for it, Bob." He paused. "That is, if that's what you really want."

Bob assured him that he did. "I'm going to give up the Highland Games circuit," he said. "That's the old me. The new me is going to be very different."

"You're going to develop a new hobby?" asked Eddie.

"I'm open to that," said Bob. "I haven't decided yet. Maybe something artistic."

"Anything will do," said Eddie. "What's important is that it takes your mind off eating. So many people think about food too much. You need to break that habit – if you have it."

"I think about bacon rolls," said Bob. "My wife, Big Lou, makes bacon rolls to die for."

"Good choice of words," said Eddie. "Bacon rolls are killers, Bob."

Bob nodded sadly. "Aye, they're not all that healthy. But . . ."

"No buts," said Eddie. "There's going to be a new you, Bob – a new you that doesn't think about bacon rolls in those terms."

Bob looked out of the gym window. There was a lochan just beyond the gym, surrounded by reeds in which birds made their nests. A line of ducks moved across the water. The surface was calm, reflecting the sky. He thought for a moment of the last games he had been at in Perthshire where, at the side of the field, there had been a piping competition. Bob knew many of the pipers, and he pictured now his friend, Charlie Macdonald, playing a pipe tune, a slow air, a lament even, the notes rising steadily; and the tune would be 'Fat Bob's Farewell to Bacon Rolls'. It would be a bit like 'Mist Covered Mountains', the pipe tune that somehow expressed all the longing and sadness of Gaelic Scotland's history; this would speak, rather, of urban Scotland's longing for unhealthy food.

He looked at Eddie. "I'm serious, Eddie," he said. "I want to make this work."

Eddie said that he understood that. "I can tell that you mean business, Bob. But let's go and have a cup of tea out the front before we begin. I need a wee bit of a break."

They went outside, into the sunlight, where a small mobile coffee bar also sold tea and energy drinks. Eddie bought them each a mug of tea and they sat down on a bench overlooking the lochan to drink it. From behind them, they heard the sound of tennis balls being pounded across the court – a cry of disappointment, laughter.

"Tell me a bit about yourself, Eddie," said Bob.

"You want my story?" asked Eddie.

Bob said that he did. "You mentioned working on the Falkirk Wheel," he said.

"It starts well before that," said Eddie.

# 26

*Sleep Deprivation*

"My father," said Eddie, "was a ship's pilot on the Forth." He glanced at Bob quizzically. "You know what a ship's pilot is?"

Bob gave him a sideways look, which prompted an immediate apology from Eddie. "Sorry, Bob, it's just that some people don't know about these things. My old man often used to have to say to people, 'Look, I don't *fly* anything – I'm a master mariner.'"

"I know what pilots do," said Bob. "They have to know the waters, don't they?"

Eddie nodded. "They certainly do. They have to know everything – what the depths are; the location of rocks; currents. They have to know how to make their way past obstacles."

"So they take the helm?" asked Bob.

"No, it's the ship's officers who do that. The pilot is there to advise. He never takes command of the ship from the captain."

Bob looked interested. "So the captain is always responsible for the ship – even when there's a pilot on board?"

"Yes,' replied Eddie. "With one exception. And that's in the Panama Canal. A captain who takes a ship through there has to hand over control of the vessel to the pilot."

"So it's almost always the captain who carries the can?"

"That's right," said Eddie. "And that's always been the rule in the Royal Navy, you know. If you're a captain in the navy and you run aground or hit another ship, you're court-martialled."

Bob thought about this. Captains had to sleep, presumably.

"How would that rule apply if the captain was in his bunk
– sleeping legitimately – and the officer of the watch hit a
sandbank?"

"Still the captain's fault," said Eddie.

"That sounds pretty unfair."

"It's the sea. It's tough – and unfair."

Bob said that he did not see how a captain could be blamed
for things that weren't his fault.

"But there will be fault somewhere along the line," Eddie
said. "If a junior officer or one of the ratings does something
wrong, then that might be because he hasn't been trained
properly – or supervised when he should have been. And
whose fault is that? The captain's."

"That's a bit harsh," Bob mused.

"It's the way it works," said Eddie. "My old man used
to say that rules like that kept captains on their toes." He
paused. "He used to take his work terribly seriously. He said
that millions of pounds could depend on his directions."

"Like air traffic control."

"Yes, a bit like that."

Eddie looked sad. "His job began to get him down, I think.
There were little signs to begin with – then it became more
serious. I was still young, but I noticed it. He often seemed absent
– staring into space, as if thinking about some great puzzle."

Eddie looked down at his hands. "When you're a child, there's
so much you don't notice – or never think too much about.
How your parents feel, for example. We never think about how
difficult it is at times for them to be them. It doesn't occur to us
that they have all sorts of things going on in their lives."

Bob agreed. "You're right there, Eddie." He thought of his
own parents: of how his father had never got anywhere in his
job with the railways; of how his mother had been obliged to
scrimp and save to keep the family going, and had never said
anything about it – to anyone, as far as he knew.

"It came to a head," Eddie continued, "when a ship ran aground near Cramond. It was a freighter coming over from Rotterdam, delivering something up at Rosyth. My dad had boarded her further out and was on the bridge. There was a thick mist, like soup. You know how it can get. Sometimes you can't see a thing in front of your nose. It was like that.

"Obviously, he was being very careful. The master was on the bridge with him and the first officer was at the helm. They were going really slowly, apparently – two or three knots at the most, against the tide. My dad gave them an instruction – he said something like 'Steer one-four-oh degrees, one hundred and forty degrees', and the first officer repeated the instruction. But then he actually steered a course of two hundred and forty degrees, which took them right into a sandbank off Cramond. The ship's screw was damaged and they had to be towed off by a tug the following day."

Bob shook his head. "It wasn't his fault."

"No, it wasn't his fault," said Eddie. "Nobody could see where they were and their radar was malfunctioning. But the problem was that the first officer said that my dad had told him to steer two hundred and forty degrees, and the master backed him up. They were cousins, and they were obviously going to watch each other's back. So to begin with my dad was blamed – quite unfairly."

"That's really bad luck," said Bob.

"Yes. There was an inquiry, though, and things changed then. They began to dig a bit deeper and they found that both of the Dutchmen had not slept for thirty-six hours. They had been on duty solidly, because two of the other members of the crew had been drinking and were incapacitated in their bunks. So although the master and the first officer were sober, they were both sleep-deprived."

"And that made a difference?"

"Yes," said Eddie. "The inquiry held that the first officer

had probably set the course incorrectly because he was half asleep on his feet. They said that my dad was not to blame, but that didn't seem to make any difference to him. He felt awful about it.

"But you know what, Bob," Eddie continued. "Years later, when I was thinking about this incident that pretty much wrecked my dad's career, I began to read up about sleep deprivation in accidents, and I'll tell you this: just about every major accident has sleep deprivation somewhere in the background, if you look for it. It's true. Sleep deprivation is one of the biggest causes of accidents, Bob. Accidents on the road. Accidents in the home. All sorts of accidents. Sleepy people cause them because they haven't had enough sleep and then they do something dangerous."

Bob listened as Eddie intoned the list. "Chernobyl – sleepy operators; the Columbia shuttle disaster – a whole lot of sleep-deprived people in NASA; that big oil spill in Alaska – sleep deprivation on the tanker. The list goes on."

"Well," said Bob, yawning.

"I should stop now," said Eddie. "Not everybody's interested in sleep deprivation."

Bob shook his head. "No. Carry on. I'm just a bit tired."

# 27

## Zen and the Art of Hydraulics

"My poor dad was never the same, you know," Eddie continued. "He was quieter. He hardly ever went out. I suppose you'd say he was depressed."

"Very bad luck," said Bob. "But I suppose this sort of thing happens."

"Yes, and we all had to get on with our lives. I left school a couple of years after that and signed up with the air force. They taught me a trade – I was a hydraulics technician. You know what they do, I take it? Of course you do." Eddie was going out of his way to be tactful, after implying that Bob might not know what a ship's pilot did.

But Bob said no, he had an idea what it might be, but he was not sure. "I haven't really thought about hydraulics very much," he said, a note of apology in his voice. "Maybe I should have . . ."

"No," said Eddie. "Here's an interesting thing, Bob: people don't think about hydraulics – they just don't. And yet they rely on them. You'd think that they'd know at least something about systems that were making a big difference to their day-to-day lives. Brakes, for example. Do people think about their braking systems?"

Bob shook his head. "They should, I suppose."

"That's what I think," said Eddie. He recollected something, and smiled. "You know, I have another client – he's an accountant – and he told me something while he was doing his workout on the cross trainer that absolutely floored me, Bob. Honestly, you could have picked me up off the floor.

He was talking about his car and how it was in the garage that day. I said, 'So what's wrong with it, Tim?' and he said, 'The brakes are playing up. I think the wire that pulls them has stretched, or something.' I'm not making that up, Bob. True as God, that's what he said."

Bob shook his head. "And we're meant to be a country known for its engineering."

Eddie gave a snort. "Used to be. We used to make ships over on the Clyde. What happened? We used to make all sorts of other things. What went wrong?"

"We took our eye off the ball," suggested Bob.

"We certainly did. We thought we'd get other people to make them and we'd do the mathematics. Ha! Look at what's happened to the schools. Fallen out of the league tables."

Eddie sighed. "Anyway, hydraulics ... I was the chap who made sure that systems that used oil to operate – to push and pull, for the most part – I made sure that they worked. Serviced them. Changed parts. Wheel systems, for example. What pushes a plane's wheels down so that it can land? Hydraulics, Bob. Hydraulics."

"I can see how important it was," said Bob.

"Thank you, Bob. It's great that you should say that – some people never thank hydraulics engineers. Not one word of thanks. They use our stuff, but *thank you?* Forget it."

"So you were happy in your job?"

Eddie hesitated. "Mostly. I'd like to say that I was entirely happy, but I wasn't. I loved hydraulics – don't get me wrong on that, Bob – I loved those pistons and cylinders – dreamed about them, you know. That side of it was fine. But I didn't like being moved around the country. I was up at Lossiemouth and then down somewhere in the south of England. Then back up, and so on. I got married, and we lived in RAF married quarters. That was all right, but Jill – that's my wife – she couldn't settle. She said the rooms were always the wrong shape. I'm not sure what she meant, but she often said that about things – and about people too. Wrong shape. If there's something she didn't like, she'd say *wrong shape*. I could always tell."

Bob thought: am I the wrong shape? Is that why I'm here, talking to Eddie?

"It was a hard decision for me to make," Eddie continued. "It was a secure job. The technical challenges were there: if you were a hydraulics man, you couldn't ask for more interesting work. Some of those systems, Bob, they were works of art. In fact, I used to say to the apprentices, 'Think of these systems as works of art. Imagine that they've been designed by that Italian guy . . .' What's his name, Bob? Leonardo . . . Leonardo da Vinci. Yes, he drew those pictures of machinery, remember? Hundreds of years ago, when we Scots were – oh, Bob, I don't like to think of what we were like when Leonardo was drawing all that stuff down in Italy there. We would have looked like orangutans. I'm not being rude, Bob, but we Scots were pretty hairy in those days, and people say that we had long arms. Back in the days of Macbeth and all those guys.

"Anyway, Bob, I digress. I decided to leave the air force, because if your missus isn't happy, then nobody's happy – know what I mean? So I took a job in Motherwell with a firm that made hydraulic gates. It was all right, I suppose, and it paid the rent. I was there for quite a few years and then I got the job in Falkirk with the wheel. You know it? The big wheel that lifts boats up to the next level of the canal? An engineering marvel, I call it. And of course somebody has to oil it. That was me.

"Then I thought: is there more to life than oil and hydraulics? I know you may think this is odd, but I had an experience, Bob. I'm only going to tell you about it because I think you're not the sort to laugh. Some people would just laugh at me – I get the feeling that you wouldn't."

Bob assured him he would not laugh.

"I went for a walk one day along the canal – near the wheel. It was lunchtime; I wanted to get some fresh air. So I went off, and you know what happened? I saw a light, Bob. There was a light, and a voice said, 'You must get fit, Eddie. And you must help others to get fit too.'"

Eddie stopped. He gave Bob a searching look – as if daring him to mock. But Bob did not. He said, "Heavens, Eddie, where do you think that came from?"

Eddie did not reply. Instead, he looked at Bob and said, "I suggest we pray, Bob."

"Right now?" asked Bob.

Eddie closed his eyes. "I ask, here in this place, that grace should descend on this fat person, our brother Bob, and that he should be helped in his quest for weight loss and overall fitness."

Eddie opened his eyes. "Well, Bob," he said. "That's us embarked on our journey."

# 28

## *Invitation to a Nightcap*

After Deep Throat had delivered his warning, Angus Lordie and Sister Maria-Fiore dei Fiori di Montagna found themselves staring at one another in frank astonishment. It was unusual for the socialite nun to be short of anything to say, and in normal circumstances a silence such as this would be an invitation for the coining of an aphorism, but on this occasion, such was the nature of her surprise that she remained mute. It was Cyril, then, who spoke first, whimpering for attention from Angus.

"It's all right, boy," Angus said quietly, reaching down to pat the dog's head. "Nothing to worry about."

Turning to Sister Maria-Fiore dei Fiori di Montagna, Angus said, "Cyril picks up human emotions quite easily. Dogs are like that – they sense tension."

"Then he must be wondering what's going on now," said the nun. "This is a situation fraught with tension, I would venture to suggest."

Angus agreed. "I must say, I'm not at all sure what to do."

"About what he told us? That bombshell piece of information?"

Angus nodded. "It would be difficult to imagine anything more controversial than what he said they were proposing to do."

Sister Maria-Fiore agreed. "In the relatively short time I have lived in this delightful country," she said, "I have picked up a strong sense of rivalry between the two cities. Naturally, I have not taken sides, and would never express an opinion on the subject, although it is clear to me that Edinburgh is the superior city. But, as I say, I would never prefer one to the other – even in the face of overwhelming evidence that one is better than the other – which evidence, of course, is there in abundance if only one looks for it."

Angus looked doubtful. "I would never accuse you, dear Sister Maria-Fiore dei Fiori di Montagna, of being prejudiced against Glasgow – of being *parti pris* – although others might say that you very obviously are. Not me, of course."

"Thank you," said Sister Maria-Fiore. "I am glad that my impartiality is widely recognised."

Angus looked at his watch. "It's getting on a bit," he said. "And I don't think our friend in the bushes is likely to return."

"That which has gone is only going to return if it has not truly gone," observed Sister Maria-Fiore.

"Very true," said Angus. "But I think we should perhaps be on our way."

"Can I not tempt you in for a brief nightcap?" asked Sister Maria-Fiore. "Antonia will still be up, and she and I often enjoy a small sherry, or a glass of Madeira, before retiring to bed. I find that Madeira settles the stomach, although there are some who say the same thing of Guinness."

Angus hesitated. He was keen to get back to Scotland Street and tell Domenica about what they had learned in the gardens, but he also wanted to discuss the matter with Sister Maria-Fiore, who, after all, had been his joint witness to the evening's extraordinary revelations.

"Perhaps a quick drink," said Angus. "You won't mind Cyril coming with us?"

"Antonia loves dogs," said Sister Maria-Fiore. "And I like them too. They are God's creatures, as are we, of course. They were placed on this earth, I believe, to provide us with company and to bark on our behalf. They are our handmaidens and our comfort."

Angus doubted this. Did Sister Maria-Fiore not understand

that dogs had evolved from wolves? And could anybody ever say that wolves were placed on this earth to provide us with friendship and companionship? That had never been in the wolf's mission statement – not at all.

"Of course, evolution may suggest otherwise," Angus said mildly. "Dogs come from wolves, you know."

Sister Maria-Fiore dei Fiori di Montagna looked at him calmly. "That's a matter of opinion," she said.

Angus was not sure what to say. Did he really want to start a debate on evolution at this hour, in the Drummond Place Gardens, of all places?

"It's science, actually," he said, as mildly as he could.

She did not hesitate to reply. "Does opinion not come into scientific observation? Do scientists not have an opinion about what they want to find out from what is before them?"

Angus shrugged. "I suppose they do."

"Well, there you are, then," said Sister Maria-Fiore.

They started to walk towards the gate and a few minutes later they were outside Sister Maria-Fiore's front door on the other side of Drummond Place.

"You see," said the nun, pointing to a light in the window. "That's Antonia's study. She'll still be up, working on her magnum opus. She is tireless in that regard."

Angus looked up at the lit window. "She shows great determination."

"She has to be determined," said Sister Maria-Fiore. "The task of a contemporary hagiographer is a lonely one. Nobody else works in the field, you see – or very few these days. And when it comes to early Scottish saints, well, Antonia is probably the only person in the world with an interest. It is a very lonely furrow of scholarship to till."

"Scholarship is a lonely business," said Angus. He was not sure whether he was at all entitled to make such a pronouncement. He had never been a scholar – he was interested in the history of art, of course, and had studied that at the art college in his day, but he would never have described himself as a scholar. Domenica was, of course, with her anthropological papers on various obscure peoples – although obscure peoples were never obscure to *themselves.*

"Let's creep in and surprise her with a glass of Madeira," she said. "She'll be sitting at her desk, her nose buried in some dusty old tome, reading about some peculiar Highland saint who took the Word to those dreadful Picts, and then she'll look up and we'll be standing there with a glass of Madeira for her. And the poor darling will be so touched – and so relieved to put all those old saints to one side."

"A lovely picture," said Angus. "And perhaps Antonia will have some ideas as to what we can do about this . . . this leak."

"I doubt it," said Sister Maria-Fiore dei Fiori di Montagna. "Dear Antonia is no plumber, I suspect. *Plumbaria non est.* Ha!"

# 29

## Telling Antonia

Antonia Collie was, as her flatmate had predicted, not unhappy to be distracted. In spite of her previously strained relations with Domenica, she had always been on good terms with Angus. The argument with Domenica had developed as a result of a dispute as to the ownership of a room, which Antonia claimed pertained historically to her flat rather than to Domenica's. This territorial dispute had bubbled away in the background for some years, as such disagreements often do, and although it was about the possession of a single, small room, it raised passions every bit as strong as those that had been involved in the long-running conflict between Ecuador and Peru over the right to a substantial swathe of the Amazon basin.

And then there had been the vexed matter of the blue Spode teacup, which Domenica had lent to Antonia, and which she believed Antonia had not returned. Domenica had eventually used a spare key to gain access to Antonia's flat in order to recover the teacup – a risky endeavour that almost went disastrously wrong. Angus had been involved in that, in spite of his reservations, and a teacup had been clandestinely removed from Antonia's kitchen. But not the right teacup, it transpired.

That was in the past, of course, but the memory of the issue lingered, as can some ancient issues in relations between warring states. Antonia, in Domenica's mind, represented a vague and inchoate danger, requiring a certain level of caution. The two women, although civil to one another, would never sit down to the sort of heart-to-heart one might otherwise have with a former neighbour of many years.

But now Antonia was clearly pleased to see Angus, and the welcome he received was a warm one.

"Dear Sister Maria-Fiore dei Fiori di Montagna is always looking for ways to prise me from my labours," she said, as she rose from her desk. "And now she brings you in as her ally, the naughty thing!"

"All work and no play makes Jack Sprat eat the fat," said Sister Maria-Fiore.

Antonia smiled. "Dear Italianate One, we mustn't mix up our sayings. The Jack who was always working and not playing sufficiently was not the same Jack as the one who liked to eat fat. Two quite different Jacks, I'm afraid. Our Jack – the conscientious one – was a generic Jack."

Sister Maria-Fiore dei Fiori di Montagna made an impatient gesture. "Men," she said, "and their ridiculous names."

Antonia remonstrated with her. "Now then, that is hardly charitable. Men can't help it. And I know you don't mean it, of course. Angus here is a man, and a most agreeable one, if I may say so. Chromosomes are nothing to do with moral worth, we might remind ourselves."

Sister Maria-Fiore dei Fiori di Montagna raised her voice in protest. "I was only joking, Antonia. Angus knows that."

"I wasn't offended," said Angus. "I know that Sister Maria-Fiore has an idiosyncratic sense of humour."

"There you are," said Sister Maria-Fiore dei Fiori di Montagna. "And have we got news for you, Antonia! Just you wait to hear what happened in the gardens this evening."

They left Antonia's study, where this encounter had taken place, and made their way into the kitchen, where they sat down with their small glasses of Madeira.

"This is Bual," said Sister Maria-Fiore dei Fiori di Montagna, holding up her glass to the light. "It's not as dry as Sercial, but I find dry wine a bit too acidic."

Antonia smiled indulgently. "Dear Sister Maria-Fiore dei Fiori di Montagna is a bit fussy." She turned to her friend. "Not that I'm criticising you, Most Discerning One – it's just that some of us are a little bit less . . . how shall I put it? A little less particular."

The nun returned the smile. "Those who discern merit are themselves meritorious," she said sweetly. "That is something of which we should remind ourselves, I think."

"I like both sweet and dry wines," said Angus, hoping to move the conversation on. "But we were going to talk about what happened in the gardens."

"Of course," said Sister Maria-Fiore. "We had an encounter, Antonia. Angus and I had an encounter with a very *shaded* man."

"Shady, rather than shaded," Angus corrected her. "Although our shady man did indeed speak from a shaded position. He was in the rhododendrons, to be precise."

"The rhododendrons!" exclaimed Antonia. She uttered the word with all the force of Lady Bracknell on the subject of the handbag.

"Yes," said Sister Maria-Fiore. "He was keen to conceal his identity."

"Although he did tell us something about himself," Angus interjected. "He revealed that he was a senior civil servant, working for the Scottish administration."

"There are quite a few of those around here," Antonia pointed out. "The other day, when I was in the supermarket, I bumped into that poor man from the Scottish Government who always looks sair hauden doon. I think he's in the Department of Unpopular Policies. It seems as if he wheels all the cares of office around in his shopping trolley."

"So sad," said Sister Maria-Fiore. "Those who care for us are themselves so frequently bowed down under cares. Only the carefree are free of cares, I believe."

Angus frowned. He suspected that Sister Maria-Fiore might just have said something profound, but it was difficult to tell. So he simply nodded, and said, "Quite so." Then he asked, "Is there really such a department, Antonia?"

Antonia said that she believed there was. "It's not a very large department, but they have a very sensitive role. They select the policies that are most likely to annoy and irritate the people of Scotland, and then they draft the legislation to give effect to these. It's a very demanding task, because they encounter a great deal of opposition from all sorts of quarters. But it has to be done. You can't have people interfering with progress." She paused. "But tell me, what did this person in the rhododendrons have to say?"

"He wanted to leak to the press," said Sister Maria-Fiore. "He mistook Angus for a well-known journalist."

"And what did he tell you?" Antonia pressed.

Angus explained the leak of the policy to amalgamate Edinburgh and Glasgow. As he spoke, Antonia's eyes widened.

"This is quite extraordinary," she said. She looked thoughtful. "If they amalgamated the two cities, what, I wonder, would they call it?"

"He didn't say," answered Angus. "But I imagine it would be . . ."

"Greater Glasgow?" asked Antonia.

Angus nodded. "Probably," he said.

Sister Maria-Fiore shook her head. "This discussion," she said, "takes me back to Italy. We have had a great deal of this sort of thing at home, with regional reorganisation."

She poured more wine into their glasses.

"These glasses are awfully small," said Antonia. "We shouldn't feel guilty about topping up."

"Those who feel guilty," observed Sister Maria-Fiore dei Fiori di Montagna, "are usually guilty, *non siete d'accordo?*"

Antonia ignored this. "We have to do something," she said.

Angus agreed. "But what?"

Sister Maria-Fiore dei Fiori di Montagna took a sip of Madeira. "Deciding what to do is, in itself, doing something," she said.

# 30

## Would Any of Us Be Brave?

"I do like your glasses," Bruce remarked to Catriona. "Those blue frames suit you. And the shape, too – it's just right – for your face, I mean."

The three of them – Bruce, Ben and Catriona – were travelling north on the motorway between Edinburgh and Stirling. Ben was driving, and Catriona was in the passenger seat beside him. This remark about the glasses came from the back seat, where Bruce was sitting. Catriona half turned her head as Bruce addressed the compliment to her, and smiled appreciatively.

"Thanks, Bruce," she said. "You're sweet."

Ben laughed. "Bruce isn't sweet," he said. And then added, "Well, he never was in the past, were you, pal?"

Catriona said, "Don't be mean to Bruce, Ben. He's your oldest friend – remember?"

"Okay, he's not so bad." Ben paused and then added, "These days."

Catriona scolded Ben. "That's very rude, Ben. Say sorry to Bruce."

"He doesn't need to say sorry to me," Bruce said. "Ben and I go back a long way. You don't have to apologise to people you've known for ever."

Ben looked in the driver's mirror. He made eye contact with Bruce. They looked at one another for a few moments.

"Sorry, anyway," said Ben. "It's just that you seem . . . well, you seem a bit more settled." He hesitated. "Is it anything to do with that lightning strike?"

Bruce shrugged. "Maybe. Maybe not."

"Is it true you went to a monastery?" Ben continued.

"Pluscarden Abbey," Bruce replied. "They were very kind to me."

"So what happened?" asked Ben.

Bruce spoke quietly. "I realised that perhaps I'd been on the wrong track. You know. Sometimes you look at your life and you think, uh-uh, wrong track."

Catriona turned round and smiled at him. "The track you're on now suits you, Bruce." She paused. "And your hair . . . Is it a bit different?"

"Maybe it was the lightning," suggested Ben. "Are you still using that stuff you used to put on your hair? I liked the smell of it. It reminded me of something . . ."

"Cloves," said Catriona.

"Possibly," said Bruce.

They lapsed into silence for a few minutes. A motorcyclist shot past – a flash of black and red and the whining sound of an engine.

"He's in a hurry," said Ben.

"Stupid," said Catriona.

"Oh well," said Bruce.

The silence returned. Then Bruce said, "This place of yours? What's it called?"

Catriona answered. "It's not ours just yet. It will be. We get entry in . . ."

"Ten days," said Ben. "We get the keys from the lawyers in Stirling. And it's called Glenbinnie. It's a house and about forty acres of land."

"What does it consist of?" asked Bruce.

Ben explained. The house had been rather more than a basic farmhouse – not large or grand enough to be a full-scale laird's house, but close to it. It had been extended over the years, and had been briefly used as a hotel. Then it had been returned to private use and had been badly neglected.

"And the land?" asked Bruce.

"A small wood," Ben answered. "Some fields that are let out to a local farmer – he runs sheep on them, on yearly lease. And a river."

"That's good," said Bruce. "A river's always good."

"It's called the Teith," said Ben. "It runs through Doune. You may know it."

"I went to a party out there once," said Bruce. "There was a girl I knew."

Catriona glanced at him over her shoulder. "Are you seeing anybody at the moment, Bruce?"

Bruce shook his head. "Not right now."

"I was always jealous of you," said Ben. "You got all the girls. They couldn't take their eyes off you. None of them looked at the rest of us."

"I looked at you," said Catriona, and leaned across and touched Ben's forearm.

Ben looked in the mirror. Bruce looked back at him.

"I'm really keen to see this place," Bruce said.

Ben smiled. "You'll like it. I know you'll like it."

"Has Ben discussed money with you, Bruce?"

"Not in detail," said Bruce.

"I'm not pressurising you," Ben assured him. "But, as I told you, I'm more or less cleaned out buying the place. Catriona's dad has put in a bit, but we'll need a bit more to bring it up to scratch. The central heating."

"The electrics," interjected Catriona. "The wiring's ancient."

"That's a fire risk," Bruce remarked.

"Well, all that needs to be done. And the plumbing too. I've got this real expert on heating systems and all that – Alex Robertson – he works in copper, he's a real artist – and I've got a joiner, a chap called Gordon MacNaughton, who's another artist. Gordon will do all the skirting boards and make new windows." He paused. "You said you might . . ."

"Invest," supplied Bruce. "Yes, I've got a bit of spare cash. And I like the idea."

"There isn't another Pictish centre in Scotland," said Catriona. "People like themed visits. They want to stay in places with a bit of a story. They'll love it."

"I think you're right," agreed Bruce. "And you can probably count me in."

"And what about Matthew?" asked Ben. "Do you think he'll join us? Do you think he'll disgorge some cash?"

"He's a nice guy," said Bruce. "He put money into Big Lou's place – you know, that coffee bar. That woman from Arbroath or somewhere up there. He helped her."

"He has a kind face," said Catriona.

"I like investors with kind faces," said Ben, and laughed, and added, "And investors who use – or used to use – clove-scented hair gel."

"Pay no attention to him, Bruce," said Catriona.

They turned off the motorway, and onto a local road that snaked its way across a brief stretch of undulating farmland.

"A few miles along here," said Ben.

They passed a statue standing on the brow of a hill, a solitary figure looking out over the strath.

"David Stirling," said Ben. "You know about him, Cat? He set up the commandos during the war."

"He was very brave," said Bruce.

"Would you be brave?" asked Ben. "Or me? Would any of us be brave?"

Nobody said yes, but then nobody said no; and the brave, of course, never say that they are brave, and those who deny their bravery are often the bravest of all.

Then Catriona said, "I'd try, I suppose. I'd try."

# 31

## *Chez the Picts*

The house itself stood at the end of an unpaved drive that was lined with tall white poplars. The trees created an avenue, on either side of which a field stretched out to a wood in one direction, and a hillock in another. Sheep grazed in one of these fields, while the other, which was unfenced, was dotted with gorse. The scent of gorse, a coconut smell, drifted in through the open windows of the car, and this made Catriona turn and say to Ben, "I always associate that smell with a holiday we had when I was a teenager. It was on a Hebridean island and there was that smell of gorse. I've never forgotten it." She did not add that it was on that trip that she had first fallen in love, with a boy she had met in the small hotel in which they had stayed. He served at tables, helping his parents, and spoke Gaelic. Since then, love and the smell of gorse were inextricably linked.

Ben was only half listening to what she said. Now he glanced at Bruce in the driver's mirror and said, "Doesn't the house look good through the trees? Can you see its potential, Bruce? Can you see it?"

Bruce said nothing, but craned his neck to get a better view. He had made up his mind the moment they had turned off the public road into the driveway. He had decided to give Ben what he was asking for. It did not matter if it cleaned out his bank account. Things like that – money and what it bought – did not seem to mean very much to him any longer. They used to, but not now. He had been left a legacy by a bachelor uncle in Melrose. It was large. He did not need it, and he would use it for this scheme of Ben's. Ben was his friend. That was what meant something now.

They drew up in front of the house.

"The lawyers let me have a set of keys in advance," said Ben. "It's unofficial, but they don't mind, as long as we don't start any works before we get title."

Bruce nodded. "That's reasonable enough." He had been a surveyor, and he remembered a case where a prospective purchaser had sent builders in before the property became his legally and the deal had then fallen through. By that time, though, the would-be owner had knocked down a wall and begun the demolition of an old conservatory. It had been an expensive jumping of the gun.

Ben unlocked the front door, and they went inside. Bruce stopped as he crossed the threshold. He lifted his head and sniffed at the air.

"The house is a bit stuffy," said Ben. "It hasn't been lived in for almost a year."

Bruce sniffed again, and frowned. "There's damp," he said. "You can smell it."

"Scotland's a damp country," said Ben.

"I'll take a look," said Bruce. "I wish I had a damp meter with me."

"We can fix damp," said Catriona brightly. "Come and see the living room, Bruce. It's really large and it has a fantastic view of the hills."

They made their way through the entrance hall and into a large room with windows that went down almost to floor level.

"Those windows aren't original," said Bruce. "These houses didn't have big windows like that. It was far too cold."

"But look at the light," said Ben. "And that fireplace – look at that."

Bruce crossed the room. Underneath his feet, the floorboards creaked noisily.

"We'll carpet this room," said Ben hurriedly. "Some of the boards are a bit loose."

Bruce reached the fireplace, a large marble construction that dominated the room. Describing the edge of the hearth was a burnished steel surround. Bruce bent down and ran his fingers along the metal.

"This was put in about sixty or seventy years ago," he said. "This is typical Bogie work."

Catriona looked interested. "Bogie?"

"Thomas Bogie," said Bruce. "He had an ironworks in Edinburgh. He specialised in fireplaces like this. Edinburgh houses are full of them."

Ben seemed pleased that this, at least, sounded positive. He had noticed a crumbling cornice, but had not said anything about it.

Yet Bruce had seen it. "That cornice is going to fall down," he said, pointing at the ceiling. "I wouldn't walk under it, if I were you."

Catriona took Bruce's arm and led him towards one of the windows. "Let's think positively," she said. "It's so easy to be negative when you see an old house of character. You have to think beyond what you see. You have to imagine how it's going to look after the work's been done."

Bruce smiled. "You don't have to worry," he said. "I'm used to doing just that. When I was a surveyor, I saw some real dumps – serious ones – far worse than this."

Ben brightened. "So, you don't think this is too bad?" he asked.

"No, I don't," said Bruce. "I like the vibe."

Ben punched the air. "The vibe!" he explained. "That was the word I was looking for. This place has a good vibe."

Catriona gripped Bruce's arm more tightly. "I knew you'd love it, Bruce. Now let's go and look at the kitchen."

"And the bedrooms too," said Ben. "Don't forget the

bedrooms. There are ten, you know. Ten. That's just what we need for all the people who are going to sign up for the Pictish experience."

"Do you think they will?" Bruce asked. There was a note of doubt in his voice.

"Of course they will," said Ben. "But we can talk about the business plan later – after we've looked around a bit more. And had a look at the grounds too. You should see the grounds, Bruce. There's an old walled garden – we can fix that up for vegetables."

"The sort of vegetables the Picts grew," said Catriona. "People can go and look at them, and then we can serve them with the meals."

"What did the Picts grow?" asked Bruce.

Ben looked at Catriona. She took off her blue-framed glasses and polished them with a handkerchief. "I'm not exactly sure," she said.

Bruce frowned. "Does anybody know?"

Ben sighed. "There's so much we don't know about the Picts. That's why a centre like this will be so important."

"Precisely," said Catriona. "I imagine that the Picts had physic gardens – you know, places where they grew medicinal herbs."

Ben seized on this. "That's what we'll do," he said. "We'll call it Pictish Physic. And we'll grow things like . . ."

"Echinacea," suggested Catriona. "And St John's wort."

"Isn't that used to treat depression?" asked Ben.

"Yes," Catriona replied. "It's still used for that."

"Did the Picts get depressed?" asked Bruce.

Ben laughed. "I bet they did. Wouldn't you if you knew you were going to disappear – and leave hardly anything behind; no buildings; no poetry; nothing but a few place names?"

# 32

## No Potatoes

Outside, they inspected the walled garden behind the main house. The walls were in surprisingly good order – Victorian masons believed in permanence, and in the use of good stone and mortar. Here and there, clumps of pointing had crumbled and fallen out, but for the most part the wall was sound. The garden itself, though, looked as if it had not been tended for decades, since the days of Dig for Victory, perhaps, when every square inch of cultivable land had been enrolled in the campaign of survival. In a far corner, pagoda-like in its construction and lacking only a few panes, a substantial glasshouse had largely survived, its door seized open, as if in invitation.

It was the raised beds that stood out. In spite of the uncontrolled spread of brambles, the shape of these beds was still clearly discernible, as was evidence of the crops they had once nurtured. What looked like a line of potato plants could be made out in the middle of a riot of flowering weeds, a dark-green, assertive tangle. Bruce noticed these, and pointed them out to Ben.

Catriona looked thoughtful. "That reminds me of something," she said.

"What does it remind you of?" asked Ben, adding, "Honeybunch."

Bruce looked away. The private endearments of married couples depressed him. What was the point of growing up, of getting away from being mother's *sugar pie* or *sweetie pants* (as he himself had been), only to become somebody's

129

*honeybunch* or something of that sort? And yet, and yet . . .
He had nobody to call him by a fond, private name – that was
the truth of the matter; and now he looked at Ben and thought
*I want to be him*. It was an odd thing to think – and Bruce
realised that. Did he really want to be married to somebody
who wore blue-framed glasses and who seemed to reach out
and pat his forearm rather often? What was wrong with
that? What was wrong with having your forearm patted all
the time? Nothing, really. Nobody pats *my* forearm, thought
Bruce. That's the bottom line, Bruce, old chap. You've got
nobody. And it's your fault for being in love with yourself for
so long.

Catriona repeated the question. "What does it remind me
of? Something I read. You know that man who writes those
books?"

Ben thought for a moment. "I'm not sure . . ."

"The one who wrote that book about India."

"Oh, him," said Ben. "Yes. I like reading him."

"William Dalrymple."

"Yes. Him. Well, he wrote a book about the Middle East
and about how he visited the farms of dispossessed people.
And he said that the prickly pears of the people who had been
there continued to grow after they had gone and the land had
been cleared. They came up through the ground, marking out
the boundaries that the original owners had set out. It showed
that you can't eradicate the past. It keeps coming back."

Ben looked at the potato plants. "Like those potatoes?"

"Yes."

Bruce looked up at the sky. He felt a heave of emotion.
There was so much wrong with the world – and he had never
thought about it. Now he did – and it had taken a lightning
strike to get him to think about these things. "That's a sad
situation," he said. "Two sets of people fighting with one
another because they won't share."

Ben made a despairing gesture. "Tell me about it," he said. "It's the same all over the world. What do men fight about? Land. Things. Who has what. Who sticks his flag on what bit of landscape."

"Men," said Catriona. "You said: what do *men* fight about. Note the *men*."

Ben shook his head. "Don't tell me that women aren't the same," he said. "Women are implicated in it. Right up to here." He indicated his neck.

Bruce cleared his throat. "The point about these conflicts," he said, "is that there are usually two sides. And each side has a claim that has at least some merits."

Ben and Catriona looked at him.

"True," said Ben.

Catriona pointed to the potato plants. "Do you think the Picts ate potatoes?"

"Probably," said Ben. "In fact, they must have. If you were a Pict, wouldn't you eat potatoes? I would."

Bruce burst out laughing. "Come on!" he said. "When do you think the potato was invented – I mean, when was it first brought to Europe?"

Ben shrugged. Catriona looked surprised by the question, and asked, "Haven't there always been potatoes in Scotland?"

"No," said Bruce. "Definitely not. There were no potatoes in Scotland until the beginning of the seventeenth century. Fact."

"Oh," said Catriona.

"And the Picts were history by then," said Bruce. "So the Picts did not eat potatoes. Fact."

Ben turned away. He did not like the way Bruce said *fact*. It was as if it were a challenge. So he knew about the history of the potato, and he made us sound ignorant because we didn't know that. I know plenty of things that he doesn't know, but I don't go round saying *fact* all the time.

But now Bruce changed the subject. "So you'll set up your Pictish Physic Garden here?" he asked.

"Yes," said Ben. "We can grow the herbs they used – as I said. And other things too. They can buy them in the Pictish Experience shop."

Bruce considered this. "Are you sure that you'll get enough people?"

Ben became emphatic. "Listen, Bruce, Scotland gets a ton of visitors. Hundreds of thousands. They come here because it's a beautiful country, number one, and because there's a lot of history, number two. So they go to Edinburgh Castle and Holyrood and St Andrews and so on, but they still want more. So they read about the Jacobites and Bonnie Prince Charlie et cetera, et cetera and they go up to Culloden. But do they ever look further back? Do they ever stop when they're playing golf at St Andrews or drinking whisky at a distillery visitor centre and ask themselves: *Did the Picts play golf? Did they have whisky?* That sort of thing."

"That's where we come in," interjected Catriona. "They see our advertisement. They read *Who were these mysterious early Scots? Who were these people who left so little behind them?* They read that and then they think it would be good to find out, to spend a weekend in a comfortable country house in the middle of what used to be Pictland. They think: now that's a really good idea."

"The Picts did not play golf," said Bruce. "Fact."

# 33

## *Mog Wept Many Tears*

Bruce wanted to look inside the conservatory.

"I love those old structures," he said. "The Victorians over-engineered everything. The Forth Rail Bridge; domestic conservatories; everything was built to be stronger than necessary. They were not great minimalists."

He pushed at the half-open door. It would not budge.

"Rust," said Ben.

"Will you keep this?" asked Bruce. "You can probably get somebody to restore it."

Ben said that he thought it would be a major attraction of the Physic Garden. "And it will be useful too. We can keep the seedlings here – bring them on before planting them out in the beds."

"So much to do," sighed Catriona.

Once Ben had forced the door, Bruce picked up a trowel that he saw lying on a bench. He brushed off an encrustation of earth, exposing the metal beneath. "Look at this," he said. "Made in Glasgow."

Bruce examined the lettering incised in the back of the trowel. "Does anybody make trowels in Glasgow? Can you imagine?"

Bruce shook his head. "No." And added, "What a pity."

"Everything comes from far away," said Catriona. "And the people who made the trowels – what do they do now? What's left for them?"

Ben looked thoughtful. "I wonder whether we aren't going to end up like the Picts," he said. "We'll simply disappear. There'll be nothing left of us."

"The days of man are as grass," said Bruce.

Ben stared at Bruce, but was distracted by Catriona, who had made her way over to the far end of the conservatory and was looking at something on the ground.

"There's an old gravestone," she called. "Come and take a look."

Now the three of them stood above the slab of stone, which was prone on the ground, half obscured by a rotting hessian sack.

"There's something on it," said Ben. "An inscription."

He bent down and, using the trowel he had just discovered, he scraped away at the combination of dried moss and crusted mud that covered most of the stone's surface. Slowly, figures and symbols, etched into the surface of the stone, came to light.

Ben stopped. Bruce, crouching beside him, heard his friend gasp. He was very conscious of Ben being so close to him – the sheer physical presence of another. They were boys again, back on that Saturday so many years ago, when they had climbed a hill outside Crieff and had then sat together on a hummock and talked until it was time to go down again.

"Am I imagining this?" Ben asked. "Am I dreaming? Tell me I'm not."

Catriona had joined them. She adjusted her blue-framed spectacles as she peered at the stone. "You're not imagining it at all. This is Pictish." She paused, and looked at Bruce. "What do you think, Bruce?"

Bruce stood up. He felt slightly giddy as he did so. That was something to do with blood draining from the head. You could faint, they said. You could keel over if you weren't careful.

"It looks Pictish," he said. "Those men on horseback. Look. And the helmets they're wearing."

"And those whirls over there at the top," said Catriona. "Those are Pictish devices. You see them on those early Pictish crosses."

Bruce bent down again. "And here," he said. "Look at this part at the bottom. That's Pictish script, isn't it?"

Ben took a handkerchief out of his pocket and used it to brush from the stone a layer of desiccated lichen. "Ogham," he said. "That's ogham. See those little lines – like matchsticks? That's ogham."

"What does it mean?" asked Catriona.

Ben sighed. "Heaven knows," he said. "People can't decipher these Pictish inscriptions. They're unintelligible."

Bruce stared at the incised marks. How many years was it since somebody had patiently chiselled these into the stone? Thirteen, fourteen centuries? Even more?

Catriona wondered how the stone had found its way into the conservatory. Had it been in the earth on which the ironwork structure had been erected?

"Who knows?" said Bruce. "They probably found it lying around when they made the walled garden." He looked about him. The conservatory was littered with odd remnants of previous gardening activity: pots, shards of pots, ancient rakes, a hoe, seed trays made of rotting wood, an outsize watering can. "They might have carted it in here and then forgotten about it."

"People were much more casual about these things in those days," said Ben. "You could go anywhere and dig up the past. You could go to Egypt and remove things. Whole mummies. There was nobody to stop you. Same here in Scotland. You could do more or less what you liked."

"But what about us?" asked Catriona. "Do we have to report this?"

"I don't see why we should," Ben replied. "There are bags of these Pictish stones all over Scotland. We haven't dug it up.

It's just sitting there, and when we get the house everything here is included. This becomes ours."

Catriona uttered a little squeal of delight. "I've always wanted to have a Pictish tablet," she said. "I remember seeing them in books at school."

"Strange ambition," said Ben, and laughed.

Bruce was still staring at the stone. "I'd love to know what it says."

"Probably nothing important," said Ben. "Something like *Og went out and smote Mog and chopped off his nose. Og carried off Mog's wife. Mog wept many tears.*"

Catriona reached out and touched Ben's forearm. "Darling," she said, "that's so, so sweet. It's poetry, you know. *Mog wept many tears.* That's so lovely."

Bruce looked thoughtful. "What if it really is a poem?" he asked. "It could be, you know."

"I wonder if anybody's making any progress with the Pictish language," mused Ben. "There have been so many arguments about what it was. P-Celtic, Q-Celtic, non-Indo-European. You name it – there's support for just about every possibility. I could ask a friend. He knows about this obscure historical stuff."

"Ask him what?" asked Catriona.

"If he can read Pictish inscriptions. It's always possible that breakthroughs are being made."

"I'll photograph it," said Ben. "Then we can show it to him. In the meantime, we'll leave it here."

He reached down and pulled the old hessian sack across the stone. "I feel as if I'm drawing a curtain across the past," he said.

They were silent. Bruce thought: somewhere in the hills the men on horseback looked down over this land, this place. Our forebears. Our earlier selves. Leading their shorter lives in forests and on grazing lands, aware perhaps of encircling others, anxious as to their fate, inured to sudden human loss, singing the songs that we would never hear, telling the tales that we would never understand.

*Mog wept many tears,* he thought.

# 34

## Safe on Board

The retrieval of a person who has fallen overboard is rarely a simple operation. As Graham Mackie, skipper of the *Aberdeen Belle*, a trawler based in Peterhead, talked his young helmsman through the manoeuvres needed to bring the boat alongside the rapidly tiring Irene, he tried to work out the best way of effecting a rescue. In such circumstances, it is vital that the engine be stopped as one approaches the casualty – to avoid propeller injuries. Graham was fully aware of that particular danger, but even as a skilled skipper he would have difficulty in positioning the boat to make the pick-up midships.

Doddie, the young helmsman, succeeded in placing the boat exactly where required. The sea was calm, in spite of the strong current that had carried Irene out from the shallows into which she had ventured. Now, with the engine barely ticking over, Graham leaned over the side and threw a rescue sling in Irene's direction. She was struggling to keep her head above water, her limbs exhausted and beginning to be unresponsive in the cold water. Encouraged by shouts from Graham, though, she managed to clutch at the sling and somehow to position it.

"Well done," shouted Graham. "Now fold your arms together over your chest, and don't let the sling ride up. I'm going to pull you out."

Winding the line round an electric winch, Graham swivelled the arm of an overhanging derrick so that it was immediately above Irene's bobbing head. Then, pressing the switch that would operate the motor, he slowly lifted her, water dripping off her as the line tugged her slowly upwards and to safety.

A large seagull glided past, silent with suspicion, eyeing proceedings with its cautious, hungry eye.

"Easy does it," purred Graham. "That's grand, just grand." Irene looked, to all intents and purposes, like a drowned rat. Her hair stuck to her face in streaks and her bathing suit was crumpled and twisted. When she opened her mouth, water dribbled out over her chin.

Graham was solicitous. "Are you all right, wifie?"

Irene's eyes struggled to focus. She did not like being called *wifie*. It might be a term of endearment in North East Scotland, but *she* was not to be endeared. "Don't call me that," she said between clenched teeth.

Graham recoiled. If *wifie* was wrong, then he instinctively used a fond term for a girl or young woman: *quine*. This was the language of Lewis Grassic Gibbon, after all, and surely nobody could object to that. "Nae offence, quine."

"Nor that either," spat Irene.

Graham bit his lip. "I'm afa sorry," he said. "I meant nae disrespect."

Irene seemed mollified. "Well, you should be a bit more careful, that's all." She paused. "But thank you for helping me."

"You look gey drookit," said Graham. "I guessed that you weren't in for a pleasure swim."

Irene wiped the hair from her face. "I was swept off the beach. It all happened a bit quickly."

"Aye, that's the sea for you," said Graham. "Things happen afa quickly."

Irene shivered. Her arms were covered in goosebumps and her feet were beginning to turn blue.

"You're chilpet," said Graham, "and nae surprise there. Come down below. I'll get you a towel."

They negotiated their way down a tight companionway

into the crew quarters. Irene looked about her, at the small saloon, with its fixed table, gimballed gas stove and chart table. There was a single cabin off this saloon and she could see two berths inside, both covered with sweaters and other garments. Graham went into this cabin and returned with a large, grubby towel.

"It's not very clean," he apologised as he handed it to her. "But it'll dry you off. You can change out of your wet things, too. We can lend you some claes."

She took the towel, and her nose twitched as she began to use it. She said nothing, though, and was silent, too, as Graham passed her a pair of rough serge trousers, a crumpled blue shirt, and a pair of thick woollen socks. He then passed her a pair of yellow rubber boots and a green woollen cap.

"I'll leave you to it," he said, and retreated back up the companionway to the deck above.

A few minutes later, Irene appeared up on deck. Her hair was less disordered now, and her expression, that had been truculent before, was now less hostile. Beckoned to by Graham, she joined him and Doddie in the cramped wheelhouse.

"I'm sorry if I was a bit abrupt," she said. "I was . . ."

"Shocked," said Graham. "And nae need to apologise. Naebody expects perfect behaviour at sea, do we, Doddie?"

Doddie smiled. "No, skip. Fit's the point of guid behaviour when there's naebody else aboot for miles?"

Graham passed Irene a mug. "Tea. And it's nice and hot."

Irene took a sip, and immediately spluttered.

Graham was concerned. "Too hot?'

"There's sugar in it," complained Irene. "You shouldn't have sugar in your tea."

Graham was surprised. "Why not?" he asked. "Sugar never hurt onybody."

Irene shook her head. "It's very harmful," she said, handing the mug back to him. "And I can't abide the taste. Sorry."

"I'll pour another one," said Graham. "Nae sugar this time."

Doddie now pointed at the radio. "Maybe we should tell the coastguard," he suggested. "They could be looking for you." He gestured towards the North Sea.

Graham nodded. "Did anybody know you were going swimming?" he asked Irene.

"Yes," she replied. "A friend was going to meet me, but she could not come."

"Meet you on the beach?"

"Yes. And . . ."

It occurred to Irene that if somebody found her towel and other possessions on the beach and then looked out over an empty ocean the conclusion might be reached that somebody was lost at sea. That could lead to a search and rescue mission being mounted.

Graham followed her train of thought even though she had said nothing. Now he turned to Doddie and told him to call the coastguard on the radio. "Tell them we've found a woman in the water. Tell them she's safe and we're taking her back with us to Peterhead."

He turned to Irene. "That'll set their minds at rest."

"Yes," Irene agreed.

Graham pointed to the aft deck. "We've got a big catch of fish out aft. I need to start gutting them. No time like the present."

Irene looked at the stack of fish boxes. "I could help you," she offered.

# 35

## *Uncharitable Thoughts*

Between the time when Irene's cold-water therapist first raised the alarm and Doddie's contacting of the coastguard to tell them Irene had been safely recovered, no more than an hour elapsed. But during that brief period, a great deal happened – not only in Aberdeen, where this potential tragedy had unfolded, but also in Edinburgh, and more particularly in Scotland Street, in the Pollock flat itself.

Edinburgh had become involved through the operation of standard coastguard procedure in checking up that a missing person had not simply gone home without telling anybody. And so, when Mark phoned to report Irene's disappearance, he had been advised that he should without delay phone her family to check that she was not with them. Mark was not sure who Irene's family were, and where they lived, and had phoned Jan, who had provided a number in Edinburgh. "This is her ex's," she said. "But I think I know where she might be – if she's not in the water, that is."

Stuart took the call in the middle of a work meeting, which he immediately left in order to return to Scotland Street. He made the short journey home in a dazed state, the dramatic news from Aberdeen barely having penetrated.

Nicola met him at the doorway. "All I know," he said to her, "is what they told me on the phone. She went swimming off the beach and . . ." He hesitated; the word *drown* was so final. "And didn't return."

Nicola shook her head. "What was she doing swimming off the beach?"

Stuart shrugged. "Why do people go swimming? Who knows?" His distress showed in the wavering of his voice. "Poor Irene . . ."

"It's very sad," said Nicola. "It's awful." She almost said *she's* awful, but fortunately did not. "I can't believe it."

"Neither can I," said Stuart. "What are we going to tell the boys?" He looked about him. "Where's Ulysses?"

"He's at the crèche."

"And Bertie's still at school?"

"I was going to collect him. I'll have to do that." She looked at Stuart. "Should I say anything when I pick him up? Or shall I wait?"

Stuart looked agonised, and so Nicola answered her own question. "I think it's best to wait," she said calmly. "We don't really know what's happened. She might simply have got out of the water further along the beach and gone for a walk . . ."

Stuart was dubious. "Or been picked up by a passing fishing trawler?" he said. "No, let's not clutch at fanciful straws. That sort of thing doesn't happen, I think."

Nicola looked thoughtful. It did happen, she thought: in fiction. Did not Mapp and Lucia, those two warring *grandes dames* in Benson's novels, get swept out to sea on an upturned kitchen table? If it could happen in the pages of a novel, then it could surely happen in reality – because fiction surprisingly often merely reflected what happened in real life. But no, straws were not to be clutched at in such circumstances – they merely delayed the acceptance of reality.

Stuart looked at his watch. "Perhaps I should go up to Aberdeen. I'll look up train times."

He left his mother and made his way into the study in which he kept his computer. Nicola returned to the kitchen, where she switched on the kettle for tea. The making of tea was a very common response to an emergency; it shouldn't make a difference to the way in which events unfold, but it did.

*I'll put the kettle on* is a powerful phrase, psychosomatically. What great international crisis might not be defused, at least temporarily, if those who determined the fate of millions sat down together over a cup of tea? As she sat in the kitchen, waiting for the kettle to boil, Nicola reflected on the range of feelings she had experienced since that fateful call had come in from Aberdeen. She felt a certain measure of shame which, as she gave matters further thought, made her feel increasingly uncomfortable. Although she had been shocked by the news, as it slowly sank in, she found herself feeling something altogether different. *She had felt a tinge of relief.* If Irene had been swept out to sea, then she would not be returning to Edinburgh as planned, and their lives, so much more satisfactory since she had absented herself, would become less complicated. And even if Irene appeared to have moderated somewhat – at least in the way she behaved at their last meeting – leopards, as the saying went, did not change their spots. And as these thoughts ran through her mind, she imagined Irene, bespattered with indelible leopard spots, prowling around the undergrowth in the Drummond Place Gardens like a real pardine denizen of the Serengeti.

She had stopped herself. It was entirely unworthy of me, she thought, to think in these terms. Irene's loss – if lost she were – would be a real tragedy, and quite undeserved. *Nobody* deserves to be swept out to sea, even those who are foolish enough to go swimming off Aberdeen beach. And it was quite wrong of her, she told herself, to entertain even the most fleeting of hopes that Nemesis would punish Irene in this way, no matter how much she deserved it, for all her hectoring and disdainful ways . . .

Again, she had to pull herself up. If Irene had been swept away, then she would have to force herself to think charitably about her and to look for good qualities by which to remember her. And there must be some.

Nicola imagined the obituary in the *Scotsman* and how it might refer to Irene's readiness to offer advice, even when unasked. No, that qualification should not be there, even if Irene had often informed Nicola of where she going wrong on some matter or other. Perhaps the way to put it was: "She was a woman of firm opinions, which she was generously prepared to share with others." That was kinder. And if one wanted to make such a reference a touch stronger, one might write: "She did not suffer fools gladly." That often cropped up in obituaries, and was a shorthand description of extreme arrogance. There were many coded messages in such apparent tributes. *He had an extensive knowledge of the more arcane aspects of his subject.* Real meaning: an obsessed bore. *He preferred his own company.* Real meaning: everybody avoided him if they possibly could.

Nicola smiled as she thought this, and was still smiling when Stuart's phone rang and the news came through from Aberdeen.

"She's safe!" shouted Stuart. "She's been picked up by a fishing trawler."

Nicola's smile faded.

# 36

*Terra Firma*

In Peterhead, on the stern coast of North East Scotland, from which the cold silver fish are hunted, halfway to Norway, Irene sat down with her new friends in front of a roaring summer fire, slowly recovering from her ordeal. Seated with her in the living room of the terraced fisherman's cottage were Graham, the skipper of the *Aberdeen Belle*, and her rescuer; Doddie, his young helmsman; and Graham's mother, Ellie Mackie, *née* Scroggie, local president of the Scottish Women's Institute, known locally as *the Rural*.

Ellie lived in the adjoining cottage, and her brother, Wally Scroggie, occupied the cottage beyond that. Wally was married to Doddie's mother, Mollie, Doddie's father, Robbie, having gone off with Ellie's cousin, Maggie, five years previously. Doddie's younger brother, Laurie, lived with his mother, brother and stepfather, but was planning to go to university in Aberdeen to study mechanical engineering.

Ellie was proud of Graham. His father, Hughie, generally known as Shuggie – the fate of many Scottish Hughs – had been difficult to live with. He, like Graham, had been a fisherman, but had grown tired of the hardships involved. He dreamed of warmer and less demanding seas, the opposite of the cold, restless expanses that girded northern Scotland. He had gone south, to Liverpool, to a job on a container ship, and had never returned. Ellie was too protective of Graham to express her satisfaction at this development: she did not want Graham to think that his father had deserted them. But that was what Graham felt, and when he was twenty, he asked a question that revealed his feelings. "Dad was selfish, wasn't he?" he asked. "You can tell me the truth, you know."

Ellie had hesitated, but then decided that he was old enough to know the truth. "Very selfish," she said. "In everything. He thought of only one person – himself."

"Poor Ma," said Graham.

"Well, there you are. Just as long as you don't grow up like him," she said. "And I don't think you will."

Ellie was concerned when Graham opted to take over the trawler in which his father had a two-thirds share. She had seen enough men lost at sea to know the risks of that particular livelihood, and she would have much preferred him to get a job on shore, or possibly on the oil rigs. But his mind was set on going to sea, just as his father and grandfather had done before him, and he would not be persuaded otherwise. So now, shortly after his fortieth birthday, he found himself in a position to buy out the other owner, to engage Doddie and one other young man as crew, and to live the life of a fisherman.

All that was lacking in Graham's life, Ellie thought, was a wife. Over the years, she had done her best to introduce him to suitable young women, but running a fishing boat seemed to leave little time for courtship, and all her candidates had ended in her finding somebody else instead.

Now she sat in Graham's living room, nursing a cup of strong tea, stealing glances at this unusual Edinburgh woman whom he had brought back from the harbour. Graham had explained the circumstances of their meeting, and the reason for Irene's odd clothing. This had elicited an immediate, sympathetic response from Ellie.

"You poor thing," she said. "You must come with me after tea and I'll lend you some more suitable clothing."

Not only was there tea to be drunk, but there were several plates of sandwiches, an array of scones, both sweet and savoury, and a plate of Aberdeen butteries, an iconic local bread roll. There were two pots of homemade goosegog jam, a pair of Finnan haddies, and two Orcadian cheeses.

"This is very kind of you," said Irene, as she surveyed the food. The cold had made her hungry and the sight of this tempting spread was making her mouth water.

"It's not much," said Ellie. "But you should tuck in, dear – after what you've been through."

Irene began with a scone, and made short work of it. Then she tried an egg sandwich, a buttery, and half a Finnan haddie.

"You'll need that to warm you up," said Ellie. "And then I think you'll need a wee rest. You can come with me and stay in my spare room. It's all made up."

Irene suddenly felt tired. She had been up early that morning, and had been late to bed the previous evening. That, along with the traumatic events of the day, was beginning to take its toll of her system.

"I wouldn't mind," she said, aware that her voice was beginning to sound drowsy.

"You should take it easy for a few days," said Ellie. "You can stay here. We'll look after you."

"Aye, that we will," said Graham.

Irene felt herself relaxing. It was a strange feeling – as if she were somehow coming off duty. The fire was warm; the food was delicious; the tea was comforting. She had been planning to travel down to Edinburgh within a few days, but now that seemed to her to be becoming a less attractive option. Edinburgh was a busy place; Peterhead was not. There was nobody to make her tea and scones in Edinburgh. Here there was, and she had just had precisely that offer from a woman who looked as if she made the best scones for miles around. And these were good people, this fisherman and his mother; why not stay a while with this good, solid family? She glanced about her. There was a copy of the *Press and Journal* on the table; there was no *Guardian*, the writ of which did not run in these latitudes. It was a different life, a different world to the one she had inhabited, and when you have been plucked out of the sea and served scones and butteries, it was a strangely attractive one.

Graham turned to his mother and said, brightly, "Irene was very handy with a filleting knife, Mother. She was a big help on the boat."

Irene looked away modestly. Ellie, though, glanced at Irene with interested, narrowed eyes. She recalled a conversation with the wife of the local minister, who had said, "Don't worry about Graham, Ellie. God may be taking his time, but he'll send the right woman sooner or later."

Had that remark been prescient? Ellie thought that it perhaps it had been. It was probably no accident that the sea should sweep Irene on a course that resulted in her being intercepted by the *Aberdeen Belle*. Some things looked like coincidences, but were, in reality, far from that. Some meetings were *meant* to be – and she felt that this might well be one of them. She looked again at Irene. She had good, broad shoulders and strong calves. She could survive the cold, as had been proved by her recovery from her ordeal, and Graham had said that she knew how to gut a fish. Who could be more suitable?

# 37

## *The Dalai Lama's Eyes*

Matthew arrived at his gallery rather later than normal the following morning. He liked to be punctual, but he had long since realised that it made no real difference when the gallery opened, as there were very few visitors until at least lunchtime. And there were days, of course, when nobody came at all.

Not that this really made any financial difference. The profitable part of Matthew's business now consisted of buying and selling at auction and in private sales, negotiated in many cases with collectors of Scottish art who lived elsewhere. The gallery, though, provided an important way of launching artists at an early stage of their careers. To have had an exhibition, even one to which almost nobody came, was an important element in any artistic curriculum vitae, and Matthew spent a great deal of time encouraging artists to work towards an exhibition. He loved discovering new talent, and made a point of attending the annual degree shows of the main Scottish art colleges. He hoped, of course, to find a new Hockney, or an emergent Fergusson or Peploe, but he never did. That was precluded by a current orthodoxy that did not countenance the rigorous teaching of the traditional basic skills of the artist. Drawing and painting seemed to be viewed with distaste, with the result that there was very little to delight the eye in an art college show.

On a visit to the Edinburgh College of Art some years earlier, he had seen the work of a graduate who had summed up four years of study by placing a broken kitchen chair in the centre of a room and placing upon it a parcel wrapped in brown paper. That was all, although a title had been added, *Parcel IV*. Nothing was said about *Parcels I to III* – and that, perhaps, was the point. What the artist was trying to do through his practice – and that was what artists had: they had a *practice*; they did not do anything as mundane as paint or sculpt – was to communicate about *sequence*. Everything was *interconnected*, and we should try to understand the connection between one moment – or one physical object – and the moment or object that had preceded it.

Matthew had left that particular show in a state of puzzlement. He had gone straight to see Angus in his studio, and had told him of what he had seen. Angus had rolled his eyes.

"Intellectual fashion," he had said. "The desire to break away from a tradition is hardly new. In fact, it's that which is tired, rather than the tradition itself."

"But," sighed Matthew, "what will happen to these people who put parcels on chairs?"

"Oh, nothing much," said Angus. "Although one or two of them may win the Turner Prize. That's always available for parcels on chairs." He paused. He was painting somebody's eye, and he needed to get the light right. Matthew peered at the canvas. He recognised who Angus's sitter had been – a prominent actress whose face was always in the papers.

"You've captured her," he said. "That tiny dot of paint says it all. Everything. Her character. The way she looks at the world. Everything."

Angus stood back from his painting. "The eyes have it," he said. "So to speak."

Matthew looked again. It was true. The rest of the face – the nose, the lips, could have belonged to anybody – but it was the eyes that did the work.

"Isn't it odd," Angus said as he cleaned his brush, "how the whole moral story is written in the face – particularly the eyes? Look at a picture of the Dalai Lama. Have you looked at his eyes? There's a wonderful humanity there – and a sense of humour. You see the man in his eyes."

Matthew tried to conjure up the Dalai Lama. Angus was right. And Matthew then thought: Buddhist monks like to laugh. That said so much about them, and about Buddhism.

"I never tire of looking at eyes," Angus continued. "I've been looking at pictures of politicians. You should look at their eyes, because they tell you so much about their motives. In fact, before you vote for anybody you should perhaps take a close look at their eyes."

Matthew smiled. "And never vote for anybody wearing sunglasses?"

Angus agreed. "Definitely not. There are occasions when you need to wear sunglasses – very bright days, for instance, or when you're skiing, but any other use of sunglasses suggests that you have something to hide. Sunglasses can be the equivalent of a mask."

But now Matthew was at his desk, looking at the morning mail, which seemed to him to be more promising than usual. There were no bills, which made for a good start to the day, and one or two invitations to exhibition openings. One of these caught his eye: "*Parcels*", the invitation proclaimed. "You are cordially invited to *Parcels VIII* and other work by Gregory Trash. Trash has devoted his recent practice to the exploration of sequence and this show contains his latest work, following on the success in London of *Parcels VII*. There will be a short talk before the opening of the exhibition in which Trash will discuss his recent collaboration with the Icelandic installation artist Helga Dóttirsondóttir, *Geyser III*."

Matthew put the invitation in a drawer. Trash was clearly doing well, although it was often difficult to separate hype from substance. He was inclined, though, to go to the show and the promised talk, in the same way as people who find bullfighting hateful are drawn to the awful spectacle of the *corrida de toros*, knowing they will detest what they see, but wanting to see just how bad it is so that they confirm their antipathy. And at the back of his mind, there was a niggling doubt. If Trash was doing so well, then there might just be something in his vision that Matthew was missing? Mind you, thought Matthew, for *vision*, read *practice*. Have I closed my mind to the broader possibilities of art? Matthew asked himself. Is Angus Lordie just an out-of-touch reactionary living in a world of tired, neoclassical attitudes, while all about him inquisitive spirits were exploring the boundaries of what it is to be human – making us look at everyday things in an entirely new way?

Possibly, he thought. And then he looked at his watch and realised that it was time for coffee at Big Lou's. Angus would be dropping in, and he could tell him about Trash's forthcoming exhibition. He knew how Angus would react, but nevertheless he might say to him, "Are you sure, Angus? Aren't you being a bit dismissive of the zeitgeist?"

He closed the gallery behind him, hanging up the usual sign: *Back in Fifteen Minutes.* That, he thought, was aspirational, rather than predictive: perhaps he should preface it with the words *Hope to be* – words that might precede much of what we said about our intentions.

# 38

## *The Nature of Normality*

Big Lou was polishing the steam spout of her large Italian coffee making machine, *La Magnifica*. It was the machine's weak point, she had discovered. It ground coffee with consummate ease, and could disgorge a stream of espresso seemingly as limitless as the water drawn from St Catherine of Siena's miraculous barrel, but the steaming of milk could lead to blockages unless care was taken to give the spout regular and thorough cleans. In the performance of that duty, Lou could not be faulted. Her childhood years on the family farm, Snell Mains, had taught her the importance of thorough washing of anything in contact with milk. The farm had run a small dairy herd, and the milking equipment had to be kept as sterile as possible – a difficult task in a building frequented by cows. Big Lou had already been able to milk a cow when she was six, and could be trusted to wash the bucket thoroughly after pouring the milk into a churn. But she knew, as any farm child knows, that milk that was spilled or forgotten about was capable within days of producing a smell that was almost impossible to eradicate.

Now, as she gave the steam spout a final wipe, she looked up to see Matthew pushing open the door at the bottom of the stone steps leading from the street. Big Lou smiled a welcome. Matthew was joint owner of her coffee bar, having invested in it when she needed to raise money, but he was the most tactful of business partners. While other investors might insist on being given an opportunity regularly to scrutinise accounts, Matthew never asked to do this, being satisfied with Big Lou's occasional reports on how the business was faring. And that, she was happy to be able to tell him, was rather better than expected.

The secret, it seemed, of Big Lou's success was her constancy. While other coffee bars employed young people who came and went, Big Lou was always there, and was, moreover, always willing to listen to what her customers had to say. In that respect, she was like one of those legendary barmen who could engage in repartee and converse on a wide range of subjects while serving martinis, or whatever it was that their customers wanted.

In a world where the number of shoulders upon which people may cry seems to be diminishing – the decline of neighbourliness being the main reason for that – having a barista or hairdresser, or somebody of that sort who could be counted on to listen, was something to be cherished. And Big Lou, although robust in her views, and not one to encourage a complaining or entitled view of life, was nonetheless a sympathetic ear.

So it was not surprising that Matthew should take a seat at the coffee bar, eschewing the nearby table at which he normally sat, and raise with Big Lou the subject that he had been thinking about since he had visited the site of the proposed Pictish Experience Centre in rural Stirlingshire.

As Big Lou prepared his coffee, he told her about the trip he had made with Bruce and his friends. Big Lou listened with interest, a worried frown crossing her brow when Matthew related the proposal that Ben had sent him the previous evening.

"He needs to raise money," Matthew said. "He's asked me for a hundred thousand."

Big Lou drew in her breath. "A hundred thousand? Matthew, isn't that a bit much?"

Matthew shrugged. "Start-ups need that sort of funding. There's quite a lot to do to the house. The roof needs attention, for starters. Then there's the plumbing, and the wiring. Ben's going to have to put more in himself."

Big Lou shook her head. "And can you be sure you won't lose the lot?"

Matthew said that he was aware of that possibility. "But you have to take risks in business," he said. "Look at the people who have done well. They've put their money on the line – and it's paid off. Those two who invented Apple. Didn't they work from their garage right at the beginning? And Mr Dyson and his bagless vacuum cleaner – he had to take a risk to pull that off. There are numerous examples."

Big Lou was not convinced. "Most start-ups fail. I read that in the paper. There was an article about them. A very small proportion of them survive – even if the original idea was a good one."

"Oh, I know that," said Matthew. "But if nobody supported these people, then would there ever be any innovation? Nothing new would ever reach the market-place."

Big Lou conceded the point. But then she said, "One hundred thousand, though . . . does Elspeth know?"

"She was there when we first heard about it," said Matthew.

"Oh well," said Big Lou. "If you think people will come for a weekend of thinking about the Picts . . ."

"They will," said Matthew. "Wouldn't you?"

Big Lou shook her head. "I don't think so," she said. "Remember: I grew up with these people."

"With Picts?"

"Well, with people who looked pretty Pictish to me," said Big Lou. She paused. "Mind you, I happen to know of one group who will be keen to make a booking. They were talking to me about the difficulty of finding somewhere for their weekend meetings. They might well come and stay at this place of yours."

"There you are," said Matthew, and then asked, "Who were they?"

"Those nudist folk," said Big Lou. "They tried to book at Gleneagles recently but they were turned down. Something about a dress code."

Matthew looked thoughtful. He knew who Big Lou was talking about. The Chairman and the Secretary of the Association of Scottish Nudists were occasional customers in Big Lou's café, and Matthew had seen them on a number of occasions. The café was convenient for their headquarters, which were in Moray Place, at the end of Heriot Row.

"They might be interested, I suppose," he said, and then added, "Of course those people are always complaining, aren't they?"

"Aye," said Big Lou. "But then, if you were a nudist and you lived in Scotland, wouldn't you complain? Temperature, rain, midges . . ."

Matthew had to agree. He sipped his coffee and glanced at his watch. He was expecting Angus and Cyril, who would be here shortly, in three minutes, to be precise, because Angus was scrupulously punctual – as much so, Matthew thought, as Immanuel Kant, by whom the citizens of Königsberg could famously set their watches when they saw him setting off on his daily walk. Did Kant suffer, he wondered, from OCD? So many people did now, ever since we learned of the condition and people were able to see it in themselves and their friends. Was anybody left to be normal these days? Was he – Matthew – normal? Or the nudists from Moray Place? Or Bruce? Was the new Bruce the new normal for Bruce? Could lightning have the effect of a massive dose of ECT? Was the new Bruce there for good, or would he revert to type?

# 39

## In a Snorl

Angus came in with Cyril, passing the small, discouraging notice that said *No dogs allowed, except Cyril*. It was a concession made grudgingly by Big Lou, who, having been raised on a farm, believed that dogs belonged in the yard. She had to admit that Cyril, with his Border collie heritage, was worthy of greater consideration than the irredeemably urban dogs to be seen in the streets of the Edinburgh New Town. Big Lou was particularly scornful of the fashion for what she called *designer dogs* – combinations of breeds with composite names: labradoodles and so on. Such dogs might have their merits, and might even represent the best of both breeds in the mixture, but she suspected that many of their owners chose them for their exotic names and fancy appearance – not a basis, in her view, on which to choose a dog.

Cyril immediately recognised Matthew, who had now moved to the table at which he and Angus normally sat. Taking up his position at Matthew's feet, he gazed longingly at the ankles he so wished to nip. It was a strange thing, this obsession that the dog had with Matthew's ankles. It was not that there was anything unusual in them – at least there was nothing that a human observer might notice – but to Cyril they represented temptation in its most irresistible form. He had once succumbed, and had nipped at the forbidden fruit, incurring the wrath of his owner. Matthew had been understanding, and assured Angus that the skin had not been broken.

"It's not as if he has rabies," Matthew joked, as he threw a reproachful glance in Cyril's direction.

"I assure you he doesn't," said Angus.

And there then followed an awkward silence, as he asked himself whether Cyril had ever been inoculated against the terrible disease, and decided that he had not. Of course, rabies was not present in Scotland and so there was no need, unless . . .

"There's no rabies in Scotland, is there?" asked Matthew, a note of anxiety in his voice.

"Not as far as I know," Angus began. "Although . . ."

Matthew waited.

"Although I think it might be present in bats."

Matthew's eyes widened.

"Scottish bats?"

Angus tried to appear nonchalant. "One or two maybe."

Matthew hesitated. Then he said, "But it's there?"

Angus nodded. "In bats," he said. "Not in dogs." He looked down at Cyril. "Cyril is weak – we all are. He knows that he shouldn't bite, but he suffers from *akrasia*, you see."

Matthew's eyes widened again. "Akrasia? How did he get that?"

Angus shrugged. "How does anybody get akrasia?" he asked. "Born with it, I suppose." He paused. "I have it myself, if I'm honest. You're probably prone to it yourself."

"Now?" asked Matthew, looking down at Cyril. "You mean I might develop it? Develop akrasia?"

Matthew was silent for a few moments. Then he asked, "How do they treat it? How do they treat akrasia?"

Angus smiled. "It's a familiar story: you can only treat akrasia in somebody who recognises that they have it – and who wants to do something about it."

"But dogs can't do that," objected Matthew.

"I suppose they can't," Angus agreed. "Dogs have no insight into their condition. They just *are*. They don't have the consciousness of self that we have."

Matthew looked down at Cyril once more. Cyril looked back up at him – and wagged his tail, in recognition, or, possibly, apology. "What does the vet say?" he asked. "What did the vet say about his akrasia?"

The question seemed to puzzle Angus. "I doubt that the vet knows what it is," he replied.

Matthew considered this. "He should," he said at last. "If akrasia is common in dogs, then surely vets should know the symptoms. Are there antibiotics? Do they help?"

Angus stared at Matthew incredulously. Then he started to smile. "I'm sorry," he said. "I should have realised . . . I should have explained what akrasia is. It's not a disease, Matthew. Sorry about the misunderstanding. I assumed you'd know."

Matthew looked askance at his friend. "How many people know what akrasia is? I'm not ignorant just because I don't know what akrasia is."

Angus reassured him that nobody was calling anybody ignorant. "Akrasia is weakness of will. It's a Greek word. Greek philosophers talked about akratic action. It's a big debate in philosophy – whether it makes sense to say that you can ever act in such a way that is against your own interests, because we always end up doing what we want to do – if you see my meaning."

Matthew looked away. "You implied it was a disease that Cyril had," he muttered peevishly.

Angus apologised. "I suggest we forget about akrasia. Cyril has it, but you can't transmit it through biting." He paused. "Rabies is a different matter, of course."

"Those bats," Matthew said. "Why don't they pass it on to other animals?"

"Because they have very small teeth," said Angus. "The bats we have in Scotland have small teeth and don't go round biting people."

Matthew looked thoughtful. "But what if a bat dies and

a fox were to come and eat it. Couldn't the fox get rabies?"

"I don't think so," said Angus. "I read that rabies is a fragile virus. I don't think you can pass it on that way."

But now, on this morning in Big Lou's café, even with his tendency to akrasia, Cyril refrained from nipping Matthew's ankles. At the table above, at the human level, the conversation turned to a more immediate concern, which was the invitation Matthew had received to invest in the Pictish Experience Centre.

"You shouldn't," said Angus. "Start-ups never work – or very few of them do." He paused. "And I'd never get involved with Bruce . . . in anything. You know what he's like."

"Bruce has changed," said Matthew. "Ever since the lightning strike, he's been different."

Angus was sceptical. "People don't change," he said.

Matthew felt this was far too bleak a view to take of humanity. "Do you really think so?" he asked. He looked at Angus intensely. "Are you saying that you've never changed? Ever? That the twenty-year-old Angus Lordie is the same as the Angus Lordie sitting here today? Are you really saying that?"

Angus hesitated, and instead of waiting for him to reply, Matthew continued, "We all change, Angus – unless we're completely devoid of self-awareness."

"We may change a bit, maybe," Angus conceded. "But Bruce . . ." He trailed off, his voice full of scepticism.

Matthew looked uncomfortable. "I think he really *has* changed," he said. "And I'm going to support him – and Ben and Catriona too."

Angus shrugged. "I've done the duty that friendship requires of me," he said.

"Namely?'

"To warn you you're being taken for a ride, Matthew. Completely. A Pictish Experience Centre? Come on, Matthew – be realistic!"

Big Lou had been listening from her counter. "I agree with Angus," she said. "You're going to get yersel in an awfa snorl."

*Snorl?* thought Matthew. But then he realised that this was one of those Scots words of which the general sense was completely clear, even if you had never encountered the word before and had no idea what it meant.

# 40

## *The Association of Scottish Nudists*

Matthew sipped at his coffee. He had listened to what Angus had to say, but it was too late, he thought, for him to go back on his offer to invest in the Pictish Experience Centre. And it was all very well, he thought, for Big Lou to suggest that he should not help his friends in their new venture, but had she forgotten that she herself had benefited in the past from his financial help? He had acquired an interest in her café, not to make money, but because he had wanted to help her in her business. Had he been more cautious he would not have done so, and she may have been obliged to close her doors. So now that he was proposing to do a similar thing for Ben and Catriona, he did not think that she should raise objections based on financial prudence. And what was money for, anyway? If everybody hoarded what they had, then the economy would seize up, and that, surely, would be in nobody's interest. Matthew was lucky, and was conscious of his good fortune. He had been given money by his businessman father, and was grateful for that. He was of a generous disposition, though, and he always liked to share what he had. It was a sign of moral failure, he had decided, to die with more money than you needed.

He looked at Angus. "I don't mind giving money away," he said, adding, "I really don't."

Angus smiled. He had witnessed – and appreciated – Matthew's generosity. "Fair enough, but you don't want to give it *all* away, do you? Not everything. You have to be careful – that's all I'm saying."

"But I'm not giving it all away," said Matthew. "I'm going to put in one hundred thousand pounds, and that's it." He lowered his voice. "I've got more than that, you know."

"This isn't small change," Angus said. "Most people don't have anything like that much."

"That may be so," Matthew conceded. "And I know that I'm really lucky to have the money I've got. But I don't want to still have it when I eventually die."

Angus looked thoughtful. "You think it's a good thing to have nothing left when you go?"

Matthew nodded. "I do." There was a qualification, though. "Provided that you don't squander it. I'm not advocating waste – or self-indulgence."

Angus grinned. "Like that famous footballer who said that that he had spent most of his money on drink, women, and fast cars – and then added that the rest he had just squandered?"

Matthew appreciated the joke. "Yes, like him."

"Or like Father John Maitland Moir?"

Matthew was not sure that he knew who this was.

"He was an Orthodox priest here in Edinburgh," Angus explained. "I met him towards the end of his life. He was a kenspeckle character around the town."

Matthew liked the word *kenspeckle,* Scots for 'well-known'. "Kenspeckle," he mused.

"He was a great man," Angus went on. "He was very eccentric. You used to see him riding his large tricycle in his black cassock. He used to be an Episcopalian priest, but he developed an interest in orthodoxy. He was proud of the fact that the liturgy of the Scottish Episcopalian Church contained an epiclesis."

Matthew was lost. "I have no idea what that is," he said.

"It's an invocation of the Holy Spirit," explained Angus. "Anyway, he decided to become Orthodox. He went to Mount Athos and was admitted to the Greek Orthodox Church."

"Is that the place where—"

Angus interrupted him. "Where monks are lowered down in baskets; where there are no women; where everybody has a beard . . . Yes. But he didn't stay there long. He came back to Edinburgh and ran a chaplaincy for Orthodox students. This is was where he was from. He had inherited a fortune, but over the years he gave everything away – everything. He ate only once a day. He fed homeless people – he offered his couch to tramps who needed a bed for the night. He helped anybody who pitched up at his door. And at the end, he had given away every penny – every single penny – and he was looked after by those nuns who had that convent near the King's Theatre – the Little Sisters of the Poor."

For a short while, Matthew was silent. Any account of a good life always moved him. He wanted to be good – he most fervently wanted to be good, but he felt that it would never be given to him, to be that which he desired to be. Now he said, in a voice tinged with disappointment, "I don't think I could do that. I don't think I could give everything away."

"Nor should you," said Angus quickly. "You are a husband and a father of three. You have to provide."

"I know that," said Matthew. "But that doesn't stop me from thinking my life is always going to be . . . dull and respectable."

Angus shook an admonishing finger. "There is nothing wrong with your life, Matthew. Nothing."

He was about to say something more, but he was distracted by the arrival of two men in dark suits, who had come into the café and sat down at a table in the far corner.

"Those two," Angus said. "They're somehow familiar."

Matthew glanced in the direction of the newcomers, now sunk deep in conversation. "I know who they are," he said, and smiled. "They're in here from time to time."

"Well?"

Matthew lowered his voice. In the background, from Big Lou's coffee maker, there came the hiss of escaping steam. "The Association of Scottish Nudists. Remember? They have their office over in Moray Place."

Angus looked at the two men again. Now he remembered. "Of course. They're the committee, aren't they?"

"They always look so miserable," Matthew said. "They sit in here and confer – and look thoroughly miserable."

Angus shrugged. "Wouldn't you? I mean, if you were a nudist in Scotland, what chance have you got? A tiny window of opportunity, so to speak, in the middle of the summer, when the temperature creeps up to . . . well, double figures . . . and then it's back to thermal underwear and Shetland sweaters."

"That's a bit extreme," said Matthew.

"But realistic," Angus responded. "You should live according to your latitude, I always say. And that means you should dress accordingly. We are a tweedy people, Matthew."

Matthew did not like that. Angus may have been tweedy, but he most certainly was not. He allowed himself another quick glance at the committee. Nudists would be used to stares, he thought, but he would not wish to be rude.

"I wonder what they're talking about?" he mused.

# 41

## *The Past, Smugness, Conscience*

The Chairman of the Association of Scottish Nudists surveyed the bacon roll on the plate before him.

"Very nice," he said to the Secretary of the Association, seated opposite him. "That woman makes very good bacon rolls, I'd be inclined to say."

He spoke in the accents of Morningside, *I'd* becoming *Aid;* and the Secretary's reply being delivered in similar tones, with *mine* becoming *main.*

The Secretary looked at his own bacon roll, and then, discreetly, at the Chairman's. It was not the first time that the Chairman had taken the more appetising of the two rolls for himself. Now he said, "My roll doesn't have quite as much bacon as yours does – not that I'm complaining, I'd hasten to point out."

The barb in this comment went unnoticed. "Bacon rolls are rarely equal," the Chairman said. "Not that I'd noticed that, in this particular case."

They each addressed their roll, taking a few bites in silence before the first sips of coffee were taken and the conversation resumed.

"Well," said the Chairman, dabbing at his lips with a paper napkin, "just when we thought we'd achieved a certain stability, this happens."

The Secretary inclined his head. "I'm afraid it's very much a requirement these days. It's called good governance. We all have to comply."

"Oh, I know that," said the Chairman. "It's just that you'd

think they'd make a distinction between public and private. We're a completely private association, and how we run our affairs should be our business, you'd think."

The Secretary sighed. "That's not the world we live in, Chairman. The boundaries between private and public are being broken down by the new" — he searched for a suitable phrase — "by the new intrusiveness." He paused. "What you say in your own house is no longer your business, you know."

"So I hear," said the Chairman.

"And the result is that people are afraid to express views on anything vaguely controversial – in case they're reported."

"So much for freedom of speech," sighed the Chairman. "But let's not dwell on such general matters. What we have to decide is how to respond to the members' demands for a governance review." He frowned. "Demands from the Glasgow members."

"Be that as it may," said the Secretary. "We shall still need to respond." He paused as he consulted a letter he had extracted from his pocket. "I see that they want us to establish an ethical investments review committee, to look at the association's endowment. They're even suggesting themselves as members."

"They would," said the Chairman.

"They want us to divest ourselves of any investments in companies that make clothes,' said the Secretary.

The Chairman considered this. "I suppose one can see the point of that," he said. "Do we have any investments of that nature?"

The Secretary looked thoughtful. "I think we may. We have one or two high street names in our portfolio. I suspect that's what they have in mind."

The Chairman was concerned. "The problem is that wherever you turn for alternative investments, somebody somewhere or other will come up with an objection to what you propose."

The Secretary looked up at the ceiling. "Frankly," he said, "I am somewhat bemused. It seems to me that we are in danger of destroying the basic confidence any society requires in order to function – destroying it by injecting excessive moral scruple."

The Chairman considered this. "Oh, I don't know," he said. "I think that people are just opening their eyes to things that they previously ignored. We're asking more questions, I agree – but perhaps we should have asked those questions a long time ago. We were too comfortable – too smug."

The Secretary stared at him. *He* was not smug, and if the Glasgow members who were raising these issues were suggesting that, then he felt they had no right to do so.

"I suppose I can see what people mean," the Chairman went on. "There are those who say that all money in the current system is tainted by exploitation, past or present – certainly by the wrongs of the past. What is the basis of such prosperity as we currently enjoy? Our imperial past? Probably. We did very well out of other people's natural resources, didn't we? Perhaps it's payback time now."

The Secretary sniffed. "My people didn't do well. We were tenant farmers in Ayrshire – in a very small way. My maternal grandfather went to school in parish boots. His father was a collier." He paused. "I'm not sure that we can unravel things. Perhaps we have to concentrate on behaving well *now*, and not pay so much attention to how things were in the past."

"Except that the ill-gotten gains of the past are still under our noses," said the Chairman. "Or so some people believe – I'm not necessarily saying that myself. But others are."

"Should we empty our museums?" asked the Secretary. "Is that what you're saying?"

The Chairman looked at his hands. Were they dirty, he

wondered, simply because they were the hands of one who lived in a society where, in the past, many hands *were* dirty?

"I wouldn't empty them," he said. "But I would look at them very carefully. I'd give back the big things – the things that mean a great deal to the people we took them from. There's a certain justice in that, I'd have thought."

The Secretary took a sip of his coffee. "Museums are one thing – stock exchanges are another. I find it difficult to identify investments that are completely guilt-free – much as I'd like to be able to do so." He took another sip of coffee. Coffee beans, he thought: how clean are they? But then he had an idea. "Actually, I can think of something. There's a new company out in Motherwell that's making outdoor heaters. I can see that appealing to the members."

"That's a brilliant idea," said the Chairman. "They'll be a great boon to mankind in general."

"And in particular to us," said the Secretary. "They make a great difference."

"And there's a firm making a new form of midge repellent," said the Chairman. "That's a natural for us."

The Secretary looked more cheerful. "These problems often go away once one starts to think about them."

The Chairman sat back. "The important thing is to be transparent," he said. "If you are transparent in your conduct of the affairs of anything, then you'll have nothing to reproach yourself over."

The Secretary agreed. "And it's very important that bodies like ours should behave with the utmost integrity. We are, after all, the Association of Scottish Nudists. People still expect Scottish nudists to behave with integrity. We are not just any old nudists – we are Scottish nudists, and that counts for something."

The Chairman nodded. He wished that certain Scottish bankers had thought that way in the past – the recent past

– but they had not. It was quite wrong, he felt, that such thinking should be left to organisations like the Association of Scottish Nudists, but there we are: the world is often not quite as one would wish it to be – nor were the barricades always in the right place.

# 42

## *Galactica Makes Her Move*

Ranald Braveheart Macpherson's birthday party would not be readily forgotten by any of those who attended it. For Ranald himself, it had been a bleak experience, doomed by its guest list to be an occasion of discord and dispute and, in its tense and thrawn closing stages, tears. Ranald had certainly cried for a full ten minutes towards the end, when a game of musical chairs had collapsed into a rugby scrum every bit as robustly physical as anything ever witnessed at Murrayfield Stadium. That had been the last straw for Ranald, whose tears had then proved contagious in much the same way as a yawn tends to be. Shortly thereafter, Moss had followed Ranald's example, shedding copious tears as he struggled to deal with the muttered threats of Socrates Dunbar. Pelion was piled upon Ossa when Pansy, unable to accept the humiliation of her patron, Olive, had joined in the sobbing. A few minutes later, the party began to break up, and the guests were removed in parental embrace, leaving Ranald to ask himself how everything could have gone so terribly wrong. It was all because of the guest list, he decided, and that, fairly and squarely, was the responsibility of his mother. If only she had not invited Galactica, then the party might not have been such a disaster. But mothers always had ideas of their own, he reflected, and one could no more influence them than one could dictate the weather.

Ranald was worried that his party would become the subject of a post-mortem at school the following Monday, but no mention was made of it beyond an enquiry by Socrates Dunbar as to when Ranald might entertain again, as he,

Socrates, had so enjoyed himself at his house. Ranald had given a non-committal answer, but had privately reminded himself of the various provocations that Socrates had offered to the other guests. If he were to hold another party, he told himself, Socrates would definitely not be invited, and nor would Moss, Tofu, Olive, Pansy or Galactica – which left only a small handful of possible guests, including Bertie, who would, of course, always be welcome.

It was an hour into the school day when Bertie became aware that tension was developing in the classroom. He had been engaged in a colouring-in exercise when he happened to look up to see Galactica staring across the room to the table at which Olive and Pansy were seated. This would not have been of any particular interest had it not been for the fact that Olive was herself staring back at Galactica, her eyes narrowed in response to the unflinching look directed towards her.

Bertie nudged Ranald Braveheart Macpherson, who was sitting beside him. "See that, Ranald," he said. "Galactica's staring at Olive."

Ranald looked in Olive's direction. "I don't think Galactica likes her," he said.

Bertie had to agree. "Why do people hate other people, Ranald?" he asked.

Ranald shrugged. "Sometimes they hate their faces," he said. "But I think there are lots of other bits they can hate."

Bertie sighed. "It's not very kind to hate other people, Ranald. And it doesn't make things better. Professor Freud says that you only hate other people if you're not very confident."

In spite of being only seven, Bertie had read Freud (and not just the Ladybird editions).

Ranald looked puzzled. "Who's Professor Freud, Bertie?'

"He's a man who lived a long time ago, Ranald," Bertie replied. "You can read him, maybe, when you learn how to read a bit better."

They became aware that something was happening on the other side of the room. At Olive's desk, Pansy was clearly becoming agitated, gripping her friend's arm to attract her attention. But Olive was not to be distracted; she was determined to outstare Galactica, even if she was finding it increasingly difficult. And now, perhaps disturbed by Pansy's anxious intervention, she was on the point of blinking – which she did, her eyes lowered in submission to the greater intensity of her rival's stare.

For her part, Galactica raised her head in triumph, a smile spreading across her face. Olive, by contrast, humiliated in the eyes of those who had witnessed the encounter, pretended to busy herself with the class reading book, *Janet and John Deconstructed*. For a few moments, she withered under Galactica's display of triumph before, goaded beyond human endurance, she acted. Brushing aside Pansy's restraining hand, she rose to her feet and strode across the classroom to stand immediately behind Galactica's chair. There, with a sudden, deft movement, she pulled the chair from under its occupant, sending Galactica sprawling on the floor.

Those in the immediate vicinity drew in their breath sharply. Pansy, witnessing this blatant attack by her friend, gasped, and put her hand to her mouth in alarm. Galactica herself was unhurt, and soon picked herself up and resumed her seat, barely glancing at Olive as she did so.

The teacher, Miss Campbell, had been looking at the blackboard, and had not seen what happened. When she turned round, she saw Pansy approaching her desk, seemingly eager to make a report.

"Galactica was staring at Olive, Miss Campbell," she said, her voice filled with righteous indignation. "I saw her. She was staring at her for ages. Olive didn't start it."

Miss Campbell made her way to the scene of the crime and addressed the two girls. "What exactly is happening here, girls?" she asked.

Galactica was quick to seize the initiative. "Olive made me fall out of my chair," she replied.

"I didn't," said Olive. "Her chair fell over – and now she's blaming me, Miss Campbell. It's not fair."

Tofu, who was seated nearby, saw a chance to settle a score with Olive. "That's not true, Miss Campbell. I saw what happened. I was right here. I saw it."

Miss Campbell turned to Tofu. Of all the children in the class, he would be the most unreliable witness, she thought. But she could hardly ignore him.

"Tofu's a liar," protested Olive. "Everybody knows he's a psychopath, Miss Campbell. He's the biggest liar in the school – maybe the whole of Edinburgh, I think. And he smells. Everybody knows that as well. He really smells."

"*You* smell," hissed Tofu.

"Please!" exhorted Miss Campbell. "Olive, you're not to say things like that."

"Even if it's true, Miss Campbell?"

"Even if it's true," said Miss Campbell, and then quickly corrected herself. "Not that it is true, of course. Tofu doesn't smell."

The teacher sighed. This was a middle-class school. These children, she said to herself, were *middle class*, for heaven's sake. What was the point of having a middle class if its offspring were going to behave like this? She thought of *Lord of the Flies*, which she had only recently read for the first time. It should be the first item on the reading list at teaching college, she thought – item number one – underlined, a *sine qua non* of any teacher's understanding.

# 43

## *Galactica Apologises*

Quite unexpectedly, but with a perfect sense of what the exigencies of the situation required, Galactica diverted attention from Tofu and brought it back to herself.

"I'm afraid it probably was my fault, Miss Campbell," she said. "I *was* staring at Olive, but only in admiration."

There were contrasting reactions to this. Olive was incredulous, struck by the unlikelihood of the claim: she, at least, would not be fooled. Miss Campbell, though, eager to defuse the conflict, after taking a few moments to gather her thoughts praised Galactica's mature reaction – a response of the sort she wished more people would adopt when confronted with their misdeeds. "It's called accepting responsibility, children," she announced. "If you have done something wrong, then it is always far better to admit to it and apologise – just as Galactica has done." She paused. "So well done, Galactica, although I take it that you will say sorry to Olive. I don't expect you to say sorry for *everything* – just for being perhaps a touch insensitive as to how other people might interpret your staring."

Galactica was reason itself. "Of course, Miss Campbell – of course I'll say sorry to Olive." She turned to face Olive, once again fixing her with a powerful stare. Olive winced.

"I'm so sorry, Olive," said Galactica. She paused as the icing was added to the unctuous cake. Then, she continued, "I didn't know you were so nervous. I'm very sorry. I won't look at you again – ever. I'll close my eyes when you're around."

Miss Campbell laughed nervously. "No, I don't think

you quite mean that, Galactica. A simple sorry will be quite enough."

Galactica nodded. "I'm very sorry, Olive." She turned to Miss Campbell. "Was that right, Miss Campbell?"

Miss Campbell was quite satisfied. "Yes, that's quite all right, Galactica. And Olive, I think you should say to Galactica that you're sorry too. And you should perhaps apologise to Tofu for calling him a psychopath. And for saying that he smells."

Olive bit her lip. At least with Tofu she was on unassailable ground. "But Tofu is a psychopath," she said. "My mummy is a psychiatrist. She knows all about psychopaths, and she says Tofu is definitely one. You ask her – she'll tell you."

Miss Campbell gave Olive a severe look. "You are not to say such things, Olive."

"Yes," said Tofu. "You should look out, Olive. You can't go around calling people psychopaths. 'Specially me."

Galactica continued to stare at Olive. "You should try to be more mature, Olive," said Galactica. "It's not hard, you know, but I'm at hand to help you."

Olive was by now flushed red with anger and frustration. Seeing this, Miss Campbell put an arm round her shoulder and whispered to her, "It'll all blow over, Olive, dear. Sometimes we feel a little bit angry because things don't work out as we want them to. The important thing is not to let oneself be upset."

Galactica smiled indulgently. "A storm in a teacup," she said. Then, turning to Olive, she said, with a condescending smile, "That expression means that it doesn't really matter, Olive."

Olive swallowed hard as she struggled with the turn that events had taken. Pansy was by her side now, and led her gently back to their desk, as might the defeated remnants of an army skulk back to their quarters.

"Well, that's that," Galactica announced to Socrates Dunbar and Moss, both of whom were now looking at her with unconcealed admiration. Her subtle techniques might be beyond them, but the two boys understood a victory when they saw one, and they were delighted that Olive, who had for so long exercised her authority with impunity, had been publicly reduced. There was no doubt in the minds of both of them as to where their loyalty should now lie: if Galactica needed lieutenants, then that is what they would be from now on.

Socrates Dunbar glanced across the classroom, to where Olive and Pansy now sat in a state of shock.

"Olive's toast," Socrates whispered.

"Big time," agreed Moss.

"And Pansy too," added Socrates.

"She's history," said Moss.

During the morning break, Bertie and Ranald Braveheart Macpherson did their best to be unobtrusive, but they were soon located by Galactica, who skipped across the playground to engage them in conversation.

"I haven't had the chance to thank you properly for your party, Ranald," she said. "I really enjoyed myself. I didn't mind your crying, you know – I always say: if you can't cry at your own party, then where can you cry?"

Ranald glanced at Galactica, and then looked away. He did not say anything.

"Ranald doesn't normally cry," Bertie said, defending his friend.

"Oh, I'm sure he doesn't," said Galactica. "And anyway, I'm not one of those people who say that boys shouldn't cry. I think they should be allowed to cry if they like. Boys can be really weak, you know – and if they're weak, like poor, sweet Ranald, then they should be allowed to cry – if it makes them feel better."

Bertie bit his lip. He wanted Galactica to go away, but he did not know how to suggest that without offending her. And something deep within him told him that Galactica was not one who anybody should offend lightly.

Galactica now changed the subject. "I'm planning a party to celebrate our engagement, Bertie," she said. "I thought I should tell you the date so that you can pencil it in, in your diary."

Bertie held his breath.

"Nothing too big," Galactica went on. "Just a few close friends. Have you got many close friends, Bertie?"

Bertie struggled to speak, but no words came.

"Oh, I know that you and Ranald are very good friends," Galactica went on. "I suppose you'll want him as your best man when we eventually get married – when we're twenty " She paused, and gave Ranald a look of appraisal. "I want you to know that I have no objection to Ranald. He'll be better than Tofu, certainly. But do you know anybody else?"

Bertie was at a loss for words. Eventually he managed, "Not really, Galactica, but I think—"

Galactica raised a finger to her lips in a gesture of silence. "I thought next Saturday would be a good time, Bertie. We can have the party at my house in Ann Street. I'll get some chocolate ice cream."

Bertie managed to utter a few words. "I never said I wanted to be engaged, Galactica. I never said I would. Honestly. You can ask Ranald if you don't believe me."

Ranald Braveheart Macpherson nodded. "Bertie never said yes, Galactica."

Galactica spun round to face Ranald. "You keep out of this, Ranald Braveheart Macpherson. This is private business between me and Bertie."

Galactica turned back to Bertie. "All right, Bertie. That's all arranged then. Three o'clock on Saturday."

And with that she left them, and sauntered over to speak to Socrates Dunbar, who had been watching this encounter from a distance, smirking.

"What are we going to do, Bertie?" wailed Ranald.

Bertie thought for a moment. His answer, when he gave it, was not a spur of the moment decision, but was the result of a long process of reflection over several years. Glasgow. He would say goodbye to Edinburgh and go to Glasgow – for good. This sort of thing rarely, if ever, happened in Glasgow – he was sure of it. There were no people like Galactica in Glasgow, in that shining city on its hill, in that dear green place.

"We're going to Glasgow, Ranald," Bertie announced. "Soon."

# 44

## *Are You Swedish?*

Eddie, having arranged to meet Bob in the Craiglockhart gym for their second intensive workout session, was already there when Bob arrived. Bob found him seated on one of the exercise bicycles, straining under the maximum setting, grunting with the effort. On seeing Bob, Eddie dismounted from the cycle to greet his client.

"I've worked out your programme, Bob," Eddie said as he wiped his brow. "Are you ready?"

Bob nodded. "I can't wait," he said. "Roll it on."

"And the carbs?" asked Eddie, throwing a glance at Bob's stomach, which protruded beyond the band of his exercise pants.

"Down to sixty five grams," said Bob. "That's the average. I've found a substitute pasta that has zero carbs per hundred grams – and only thirteen calories."

"I know that stuff," Eddie said. "It's made of konjac root, isn't it? Also, it has no taste, and has an offensive smell before you wash it."

"That's it," said Bob. "I'm persisting."

"That's the only way," said Eddie. "You'll achieve keto before you know it."

"I'm on the way," said Bob. "I'm going to do this, Eddie – I really am."

Eddie reached out and patted Bob's shoulder in a friendly manner. "I'm sure you will, Bob," he said. "And remember: I'm here to help you. If ever you feel tempted by carbs – any time, and I mean 24/7 – then all you have to do is call me. I'm your low-carb brother."

Bob smiled. "You're very kind, Eddie."

"I do my best," said Eddie. "And with a bit of effort on your part, you'll make it. We'll see a new Bob shortly, I believe."

Bob grinned. He liked Eddie. The personal trainer was enthusiastic, and not ashamed to display his enthusiasm. There was far too much defeatism abroad, and it was refreshing to encounter this brisk optimism. It was a great pity, he thought, that so many people who embarked on a diet had nobody like Eddie to motivate them.

Eddie suggested a gentle start. "I know that you're keen to get onto the weights," he said, "but it's important to warm up first. And there's nothing better for that than the running track. A couple of notional miles on that should set you up nicely for a bit of heavy lifting afterwards."

They crossed the floor of the gym to the line of machines positioned before the large windows looking out onto a small lochan and, beyond it, the lower slopes of Craiglockhart Hill. A small flock of geese had alighted on the edge of the lochan, and was investigating such scraps of food as could be found on the grass and in the reeds.

"It's a great gym for birdwatching," said Eddie.

"So I see," said Bob.

Eddie pointed to one of the machines and invited Bob to step up onto the belt. He took the machine next door, and soon busied himself with adjusting settings. Bob chose a programme accordingly, and together they set off at a brisk walk. After a couple of minutes, the walk became a trot, and then a full-blooded run. Bob was considerably heavier than Eddie, and far less fit, with the result that although Eddie's breathing could barely be heard, his own panting was embarrassingly obvious.

After five minutes, Bob felt that he would need to call a halt. Reaching forward to set the machine to *Train Down*, he inadvertently increased the speed of the revolving belt beneath his feet. The increase was by a good ten miles per hour, and was enough to carry him backwards and then off the belt altogether. He gave a cry, and Eddie immediately pressed the emergency stop on his own machine. But it was too late for him to prevent Bob's ignominious toppling.

Down went Fat Bob, like a felled tree. And as he fell, his head came into contact with the floor, with an alarming cracking sound. Thus did Humpty Dumpty meet his end, and although Bob was not so fragile as to shatter as Humpty did, a consequence of this blow to the head was still a loss of consciousness.

Eddie was by his side, and was soon joined by two members of the gym staff, one of whom was already calling an ambulance on his phone. By happy coincidence, an ambulance was making its way down Colinton Road on its way back to the Royal Infirmary, and the crew of this vehicle were soon on the scene. Bob was still unconscious when they arrived with their stretcher, and he was still in that state when he arrived at the Accident and Emergency department. There, while being wheeled on a trolley to the X-ray department, he awoke, and looked about himself with the puzzlement that might be expected of one whose last conscious memory had been of Craiglockhart Gym, but who now found himself in the Royal Infirmary, staring into the face of a concerned nurse and a hospital porter.

"Don't try to sit up," said the nurse, pressing Bob back onto the trolley.

"I don't know what happened," said Bob. "Did I have an accident?"

The porter answered. "Bumped your heid, it seems," he said. "There's a big swelling. Nasty."

Bob reached up to feel the back of his head. "You're right," he said. "Very nasty. I was on one of those running machines."

The porter nodded. They were nearing the X-ray department now, and he was preparing to push Bob down a corridor
that led off to the right.

"You Swedish?" the porter asked.

Bob looked puzzled. "No."

"You sound it," said the porter.

Bob frowned. It was difficult enough to make sense of what
was happening without strange comments like this.

"John's right," said the nurse.

"Well, I'm not," said Bob. "I'm actually from Canonmills,
as it happens. And Leith before that."

The porter and nurse exchanged glances.

"Of Swedish extraction, perhaps?" suggested the nurse
brightly.

"I'm not Swedish," Bob insisted. "I already told you – I'm
Scottish. I've never been to Sweden in my life."

"I'm sorry," said the porter. "I don't want to upset you –
it's just that you sound very Swedish to me."

Bob closed his eyes. He had a headache, although it was
not much more than a dull throb. He felt tired, though, and
the last thing he wanted to do was to discuss with these people
whether or not he was Swedish. Of course he was not Swedish,
and it was bizarre that they should think that of him.

He opened his eyes. "I'm definitely not Swedish," he said.
"I'm not saying there's anything wrong with being Swedish –
it's just that I'm not Swedish at all. Sorry to disappoint you."

The nurse laughed. "We'll take your word for it," she said.
"But there you go again. You're sound exactly like a Swedish
friend I play tennis with. You're speaking just like him."

"I told you that you sounded Swedish," said the porter. "I
wasn't imagining it."

They had reached the Radiology department, where a
radiographer helped Bob off the trolley and invited him to
stand in front of a large X-ray machine. She asked Bob how

he was feeling and whether he could stand unaided, and he replied that he was quite capable.

She looked at him. "Are you Swedish, by any chance?" she asked.

# 45

## *An Interesting Syndrome*

That evening, Angus told Domenica about Bob's accident. He had accompanied Big Lou to the infirmary after she had received the call from a nurse to tell her that her husband had been admitted. Big Lou had asked him to go with her for company, and he had readily agreed. "You say they're going to discharge him tomorrow," said Angus. "That means Bob's fine, Lou. You needn't worry. They would be keeping him in if it were serious. And remember: he's as strong as an ox."

They had visited Bob in the ward, and were at his bedside when one of the doctors arrived. This doctor drew them aside and assured them that there appeared to be no fracture of the skull, and that although they liked to watch people who had been concussed, it looked as if Bob was largely unharmed.

"Largely?" asked Angus.

"Well," said the doctor, "largely means not entirely." She paused. "There is one rather odd thing. Perhaps we'd better go off and discuss it in the office."

Now, having returned from the infirmary, Angus told Domenica about the curious issue that the doctor had raised with them.

"I must say I had noticed the same thing myself," Angus said.

"What thing?" asked Domenica.

"He sounds odd," said Angus. "I noticed it the moment we arrived in the ward. There he was, sitting on the edge of the bed, talking nineteen to the dozen with one of the other patients. And then, when Big Lou and I arrived, he started a long explanation about how he had fallen off the end of one of those running machines you find in gyms."

"You say he sounded odd?" asked Domenica.

"Yes," Angus replied. "He did not sound himself at all. He sounded . . . Swedish."

Domenica frowned. "Shades of Bruce? Didn't he undergo some sort of metamorphosis after he was struck by lightning?" She paused. She was one of those who was sceptical about Bruce's apparent change – even if genuine, it would not last, she thought. Lightning, after all, was an extremely transient phenomenon. And how could something as deeply engrained as character be changed by a mere charge of electricity?

Angus took a different view. He remembered a conversation he had had with his neurologist friend, Colin Mumford, in the Scottish Arts Club. Colin had spoken of personality changes that could result from an injury to the brain. "Don't imagine," Colin had said, "that behaviour is independent of what's happening – physically – to the brain or, indeed, the body. You might have heard of Phineas Gage."

"Phineas Gage?"

Colin explained that Gage was an American railway worker who'd had a metal bolt go through his head, but who had, miraculously, survived. His personality, though, was completely different after the accident. His case became very well-known and made people think about how behaviour may be physically determined.

Angus sighed. "We're physical creatures. We like to think mind and body are quite distinct, but they aren't, are they?"

Colin smiled. "No. And it doesn't need an iron bolt through the skull to change us. All sorts of conditions can have an effect on how people behave – and speak."

"How they speak?"

"Yes," said Colin. "Listen to the speech of somebody who's had too much to drink. The words are slurred. They may not make much sense. And there are other ways, too, in which speech may be affected. There's something called foreign accent syndrome. That's pretty odd. There are about sixty recorded cases, which makes it very rare, but it's there – in the neurological literature."

"What happens?" Angus asked.

"For one reason or another – a lesion, perhaps, or a blow to the head – people suddenly start talking with a foreign accent. So they speak with a standard Scottish accent and then suddenly they open their mouth and they sound German or Dutch. They really do. It's very strange, but there are these cases in which it seems to happen."

"Peculiar," said Angus.

"Very," agreed Colin. "What appears to be happening is that there is some interference in the person's sense of the prosody of language. Every language has an inbuilt music to it – and that becomes deeply embedded somewhere in the brain of the speaker. Then something comes along to change that, and everything sounds different. That's a possible explanation. Or, more prosaically, perhaps, what happens is that people feel a subconscious desire to imitate, and that leads to the adoption of a foreign accent. You may have heard of people going to live abroad who eventually start speaking their native language with the accent of those amongst whom they've gone to live. It might be an imitative strategy connected with our desire to merge into our surroundings – to be taken for one of the group. After all, who amongst us doesn't want to do that?"

Angus looked thoughtful. "We don't want to appear different?"

"No, we don't – by and large. We look for protective colouring."

"Because?"

"Because at heart we want to be accepted by those around us.

We can't bear too much difference – perhaps for sociobiological reasons. In earlier societies we needed to recognise members of the group, because everybody else was a threat." Colin paused. "And some people are still a bit like that."

Angus sighed. "I suppose they are."

"And then, while we're thinking of language, there's xenoglossy."

"Another strange syndrome?'

"Technically not a syndrome, but an odd phenomenon. I don't think there's much to it, but some people seize upon it as evidence of what they want to believe in. There are people, you see, who believe in things because they provide evidence for something else they'd like to believe in."

"I see," said Angus, and, as he said this, he wondered whether he sounded at all different from normal. He decided he did not.

# 46

## *Xenoglossy*

"If you think foreign accent syndrome is strange," Colin continued, "then xenoglossy is even odder. I happen to have a book on the subject – *Unlearned Language*. It's by a psychiatrist at the University of Virginia."

"I enjoy the occasional offbeat book," Angus admitted. "I have one that argues that Homer's *Odyssey* doesn't refer to a journey in Greece at all, but takes place in, of all places, the Baltic. The author was an Italian nuclear physicist who made it his life work to relocate the story of Odysseus to the north – basing the whole thing on the argument that northern European geography suits the epic much better than does the topography of Greece. Remember the Wandering Rocks so feared by Odysseus and his crew? Those are apparently to be found in one of the dangerous passages in the Lofoten Islands, of all places. And Ithaca is all wrong if you look at the current island of that name – it's really the island of Lyø, off the Danish coast."

"I'd not heard that before," said Colin. "This book I mentioned looks at some rather puzzling cases of people who are claimed to have spoken a language they could never have learned. This isn't just about accents – this is about actual languages."

Angus laughed. "*Man wakes up from coma and discovers he can speak Mandarin*? There are headlines like that every so often, aren't there?"

"Unfortunately, yes," said Colin. "The public appetite for sensation is—"

"Never satisfied? No, it isn't, is it? This book, though . . .

Does it seriously suggest that anybody can speak a language they've never consciously learned? Or, should I say, been exposed to, because I suppose we don't consciously learn our native tongue."

Colin explained. "The cases he deals with are ones where either the foreign language is spoken by somebody in a state of hypnosis-induced dissociation, or where another personality suddenly emerges, so to speak."

He looked at Angus, who was rolling his eyes in disbelief.

"I'm rather inclined to agree with you," Colin said. "Nobody has yet to demonstrate conclusively that these people could not have been exposed to the language in question. There's no satisfactory proof."

"Well, there you are, then," said Angus. "Reason asserts itself. Triumph of the scientific method."

"In one of the cases it looks at, the case of an Indian woman who laid claim to reincarnation, the personality asserting itself chose to speak in Bengali – not the home language of the family. Various Bengali speakers were wheeled out to confirm that she spoke the language – and, for the most part, they agreed that she did. Some had reservations, though. One said that she spoke an odd form of the language, and another said that she spoke it with the accent of one who had learned the language as an adult. It was also pointed out that although her parents denied that Sharada had ever been given any lessons in the language, she nonetheless lived in a city where there were quite a few Bengali speakers. Children can pick things up, of course, and that might explain the whole thing. Yet she did give details," Colin continued, "of what she claimed was a previous life in another family, and investigations revealed that such a family could have existed."

"Coincidence," said Angus.

"Probably," said Colin. "We have to be extremely cautious about this sort of claim."

Angus remembered something. "Wasn't there a Scottish case a few years back? A small boy in Glasgow claimed to have had a previous life in a family that lived on an island. He gave very detailed descriptions of the house in which he had lived. He said it was on an island where planes landed on the beach . . ."

Colin smiled. "Sounds like Barra."

"Yes, so it seemed. And a Scottish television crew took them all to Barra to look for the place he described – and they seemed to find it. The house fitted the description – and the garden gate too. And the neighbour's dog."

"Children can be inventive."

"Yes, they are. But it was an odd case – and people are always looking for proof of reincarnation. They seize upon such things."

For a few moments, they were both silent. Then Angus remarked, "I remain sceptical about this sort of thing. I don't think one should believe anything unless one is capable of finding grounds to believe it. Evidence is what is needed for any belief. Evidence. Old-fashioned, rigorous evidence."

"I agree," said Colin. "Wishful thinking is a great distorter of reality."

"But not optimism?"

Colin was cautious. "That's different. You can be optimistic and yet still require evidence for your beliefs. Optimism doesn't involve any manifest untruths. An optimist hopes that something will prove to be the case; he doesn't say it is the case if he has no evidence."

Now, as he sat in their kitchen with Domenica, Angus thought about Bob and his peculiar complaint. Would it matter if he continued to speak with a Swedish accent? It might surprise people who knew that he was not at all Swedish, but apart from that, it would have no real consequences one way or the other. If to sound Swedish was the only lasting effect of a bad bang to the head, then that was no cause for dismay. There were worse things than that, after all – and, in general, people rather admired the Swedes. A Swedish accent, indeed, might incline others to listen to what one had to say, and to endow one with a certain stylishness. A Scottish accent, of course, inspired confidence – or so Angus had been told. Bank managers or financial advisers who spoke with a Scottish accent were considered, it was said, to be more trustworthy than those who did not.

Angus thought of Bob. A pronounced Swedish accent would get you nowhere in Canonmills or Leith. He hoped that the phenomenon was a passing one, and that Bob would recover. Did people sound Swedish for the rest of their lives? Swedes did, of course, but that was another matter altogether.

# 47

## *Names on a Plate*

After Angus finished telling Domenica about his visit to Bob in the Infirmary, he made his way to the flat in Drummond Place occupied by Antonia Collie and Sister Maria-Fiore dei Fiori di Montagna. It was almost nine o'clock in the evening, and he and Sister Maria-Fiore had agreed to meet their informant in the Drummond Place Gardens at nine thirty. Nothing had been said about the purpose of the assignation, although Angus assumed that it was to receive more disclosures. They had yet to decide what to do with the information they received, and he was tempted simply not to show up for the meeting. Sister Maria-Fiore, though, was keen for it to take place, and he had agreed to go for her sake.

Now he stood, with Cyril on his lead beside him, outside the door of the Drummond Place flat. A small brass plate on the doorbell announced *Collie/Fiori di Montagna* – a wording that made him reflect on the fact that he did not know Sister Maria-Fiore's real surname. *Fiori di Montagna* was, he thought, the equivalent of a Scottish territorial designation, of the sort that indicated the bearer's association with a particular piece of land. There were many of these, some obscure, others laden with historical significance. Cameron of Lochiel was one example: that branch of the Cameron family had played a major part in the 1745 uprising against the Hanoverians, and still maintained a presence around Loch Eil in Argyll. Others may have lost that connection, except in a historical sense.

Antonia answered the door. She was dressed in casual slacks and a white Aran sweater, reading glasses perched on the end of her nose to suggest that she had been disturbed in the middle of her researches into the lives of the early Scottish saints.

"Maria-Fiore has been expecting you," she said. "I gather you're going to meet our secretive friend again."

"That's the general idea," said Angus. "Although I must admit that I'm not sure what we're going to do with what he proposes to tell us."

Antonia laughed. She did not appear to take the whole matter seriously, thought Angus. It was all very well for her, living as she did in the world of those early Scottish saints, but he and Sister Maria-Fiore had to make decisions about what to do with the information that was very much about the here and now. They had come by information that was political dynamite – and they had received it illicitly. They knew that it was not intended for them, which somehow compounded the offence. It was as if they had chanced upon nuclear secrets left behind on an Edinburgh bus, and had no idea what to do with them.

Before he was admitted to the flat, Angus pointed to the brass plate. "I couldn't help but notice the wording of your name plate," he said.

Antonia glanced at it over the top of her spectacles. "Well?" she said. "It says what it needs to say. We share the flat."

She gave him a defensive glance, and he was quick to reassure her that he was not disapproving in any way. "It's just curiosity about the name," he said quickly. "I mean, Sister Maria-Fiore's name. Normally one would put a surname – as you have done with Collie. But what's her surname? I realise that, as well as I know her, I have no idea what it is."

Antonia stared at him. "Fiore," she said.

Angus shook his head. "No, that's her . . . well, I suppose it's the religious equivalent of one of our Scottish territorial designations."

Antonia smiled, as if explaining something very obvious to one who was missing something. "No, Fiore is her family name. Her father, I imagine, was Mr Fiore. In fact, I know he was. She showed me a picture of him in an Italian newspaper. He was Filippo Fiore, now that I come to think of it. Phil Flower, in English." She laughed. "You get some odd-sounding effects once you start translating Italian surnames – and others too. I came across a reference to one Herr Bierhals the other day – which means beer-neck. Why would somebody be called that, I wonder? Or Schweinfest – which means pig festival. There are people who are actually called that, would you believe?"

"Oh, I can well believe it," said Angus. He thought of Parsi names, which, like many names in other traditions, tended to be occupational.

"You will have come across names with *wala* as a suffix?"

Antonia thought for a moment. She had seen names like that, but could not recall exactly what they were.

"Mr Hotelwala," Angus said, "would be in no doubt about the occupation of his ancestors. Nor would anybody called Mr Engineer. These are real names, you know. And Sodawaterwala is an actual Parsi name – as is Sodabottleopenerwala."

"Most interesting," said Antonia, dryly. "But, as I said, Maria-Fiore is really Maria-Fiore Fiore. Not that I'm suggesting that she should not be Maria-Fiore dei Fiori di Montagna. She's entitled to call herself that too."

"There seem to be a lot of floral references in her name," said Angus, adding, "Let a thousand flowers blossom, and all that."

Antonia invited him in. "Actually, while we're on the subject, I don't have to be just plain Collie, you know. I could be Collie of Coll," she said. "I don't call myself that, as you know – but I believe I would be entitled to the name."

Angus hesitated. He did not think that Antonia was entitled to call herself Collie of Coll. And that made him wonder whether he should say something. Harmless affectations were just that: harmless affectations. On the other hand, what was the point of having rules if people were just going to disobey them, and moreover, if those observing the breaches never said anything? Angus believed in tolerance – as far as it was compatible with the rights of others; he had read John Stuart Mill at sixteen and had never forgotten the message. Yet there was something to be said for zero tolerance, which had to be asserted in certain circumstances, such as protecting vulnerable staff from violence of one sort or another. How sobering to think that firefighters and nurses and others who looked after or served the public should be subjected to insult and assault. All of that arose, Angus thought, from excessive tolerance of small wrongs that could suddenly become much bigger. You might start off by calling yourself something you were not entitled to call yourself, and then end up robbing a bank. But that, he thought, is absurd, and it made him break into a smile – that Antonia noticed.

"Just what are you smiling at, Angus?" she asked.

# 48

## *The Official Secrets Act*

Angus repeated Antonia's question. She always spoke to him in a rather peremptory tone, he had noted – as if he were a ten-year-old boy. Did she realise how she sounded? "What am I smiling at?"

The schoolmistress again. "That is what I asked you."

"I was thinking of John Stuart Mill," answered Angus. That would teach her to condescend. How many people could give that riposte?

But Antonia did not see the relevance of Mill. "You might think of Rawls," she said cuttingly. "Or Feinberg's work on offence, perhaps."

Angus bit his lip. He had not been intending to raise the matter, but her haughty attitude had irritated him. He happened to be on firm ground here – firmer than the ground she stood on, because he had once discussed the issue with David Sellar, who had been Lord Lyon, and who knew about these obscure matters. "This business with Coll," he said. "Can you use the name of the whole island? Aren't these things usually more specific?"

Antonia glowered at him. "I don't see why not," she said. "My forebears came from the island. They had been there for centuries. We have plenty of evidence of that."

"That may be so," said Angus, "but plenty of other people are in the same boat, so to speak. You couldn't have everybody claiming to be this, that and the next thing of Coll, could you?"

Antonia gave a wave of her hand. "They had quite a bit of land," she said. "They weren't just anybody."

"But I was told that the rules are quite clear," Angus insisted. "You have to own a piece of land that has always had the name in question attached to it for some time. It has to be a farm or estate, or a house with at least five acres attached to it. David Sellar said that, when he was Lord Lyon. He specifically mentioned the five-acre requirement in the case of people who have acquired a new property and want to add a territorial designation to their name."

Antonia gave another wave of the hand, more airily this time. "I wasn't proposing to call myself Collie of Drummond Place."

Angus thought: *Cyril could.*

He smiled. "Of course, there are plenty of people who fancy a Scottish title. There are firms that will sell you a square foot of some Highland glen. People think that makes them a Scottish laird or grandee – which it doesn't." He paused. "Why would people want to own a couple of square feet of Scotland? Romantic attachment?"

"Probably," said Antonia. "Remember, Scotland is perhaps the most romantic country in Europe – or anywhere, for that matter. It always has been. Ossian, Walter Scott . . ."

"Shortbread," said Angus. "Highland cattle. The skirl of the pipes. Mists. Mountains. These are powerful things."

"One might become cynical," said Antonia. "But I'm not sure where the harm is in perpetuating that vision of Scotland. After all, people need comfort, don't they? We need to believe that somewhere there's a place like the Scotland of our imagination. And I'm not sure there's anything wrong with yearning for a lost Eden."

Angus sighed. "Is there anything left of Eden? Anywhere?"

Antonia did not answer. She looked down at the floor. Angus looked up at the ceiling. Then he said, "Sister Maria-Fiore dei Fiori di Montagna?"

Antonia gestured for him to follow her into the kitchen, where Sister Maria-Fiore was seated at a table, applying varnish to her nails. She greeted him warmly. "I'm almost ready," she said.

Angus glanced at the bottle of nail varnish. Had she not taken a vow of simplicity, he wondered – or were these things selective?

Sister Maria-Fiore slipped the bottle of nail varnish into a pocket somewhere in the folds of her habit. Rising to her feet, she announced that it was time for them to set off for their meeting.

Angus said, "I'm worried about this."

She stopped, and looked at him. "We have to be there. *Pacta servanda sunt.* We told him we'd be there." She paused. "Are you frightened? Is that it?"

He hesitated. Cyril looked up at him, as if he had understood the implicit reproach.

"I'm not frightened," he replied. "It's just that I'm not sure where this is leading us. There are things just below the surface, I think. There are murky pools in public life, and I feel that we're about to dip our toes into one of those."

Antonia turned to Sister Maria-Fiore. "Angus has a point, Floral One. This is politics. This is a leak of government information. This is serious stuff."

Sister Maria-Fiore considered this. "True," she said at last. "This is not something to be entered into lightly. But we're already involved, aren't we? The leak has taken place. We've been given the information – or some of it. I imagine there will be more."

"I think we should come clean," said Angus. "I think we should meet this man as planned, and then we should explain that he has chosen the wrong people to whom to make his disclosures. Then we can withdraw."

Sister Maria-Fiore looked to Antonia for guidance.

"That seems reasonable enough," said Antonia. "Extricate yourselves, and no harm will be done. There is always a case for honesty."

Sister Maria-Fiore dei Fiori di Montagna appeared to be torn. But then she shrugged her shoulders and said, "No, there is no harm in telling the truth. I agree. Let's do that." She glanced at her watch. "We need to go."

"Be careful," said Antonia from the door behind them as they stepped out onto the pavement.

Angus laughed. "Let's not be too melodramatic. This is the middle of Edinburgh." He gestured towards the trees in the garden, a presence behind him. A line of poetry came to him, about woods, and whose they were . . . "It's just short of nine thirty on a summer evening, and it's still light. There's no danger. The man we're going to meet is a civil servant, after all; he's probably keeping a minute of our meetings."

His own words made him feel more confident, and yet, as they approached the entrance to the gardens, he felt a niggling feeling in the pit of his stomach; a touch of fear, perhaps. He had never broken the law deliberately, and yet here he was becoming involved in a breach of confidential information. There was something called the Official Secrets Act, and you could be sent to prison for being party to its breach. And the man who was passing this information on to them was very probably on the wrong side of that very Act. It did not matter whether you felt a moral right to bring particular facts to public attention – it did not matter that you were a principled whistle-blower, acting for the greater good – all that mattered for criminal purposes was that the information was covered by the Act and had been disclosed.

He stopped at the gate. It would be possible to turn round now and go home. But Sister Maria-Fiore dei Fiori di Montagna was looking at him suspiciously – she knew weakness when she saw it – and so he sighed, and complied, following the unusual nun into the gardens where, in the depths of the rhododendrons, their informant lurked.

# 49

## *Deep Thrapple Speaks*

He was punctual, as befitted a senior civil servant, thought Angus. As on the last occasion, he was largely concealed by the foliage of the rhododendron bushes, although Angus had a glimpse of the features – the intelligent eyes, the high cheekbones, the unmistakeable look of a public servant mandarin. He had been thinking of him as Deep Throat, the mysterious informant of the Watergate affair, although now he fancied that *Deep Thrapple* would be better, *thrapple* being the Scots for throat. Yes, Deep Thrapple was a very suitable name for this half-concealed confidant.

The foliage spoke. "Good evening."

Sister Maria-Fiore dei Fiori di Montagna took it upon herself to reply, with a *buonasera*. This was delivered with all the courtesy and style of a greeting delivered during some evening *passeggiata*.

"Thank you for coming," said Deep Thrapple. "I was worried that you might have lost interest."

"*Al contrario*," said Sister Maria-Fiore. "We are very interested."

"Yes," said Angus. "We are." He felt slightly irritated that the nun was being so forward here. This was *his* leak, he thought.

Deep Thrapple now addressed Sister Maria-Fiore. "You are Italian?" he asked.

That, thought Angus, must have been obvious, but senior civil servants were perhaps unduly cautious about drawing conclusions.

"I am indeed," said the nun. "Although Scotland is now my adopted country." She paused. "My father was a bureaucrat – as you are, I believe. He worked in the local administration. He did not report to Rome."

"Then he would have known how frustrating it is," said Deep Thrapple, a note of bitterness in his voice. "As an official, you see all sorts of things, and you can't do anything about them."

Sister Maria-Fiore laughed. "That never worried my father. No, not in the slightest."

Angus looked at her inquisitively. Surely Filippo Fiore would not have been *that* insouciant.

An explanation followed. "He ignored Rome," Sister Maria-Fiore continued. "My dear father said that they received memoranda from Rome virtually every day – memoranda and instructions – but they simply tossed them in the wastepaper basket. That gave them greater freedom, he said."

Deep Thrapple drew in his breath. They heard it – a rustling sound in the leaves of the rhododendrons. Such a cavalier attitude, Angus thought, must be anathema to a senior civil servant in the Scottish Government.

But there was more to come. "And then they started to receive instructions from Brussels," Sister Maria-Fiore continued. "All sorts of directives on any number of subjects. They didn't even bother to read most of these. Sometimes they laughed. Sometimes they just shrugged. But they never paid any attention. That is how Italy is governed, you see. You can't interfere with long-established traditions."

Deep Thrapple now spoke. "I can't say I approve of that sort of thing," he said. "What is the point of having regulations if nobody is going to pay any attention to them?"

"But that's exactly what my father said," replied Sister Maria-Fiore dei Fiori di Montagna.

There followed a brief silence. Then Deep Thrapple

continued. "My department," he said, "is the Department of Unpopular Policies. Our overall responsibility is to implement the policies that the government knows the people of Scotland will not like."

Angus could contain himself no longer. "Then why do it?" he asked. "Why have policies like that in the first place?"

Deep Thrapple laughed. It was a thin, bureaucratic laugh. "Good question," he said. "It is mainly because we understand the people of Scotland. If something is popular with the public, then it is by definition likely to be the wrong policy altogether. People want an easy life. They want to be left alone. They want to run their lives without assistance from those who know better. That is where unpopular policies come in – they make the point that you are not necessarily going to like the things that are good for you."

Angus reflected on this. There might be a modicum of truth somewhere in there, and yet . . .

"But I don't want to go too deeply into matters of administrative policy," Deep Thrapple went on. "I don't object to the principle of unpopular policies – it's just that I think these things should not be done in secret. The public has a right to know. That is why I am prepared to leak these matters."

"You mentioned the plan to amalgamate Edinburgh and Glasgow," said Angus. "Is that proceeding?"

"It is at a dangerously advanced stage," came the reply. "I foresee considerable opposition."

"So do I," said Angus.

Cyril growled.

"But there are other things I should like to tell you about," said Deep Thrapple. "For instance, there is a plan to spin out the construction of the Edinburgh tram system for a further forty-two years. You won't have heard about that, will you? And then there is a report into the building of new ferries.

This is not about those ferries they've been building for the last six years or so – it's about another two that the public doesn't even know about. They're being built and designed by different people. But do you know that those ships have been built without a reverse gear? Did you know that?"

"So they won't be able to go astern?"

"Precisely," said the voice. "That will give rise to serious issues of navigation. And there are other design issues as well. The ships are roll-on, roll-off car ferries, and yet they have doors only at one end. That means all the cars will be facing the wrong way when the ship docks. The only way of getting off will be for the cars to be reversed. But what if the single door is facing out to sea? What then? The ship will have to turn round and approach the ferry dock backwards. But how do they do that, if they can't go astern because they have no reverse gear?"

"Difficult," said Angus.

"My view entirely," said Deep Thrapple. "The engineers have been looking into it, to see if they can devise a solution, but all the instruction books for these ferries are in Gaelic, and that makes it difficult. It is all very delicate."

Angus whistled with surprise. "My goodness," he said. "It's just as well that we have brave people like you, who are prepared to risk their pensions by telling the truth."

There was a complete and sudden silence. Then, in a voice that was raised barely above a whisper, Deep Thrapple said, "Risk my pension? Who said anything about that?"

"Well," said Angus, "I thought that if anybody found out . . ."

There was a sudden commotion in the rhododendron bushes as leaves parted and twigs cracked. Then silence. The man within had disappeared. Gone. The source had dried up.

# 50

*Banks of Sicily*

"Books," said Bruce, glancing around him. "Look at all these books."

He was standing with Ben in the study of a house in Morningside. Three of the walls of the room were lined with bookcases reaching from floor to ceiling. In the remaining wall, a large window gave a view of the slopes of Craiglockhart Hill and of the city beyond. In the distance, on the other side of the Firth of Forth, the low hills of Fife rose against a cloudless sky.

Ben glanced at the books, and then turned his gaze towards Fife. "Sir Patrick Spens," he muttered. "*The King sits in Dunfermline toun, drinking the blude-reid wine . . .*"

Bruce smiled. "I remember that. A shipwreck, wasn't it?"

"Yes. It's just whenever I go over to Dunfermline, I think of it. It's . . . what do you call it? An earworm."

They were waiting in the room for the return of Donald Macdonald, the professor to whom they had sent a photograph of the Pictish stone they had discovered in Stirlingshire. He had shown them in and gone off to the kitchen to make tea. Now they heard the rattle of cups as he made his way back to the study.

"This is very kind of you," said Ben.

Donald passed them each a mug of tea. "Mugs, I'm afraid – not teacups. More practical, I find."

He looked at his visitors. He knew Ben slightly through a family connection, but he had not met Bruce before. He tried not to stare at Bruce's hair. It was an unusual hairstyle, he thought – as if somebody had applied electricity to the scalp and made the hair stand up.

"Bruce and I were at Morrison's Academy together," said Ben as he took his first sip of tea. "Up in Crieff."

"That's right," said Bruce. "Ben's much more academic than I am, though. He got a History Higher with distinction . . ."

Ben made a modest gesture. "You were really good at long jump, Bruce. He almost jumped for Scotland, you know, Prof."

"That's quite an achievement," said Donald.

"And he played cricket too," added Ben.

Bruce waved aside the compliment.

"He scored fifty-two runs against Heriot's once," Ben continued.

"Very interesting," said Donald. "I played for Heriot's back in the day. You may have seen Hector MacQueen's book on the history of the Heriot's Cricket Club. Not his major work, of course, but of interest to some. Very few, perhaps, but there we are."

Bruce, still standing next to a bookcase, glanced at a shelf of books. He reached forward, picked out a small black-bound book, and opened it at the title page. "Is this by him, Prof?" he asked. "*Numerology* by John MacQueen."

Donald smiled. "No, that's one of his father's books," he said. "He wrote that when he was in the School of Scottish Studies here in Edinburgh. He was there for years, along with those great men, Hamish Henderson and Sandy Fenton." Donald hesitated. He should not expect these young men to know too much. And yet they were clearly interested in Pictish matters.

"Hamish Henderson was a folklorist," he went on. "He collected songs and stories from all corners of Scotland."

"Bothy ballads?" asked Ben.

Donald brightened. Morrison's had been teaching its students something. "Yes, he certainly collected a lot of those – the songs agricultural workers sang. Ploughmen, shepherds and so on. He also wrote some lovely songs too. Have you heard 'The 51st Division's Farewell to Sicily'?"

Ben shook his head. "I don't think so."

"Would you like to hear it? You may recognise it."

Ben nodded, and Donald went to a small iPad on his desk. "It's in here somewhere," he said, adding, "Guid gear gangs in sma' buik."

He found what he was looking for, and prepared to play the tune. "He set this to a well-known pipe tune," he said. "'Farewell to the Creeks'. He was with the 51st Highland Division when they went into Sicily to liberate it from the Germans. They were welcomed, you know – the people had had enough of fascists. There are newsreels to show the Jocks being kissed in the streets, given flowers and so on. And the people meant it." He paused. "In this recording, Hamish is singing this himself. Recorded in Sandy Bell's pub in Forrest Road. You may know it. It's still a great folk music place."

The two young men listened. Bruce glanced at Ben, and saw a strange expression on his face. He turned back to gaze out of the window as the song was played.

*The pipie is dozie, the pipie is fey,*
*He winna come roon' for his vino the day.*
*The sky ow'r Messina is unco an' grey,*
*An' a' the bricht chaulmers are eerie.*

Ben swallowed. It was a song suffused with sadness and he felt it, suddenly and unexpectedly, the sadness of what had happened – and was still happening.

Donald picked up the effect the song was having. "Those men were about your age, you know."

"Yes," said Ben.

"They went from their farms and glens in Scotland without complaint. They knew the nature of the battle they were caught up in, I believe."

Bruce glanced at Ben again, and saw the tears in his eyes. He reached out and put a hand on his friend's arm.

"I don't know why . . ."

Bruce silenced him. "It's all right, Ben."

Donald waited for the song to finish, and then switched off the iPad.

"It's very moving," he said. "But there's a lot of Scottish history that can reduce one to tears, you know."

"I hate the thought that it's still going on," said Ben, wiping at his eyes. "Different battles, of course. Different places. But it's still happening, isn't it? There are still young guys . . ."

"Fighting old men's battles?" said Donald. "Yes. Humanity doesn't exactly learn quickly – if at all."

"Why do pipe tunes have that effect?" Bruce asked. "When I hear 'Mist Covered Mountains', I . . . well, I choke up a bit. I can't help it."

"The particular pitch, I suppose," said Donald. "The plaintive note. All music has an emotional register." He paused. "Perhaps we should talk about that photograph you sent me. It was an old stone near Doune, you say?"

"Yes," said Ben. "I've bought this old house, you see, and there's a walled garden. The stone was there. It had been moved into a greenhouse. We left it there after taking the photograph."

Donald shook his head. "Our treasure lies around us," he muttered. "Unnoticed. Unprotected."

"Nobody's going to take it away," said Bruce. "It weighs a ton. More, probably."

"I'm glad to hear that," said Donald. "Because that inscription, you know, may be of immense importance." He paused, as if waiting for his assessment to sink in. Then he continued, "Immense."

They waited.

"Let me tell you," Donald continued. "But let's sit down first."

# 51

## *An Authentic Voice*

"There's something I've been wondering about," said Donald. "Why the Picts?"

Ben nodded. "A perfectly reasonable question," he said. "What did Mallory say about Everest when they asked him why he climbed it? Because it's there. Isn't that what he said?"

Donald smiled. "So you're interested in the Picts because they're there?"

"*Were* there," said Ben. "They're not there any longer. *Ergo*, *were* there. There's a certain fascination in things that have simply disappeared. And that applies to the Picts. We know that they existed – the Romans were aware of them, and indeed gave them their name – 'painted people'. But what do we know about them? Very little." He paused. "Of course, we know that they painted their faces, which some of their descendants still do. Have you been to a rugby match at Murrayfield recently? You see quite a few people there with their faces painted blue. And political rallies too. A lot of blue facepaint in evidence on such occasions."

Bruce gave a dismissive laugh. "Is there something vaguely sinister about that?" he asked. "Why paint your face blue? To intimidate the opposition? To protest your membership of the group?"

Donald shrugged. "Flags come into it, I imagine. Political rallies involve the waving of flags. Flags encourage enthusiasm for the cause – whatever the cause may be. But let's not get too involved in the psychology of political attachment. Let's return to the Picts. You'd argue, I take it, that what makes the

Picts of interest is their mystery. What intrigues people is the fact that we don't know how the Picts led their lives. What did they believe in, before they became Christian? Who were their gods? What did they eat? We don't really know what language they spoke – although there have always been theories about that."

"Gaelic?" said Ben. "That's what we were taught at school back in the day." He turned to address Bruce, "Remember Mr Stoddart, Bruce. Remember his history lessons? He had latched onto the idea that the Picts spoke a non-Indo-European language. He used to say that there was a great deal of evidence to that effect, but when you asked him what the evidence was, he simply closed his eyes and shook his head. We laughed at him, and I think he knew that. Teenagers are cruel, especially when they sense blood."

Bruce remembered. "Yes," he said. For a few moments he was silent. I have been so wrong, he thought – so wrong about everything. But at least I am being given a chance to be better, which not everyone gets. I should be grateful for that.

They had given Donald a photograph of the inscriptions etched into the surface of the stone tablet. He now reached for this and pointed to the symbols that ran across the base. "This is ogham," he said. "You'll know that, of course. It's a very old script."

Ben nodded. "We were hoping you'd translate it for us."

Donald sighed. "It's not always easy to decipher. We're learning more and more about it, but many of these early inscriptions are somewhat opaque, I'm afraid. Often they're simple lists – so-and-so owes a local potentate two cattle, or something of that sort. Early laundry lists, in some cases."

"Every society needs its records," said Ben. "They meant something, I suppose. But eventually they started to tell stories."

"Precisely," said Donald. "And then literature begins."

He looked at the photograph with admiration. "And do you know what I think this is? I think this might be the very first work of Scottish literature – ever."

For a few minutes nobody spoke. Then Ben said, "Even earlier than 'The Brus'?"

"Oh, much earlier than that," said Donald. "'The Brus' was written in the middle of the fourteenth century. That's yesterday, really. This is earlier even than 'The Gododdin', which dates back to the second half of the sixth century."

"I thought that was Welsh," said Ben.

"They spoke Welsh in the Lothians," said Donald. "The boundaries between the various kingdoms were fluid. 'The Gododin' is definitely a work of Scottish literature in the geographical sense. But this is earlier than that. I think that this dates to the fourth century,"

"Amazing," said Bruce. "And do you know what it means?"

Donald looked thoughtful. "I'm getting there," he said. "I'd like to have a few more weeks to give it further consideration. It doesn't do to commit to a meaning too early. But what I can say is that I think this is a poem – in fact I'm sure it is."

This suited Ben. "It will be such wonderful publicity," he said. "For our Pictish Experience Centre, that is. We can have a press conference to announce the discovery. We can get Creative Scotland on board."

Donald nodded. "The content is interesting," he said. "It feels that there's an entirely authentic voice speaking to us across the centuries."

"Authentic?" said Ben.

"Very Scottish," said Donald.

"Very exciting," remarked Ben.

They spent another half hour in conversation with Donald before saying goodbye. Then they walked together down Morningside Road. Ben wanted to call in on the cheese shop, where he chose a cheese for Catriona.

"A Mull cheddar," he said. "She likes that sort of thing."

He pointed to a small slice of cheese on the edge of the counter. "That's a rather unusual cheese," he said. "It's made in Orkney, in very small quantities. The woman who makes it has only one cow, I'm told."

Bruce looked at the cheese. He was tempted to buy the single slice on display, but resisted the temptation. It seemed almost indecent, he thought, to buy an entire production of anything. So he bought a small quantity of a powerful-smelling French soft cheese and then they resumed their journey.

"What do you think people like the Saltire Society will say about our discovery?" Bruce asked.

Ben was in no doubt about that. "They'll be thrilled," he said. "And why wouldn't they? They want Scottish letters to flourish."

"But what if it's inappropriate?" asked Bruce. "What if it says the wrong thing?"

Ben hesitated before he replied. "Nobody's going to judge it outside its historical context."

"Let's hope not," said Bruce. "But perhaps we should not be too sure about that. There are plenty of people who are only too happy to judge the works of the past by the standards of today."

"We can always publish it with a warning," said Ben. "That's the way most things are published these days."

Bruce thought about the cheese he had just purchased. There were some cheeses, he believed, that should be sold only with an olfactory warning. This was not yet the case, but he was sure that such warnings would soon become standard practice.

# 52

## *The Private Life of Miss Campbell*

Miss Campbell had been teaching for twelve years. She had graduated from Moray House as a fully qualified infant teacher at the age of twenty-three. She had subsequently undertaken training in Steiner Waldorf educational methods, and had studied, part-time, for an advanced certificate in the psychology of early years, awarded by the University of Stirling. She was a keen tennis player and a member of a hill-walking club called the Pentland Wandering Society. She had had the same boyfriend for eight years. He was called Andrew Macdonald Henderson and he, too, was in the Pentland Wandering Society. She was hoping that he would ask her to marry him. He had yet to do so, although once, when they were on a walk to Balerno, on the south-west outskirts of Edinburgh, they had stopped briefly at Spylaw House where, while seated on a bench in the gardens, Andrew had suddenly said, "Isn't this romantic?"

Her heart had stopped. She subsequently wished that she had responded more directly. I let my golden chances pass me by, she thought. But we all did that; we all let that happen, and we often had a lifetime – a whole lifetime – to reflect on that fact. For what she had done was to say the first thing that came into her mind, which was, "Yes, old houses are definitely romantic", which had set Andrew off on the subject of Spylaw House. He was an enthusiast for local history, and there was scarcely a building in Edinburgh whose past he did not know something about – and Spylaw House was no exception. "This was where James Gillespie lived," he said. "He built this place in 1773, as you probably know."

Miss Campbell sighed. She did not know that, and she wanted to talk about the romance of being so close to the Water of Leith, about the towering trees on the skyline not far away; about the sky that was so filled with sun, but so northern too, and about the fact that she and Andrew could so easily set up in one of those new flats beside the river, and go for walks together back into Colinton village, in summer, before anybody else got up; and that all this could happen if only he would get round to asking her.

But he was clearly not thinking of any of this, for men often did not think about the things that women thought they should think about. And so he said, "He was a snuff manufacturer, you know, and you can still see the snuff mill at the back of the house, because it was powered by the Water of Leith. Imagine that!"

"And then," Andrew continued, "when he died, he left all his money – from the snuff, you see – to set up a hospital 'for the care of aged men and women' and a school 'for the education of poor boys'. The wording of some of these provisions sounds so quaint to the modern ear."

She had found herself looking at Andrew's ears. Were modern ears all that different, she wondered – and sighed again, because it had suddenly clouded over and the romantic moment had passed.

Miss Campbell was friendly with Andrew's sister, Sheila, who was an interpreter at the Conference Centre. She spoke Spanish, Portuguese and Italian. She had been married for five years, to a chemist who worked on battery research. Sheila was careful not to contrast her own settled domestic status with Miss Campbell's uncertain position, but every so often the subject arose, and a painful exchange took place.

"I know you don't like to discuss it, Jean," said Sheila. "But it's the elephant in the room, isn't it? And sometimes it helps to articulate these matters."

Miss Campbell had looked away. Sheila was right, but the problem from her point of view was that when they discussed these matters, the conversation ended in an impasse: there was nothing more to be said; there was no way out. Ultimately, she and Andrew would have to reach an understanding, but she feared that if she pushed him too hard, he would simply opt for freedom and she would lose him. She had seen that happen to others, and she did not want to take the risk. And there were times when she accepted that this was her lot – and that she should accept it as such. Not everybody needed a whole other person in their lives: one might be perfectly happy with having part of another; sharing another life, say, between Friday and Monday, and then being by oneself on Tuesday, Wednesday and Thursday.

"I've spoken to Andrew, you know," Sheila went on. "Only three weeks ago, I said to him, 'You can't expect people to wait for ever.' I said this apropos of nothing – we weren't talking about you. I just let the remark hang in the air, but he knew what I was talking about – oh yes, he knew it was about the two of you, all right. You know how he can suddenly become silent."

Miss Campbell did.

"And he looked at me," Sheila continued. "He looked at me with that look that men have when you have them cornered. And he said, 'People have different priorities in their lives.' And he left it at that."

"Oh well," began Miss Campbell. "We need to cultivate acceptance in this life, although . . ."

Sheila looked at her expectantly.

"Although it's often women who have to do all the accepting," Sheila concluded. "Men talk about acceptance, but they can often arrange matters to suit themselves, and then they say that they accept things." She paused. "It's an old trick."

Miss Campbell agreed that it was. And if you pointed it out to men, they looked at you in an injured way and said that that sort of strategy may be used by some, but never by them. And so it continued in that never-ending, apparently unsolvable way.

"At least I have my job," Miss Campbell said. "I have the children."

"Of course," said Sheila. "The children."

She waited. She felt her friend wanted to tell her something.

# 53

## *Down Among the Children*

"I would never complain about my job," said Miss Campbell. "I think that if you don't like your job, you should do something about it. It's always possible to retrain as something else – if you're reasonably flexible."

Sheila agreed. She had thought about doing just that herself – especially after a tiresome conference at which people were arguing about something and there was tension just below the surface. There were times when the strain on the interpreter was just too much, and one had to resort to saying things like *The speaker has just expressed extreme displeasure, and the remarks are untranslatable.* That was an admission of failure, but sometimes there was nothing for it but that. She and her colleagues called those *white flag* moments, and although it was unprofessional to give up *in extremis*, you had to preserve your sanity.

And interpreters, she reminded herself, were only human – as were the speakers themselves – as events in the United Nations all those years ago confirmed. Harold Macmillan had been speaking and was interrupted by protests from Nikita Khrushchev. Khrushchev took a shoe off and started to bang it on his desk. Macmillan, the embodiment of suavity, paused, and then said, "Could we have a translation of that?" The effect of an interpreted joke is like a Mexican wave: the laughter runs slowly round the room as it is rendered into languages of varying complexity and brevity.

"I've been tempted from time to time," Miss Campbell went on. "I almost applied for a job in the educational arm of an arts organisation, but I decided against it. And I was once offered a position teaching grammar to . . . Well, I shouldn't say to whom, but I turned it down, anyway."

"And are you pleased that you did?"

This required a moment's thought. But then Miss Campbell replied, "I'm glad I didn't make the change. Teaching is my vocation. It's not just any job – you have to believe that it's worth doing. And obviously it is. Ignorance is one of the worst things there is. Wars occur because of ignorance, after all. People *die* of ignorance. It's probably the biggest cause of death there is."

"Then you should stick to teaching," said Sheila. "It's really important work."

Miss Campbell sighed. "True," she said. "But we're going through a rough patch at the moment. It's most trying."

Sheila reached out to place a hand upon her friend's wrist. "Tell me about it," she said.

Miss Campbell hesitated. Technically, a teacher shouldn't discuss her charges – not by name – but there were times . . .

"I've got some lovely children in the class, you know. There's a little boy called Bertie – I've probably mentioned him."

"The one with the mother?" asked Sheila.

"Yes. I suppose you might describe him that way. She, by the way, went up to Aberdeen. I almost couldn't believe it. She upped and offed, leaving not only Bertie, but his little brother, Ulysses, with the poor father. Fortunately, there was a grandmother in the background, and she took over, and I believe the mother has condescended to come back – dividing her time between Aberdeen and Edinburgh. But . . ."

"I've heard she's difficult."

"Well, Bertie has survived the whole thing because he's composed of pure goodness. He puts up with all sorts of things. He has a close friend now, of course, who's very good for him. Ranald Braveheart Macpherson looks up to Bertie. His mother is fine – quite a nice woman, in fact, but the father is a bit iffy. He's works in finance somewhere and was up in front of the Sheriff Court recently – for some Companies Act offence. He was given a community payback order – over one hundred hours of Scottish country dancing. There was something in the papers about it. Enough to deter anybody, I'd have thought."

"But once you move on from Bertie and Ranald Braveheart Macpherson, it becomes a bit more complicated. The other boys are a mixed bag. One of them is a real little operator. He's called Tofu. Yes, that's his name – these kids have got the most extraordinary names – and it's getting worse. Tofu's parents are both prominent vegans, but Tofu himself doesn't sign up to that – at least when he's at school. He bribes the other children to bring sausages into school for him. And they do, although they're not above spreading the rumour that Tofu's mother has died of starvation. I try to suppress that one – she looks very peely-wally to me, but it's none of my business.

"Tofu has an enforcer. He's called Larch, and he has a broken nose. He throws his weight around and I have to watch him like a hawk. He likes pulling girls' hair. He's the closest thing we have to anything feral."

Sheila was fascinated. "It must be grim down there," she said.

"Down among the children? Yes, you're right. One or two of the boys are all right – in small doses. There's a boy called Moss, who has some artistic potential that we might be able to bring out. And Socrates Dunbar . . . He falls into the Tofu camp, I'm afraid, but we shall see."

"And the girls?"

Miss Campbell winced. "They're less physical than the boys, but they have their little campaigns on the go, and I think that some of them make the boys' lives a misery. And vice versa, of course." She paused. "It all starts so early, doesn't it? The jockeying for position, the psychological power plays – it all starts so early. And if anything, it's more overt with the girls, it's more dramatic. We have our real little drama queens, you know."

There was a short silence while Miss Campbell reflected on the children under her charge. How could she describe Olive and Pansy, in order to convey the subtleties of their characters? She closed her eyes briefly, and pictured Olive, in imperious pose, with Pansy, her faithful lieutenant standing behind her. Olive's look was a familiar challenging one – the look of one who knew that her vision of the world was completely right, and completely defensible.

"The point about Olive," Miss Campbell said, "is that she *prevailed*. She wanted things to go her way, and she kept a sort of control over what was going on in the playground. Even Tofu respected her – in his way – and none of the girls would have dared to question her authority. So there was peace of a kind, I suppose – as long as nobody stepped out of line. But then . . ."

The pause was ominous.

"Galactica MacFee arrived."

"Galactica?"

"Indeed. Galactica MacFee."

# 54

## The Defining Moment

That conversation was helpful to Miss Campbell, as it gave her the chance to express her growing frustration over the series of contretemps that had followed Galactica's enrolment in the class. The old order had had the merit of predictability: it was always possible to work out how Olive would behave, but now all that had been replaced by uncertainty, as Galactica MacFee established her ascendancy. What she was witnessing, Miss Campbell told herself, was a form of regime change and regime change, at whatever level it occurred, was always unsettling. But recent incidents, Miss Campbell decided, were just the first salvos in a campaign that was to fail as quickly and precipitately as it initially succeeded. And the play, as it happened, was the thing, as it so often is . . .

One of Miss Campbell's responsibilities at the school was drama, and she usually produced a play for each class to perform in the summer term. Over the years, the offerings had varied, but one thing united them all – and that was a bold vision unusual in school dramatic productions. There had recently been a production of *Waiting for Godot* – to which the response of the audience had been mixed – and an adapted version of *Who's Afraid of Virginia Woolf?* which had caused undisguised mirth in the audience of parents and other relatives. The intention behind that production had not been comic, and yet people had clearly enjoyed themselves – and that was something. "There is nothing funny about Virginia Woolf," Miss Campbell had muttered to her friend Sheila, as the house lights went up. And Sheila had said, "No, there isn't," but had immediately been consumed by an attack of giggles.

Now she had decided to go for something a bit more conventional, and had alighted upon *A Midsummer Night's Dream*. There was enough comedy in that play, Miss Campbell had decided, to appeal to the children – and of course the names of some of the characters would be sure to appeal to the immature instincts of the age group.

"Now, children," she announced to the class. "This term we are going to do something from William Shakespeare. Do we all know who Shakespeare was? I'm sure we do. Can anybody tell me something about William Shakespeare?"

Galactica's hand shot up, and for a few moments Miss Campbell pretended not to see it. But in case there should be any failure in communication, Galactica now said, "Me, Miss Campbell. I know all about William Shakespeare. Me. I do."

From the back of the class, Tofu called out, "He's dead, you know. He died a long time ago. At least fifty years."

Galactica looked at Tofu with scorn. "Of course he's dead," she said. "Writers are usually dead – not that I suppose you know that sort of thing, Tofu."

Miss Campbell sighed. "There's no need to be rude to Tofu, Galactica," she said. "He's doing his best, you know. Let's think about this particular play. Does anybody know the names of any of the characters?"

There was the shortest of silences, and then Galactica once again called out, "Me, me, Miss Campbell."

There was no time for permission to be given before Galactica reeled off a list of names. "There's Puck," she said. "He's a sort of fairy. And Titania, who is queen of the fairies. And Oberon. And an actor called Bottom."

This brought a whoop of delight from Socrates Dunbar. "Bottom," he shouted out. "Bottom."

General mirth swept round the classroom.

"You are *so immature,*" said Galactica.

Socrates was not deterred. "You could be called that," he said. "You can be Bottom."

Miss Campbell decided to intervene. "It's not very clever to laugh at somebody's name," she said. "And we mustn't lose sight of the fact that this is one of Shakespeare's most popular plays."

Bertie thought of something. "*If* William Shakespeare wrote them," he said.

Miss Campbell gave Bertie an astonished look. "What was that, Bertie?" she asked.

"A lot of people think somebody else wrote Shakespeare's plays," he said. "There was a man called Mr Bacon, and some people said he wrote them."

"So Shakespeare *copied,*" said Pansy.

"We can't be sure of that," said Miss Campbell. "But that shouldn't really concern us, boys and girls. What we need to do now is choose a director and decide who's going to take which part. That, of course, is usually the director's decision."

"I'll do that," said Galactica.

Olive glowered. She conferred *sotto voce* with Pansy, and as a result did not hear Miss Campbell ask – in a rather hopeful tone – whether there was anybody else who might wish to be considered for the job of director. Had anybody else offered to do it, then he or she would have been chosen immediately, but nobody did.

"In that case," said Miss Campbell wearily, "you can be director, Galactica, dear."

Galactica nodded, as if this were simply her due. "May I ask, though, Miss Campbell: can the director also be an actor?"

Miss Campbell's heart sank. She could see what was coming. "I suppose so," she said. "Although it's very unusual."

"No worries," said Galactica. "I don't mind. So, I'm going

to be Titania – queen of the fairies. And Olive, you can be Bottom. In Shakespeare, boys can be played by girls – and girls by boys. You probably don't know that, Olive, but I assure you it's true. I know quite a lot of things, as it happens – and that's one of them." She paused. "Bertie, you can be Oberon, and Tofu, you can be the Wall. That's a good role for somebody who's a bit stupid – no offence."

Miss Campbell listened to all this. It was, she sensed, a defining moment in the power struggle between Olive and Galactica, and there was no doubt in her mind that Galactica would emerge the victor. But as things transpired, she was wrong. The vagaries of power can surprise even the most seasoned observer, and now, in this first rehearsal, as the children were presented with the simplified script that she had prepared for them, she realised that the authority that any director needs was simply vanishing from Galactica's grasp. The cast of any play must believe that the director has the power to make things happen in the way envisaged by the script. That belief had evaporated, and nothing was left. Disorder broke out; there were tears of rage, resentment, and embarrassment. The papier mâché ass's head lay abandoned on the floor. The Wall collapsed. Oberon's love had leaked from the water bottle, into which a small quantity of orange juice had been poured.

"This is a stupid play," announced Olive, to be immediately, and vocally, seconded by Pansy.

Only Bertie made a conscientious effort, but he was unable to do much to save the production.

Miss Campbell closed her eyes and sighed.

"Miss Campbell," asked Olive, "couldn't we do *Waiting for Godot* again? I could be the director, if you like."

It was the defining moment of the revolution.

# 55

## *At Stan's Place*

Fat Bob was given extensive tests to determine what, if any, brain damage had occurred as a result of the gym incident. Scans of his head and neck revealed nothing abnormal, and after a few follow-up consultations he was discharged from hospital. All there was to remind him of the occurrence was a persistent Swedish accent. This symptom, though, attracted some medical attention, and even became the subject of an article in neurology journals, as well as a poster presentation at a conference in Berlin. There was an article in the news section of *New Scientist*, and a short report in the Matters of Interest column in *Men's Health*.

Initially, Bob had been indifferent to the phenomenon, but as interest in his case widened, he began to be amused by the fact that he had become something of a living curiosity. Not that he was corrupted by fame: Bob was the most modest of men and would not normally talk about his experience, unless somebody remarked on his Swedish accent. Then he would open up about what had happened, rather enjoying the astonishment that people would express over the very idea of foreign accent syndrome.

Eddie was exceptionally supportive. He felt guilty about his role in the accident, in spite of Bob's assurance that none of it was his fault.

"Listen, Eddie," Bob said. "It was nothing to do with you – and I mean *nothing*. Who got on the machine and then fell off? Me. I did it. It was my fault – end of story."

Eddie was still concerned. "Your fault? No, Bob, it was

mine. You were my client. I should have known that you didn't know how to use the equipment. It's the same with the captain of a ship. Remember? We talked about that."

Bob again tried to reassure Eddie, but it proved impossible. "I'm giving up," Eddie told him. "Your accident has shaken me. I don't think I should be doing this. In fact, I've already decided. I've told the gym."

"But what will you do, Eddie?" asked Bob. "Will you go back to oiling the Falkirk Wheel?"

Eddie shook his head. "You have to move on in this life, Bob. If you stay in the same place for too long, then you'll never get anywhere."

Bob thought about this and then, eventually, said, "That's true, I suppose."

He thought of himself. What had he done with his life? He had made his mark on the Highland Games circuit, but where had that led? In tossing the caber, you were only as good as your last throw – everybody knew that. And there was something rather sad in being a veteran, sitting on the sidelines while younger men in kilts threw telephone poles about. Where was the dignity in any of that?

"So what will you do, Eddie?" asked Bob.

Eddie leaned forward, as if he was about to impart a commercial secret. "I'm not going back into hydraulics," he said. "Too much pressure. I'm going to build sheds. I've always liked working with timber, and I've got access to an old building on my brother-in-law's smallholding near Bathgate. It needs a bit of work, but the roof's sound enough."

"And you'll make the sheds there?"

"That's the plan," said Eddie. "I'll construct the walls and roofs as separate units, you see, and then I'll erect them on site. I've designed four different sorts of shed – so far." He paused. "You could come out and see the set-up, if you're interested."

Bob was, and the following day Eddie picked him up and they drove out to Eddie's brother-in-law's place. Introductions were made.

"This is Stan," said Eddie. "And this is Stan's place."

Bob looked about him. They were standing in front of a modern, unassuming bungalow with cracked, discoloured harling. Several rundown-looking vehicles were parked beside the house, and beyond that, behind rickety fencing, growing tunnels stretched out in every direction.

"Stan grows onions," said Eddie. "And other things too."

Stan nodded proudly. "Some of the big supermarkets take my stuff," he said. "In fact, I get more orders than I can fulfil. That's a healthy sign, I always say."

"That's the way to run a business," said Bob.

Stan looked at his visitor with interest. "You from Sweden?" he asked.

Bob glanced at Eddie, who was looking down at the ground. "I sound Swedish," he said. "But I'm not." And then, to divert attention from a potentially awkward subject, he pointed to a shed behind the house. "Is that one of yours, Eddie?"

Stan answered. "No, I had that put up three years ago. Eddie's sheds will be a cut above that one."

"That's where Stan keeps his ferrets," said Eddie.

"I'll show you," said Stan. "You like ferrets, Bob?"

Bob had never touched a ferret and was not sure how one might tell the difference between a ferret and a mink. Then there were pine martens – where did they fit in?

"I'll let you hold one," said Stan, as they made their way into the dimness of the shed. He reached forward and extracted a writhing creature from a hatch. "This is Alastair," he said. "You won't get a better ferret anywhere in Eastern Scotland. His mother was a champion. In her day, she was the best ferret in Scotland. No argument."

He held the creature out to Bob, who instinctively drew

back. Alastair's tiny black eyes were watching him. Stan was bemused by Bob's hesitation.

"What do you use them for?" asked Bob.

"I send them down rabbit holes," came the reply. "Then they come up with a rabbit, and I take it from them."

"Sometimes they want to hold on," said Eddie. "Alastair's father was a bit like that, wasn't he, Stan?"

Stan laughed. "That was Edgar. Yes, he knew his rights, that boy. But they always give it up when I give them a nip."

Bob was open-mouthed. "*You* bite *them*?"

"Yes," said Stan. "It's the only way to get a ferret to let go. They're so surprised. They give the rabbit up."

Bob was silent. He had noticed a small scar on Stan's right cheek. Sometimes, these things could be clues, he told himself.

"That's enough ferrets," said Eddie. "Sheds now."

They crossed a small field to an old byre, whitewashed and slated – typical of the old agricultural buildings on any number of Scottish farms. Once inside, Eddie showed Bob the large power saws and planers positioned beyond several large stacks of timber.

"You've got everything you need here, Eddie," said Bob. He sniffed the air appreciatively. "I love the smell of worked timber."

"I do too," said Eddie. He paused, and then said, "I need to find somebody to work with me, though."

Bob understood. "Me?"

"This is our chance, Bob," said Eddie. "And it's physical work, too. You'll shed the pounds making sheds. I can pretty much guarantee that."

# 56

*Fishing at Ratho*

Big Lou listened sympathetically to Bob's account of his visit to Eddie's workshop. When her husband had finished, she continued to gaze at him in her calm, no-nonsense way.

"And you say that he wants you to go into partnership with him?" she asked "Is that definite?"

Bob inclined his head. "Yes, he made a firm offer. And he said that I can acquire shares in the business as I go along. Some of my wages each month will be used to buy my stake. After three years, I'll be the joint owner. It'll be fifty-fifty."

Big Lou said that this arrangement seemed fair to her. "And it's what you want to do, isn't it? I've always thought you wanted a business of your own."

Bob looked relieved that Lou understood; he should never have entertained the possibility that she might not.

"I've always liked the idea of being my own boss, Lou – just like you. You don't have to report to anybody . . . except Matthew, I suppose. But even Matthew can't tell you what to do – just because he owns part of your café. That correct, isn't it? You have everyday responsibility for how things go. You're the CEO, I suppose."

Big Lou protested. "I'd never call myself that. This is just a wee business, Bob. I'm just the person who makes the coffee. There are no great decisions to be made. How many rolls to order, I suppose. How many rashers of bacon we need. That sort of thing. You don't have to go to the Harvard Business School to learn how to do any of that."

"But it's the small businesses that keep the country going,

Lou," said Bob. "It's people like you who . . ." He shrugged.
He was finding it difficult to express what he was thinking. He
admired Lou, not only because she was big-hearted, but also
because of what she stood for. Big Lou belonged to a face of
Scotland that was fading away: the old, rural Scotland, where
people were direct and courteous; who did not judge others on
the basis of what they had, but valued them according to what
they *were*; that old, vanishing Scotland where people treated
one another with decency and respect, and where they didn't
litter their every sentence with obscenities. Some people said
it was never like that, but there used to be such a country, Bob
thought, although it seemed to be getting smaller every day,
as if viewed through the wrong end of a telescope. Bob was
not a sophisticated man; he had not had many educational
advantages, but he could sense what was happening to the
country, to so many countries – everywhere, in fact – and he
had no difficulty in identifying it for what it was.

"I'm nae better than anybody else," said Big Lou, thereby
proving that she *was* much better. "I don't deserve any special
praise, Bob." Once again, that meant that she did. "Anyway,"
she went on. "If you want to make sheds, you should make
sheds. It's decent work, Bob."

He stood up and kissed her. "I love you so much, Lou,"
he said. "I'm not the sort to go on about that sort of thing,
but it's true. I know it's not necessary for me to say it, but I
wanted you to know."

She kissed him back. "They'll be lining up for these sheds
of yours, Bob, so they will."

With Lou's blessing, he started work with Eddie two days
later. Eddie showed him the power equipment, and made sure
that he understood the safety procedures to be observed when
using the large circular saw. "Be careful," said Eddie. "I know
somebody who lost three fingers on a machine like that."

"I will," said Bob. "I promise you."

They designed a shed together, and Bob made the shelves. Eddie said that he could tell that Bob was a natural wood-worker. "You've got it, Bob," he said. "Not everybody has it. You have."

Bob relished the praise. Few people had praised him before, and he basked in the warmth of the compliment. And once they had their website up – a simple affair, headed: *Need a shed? Contact Eddie and Bob for the best sheds in Scotland. Nae messing.* – orders came in for sheds of all shapes and sizes. A farmer in West Lothian ordered three large sheds for his turkeys. Bob designed special anti-fox provisions, which involved wire mesh being dug into the ground to a depth of three feet.

At the end of their first week in business, when they had prepared the timber for the first two turkey sheds – erecting them would be another matter – they decided to take a day off. They had been working long hours each day – almost sixteen hours, on average – and Eddie's wife, Jill, who worked for a nursing agency, insisted that they take a break. "It's no good being successful in what you do if it ruins your health," she said. "Go fishing before you start the next order."

Eddie consulted Bob, who suggested that Eddie should come into town for breakfast at Big Lou's, and then they would drive out to Ratho and fish from the canal bank. "You never know," he said. "A cousin of mine caught a muckle old pike out there. A monster. Big teeth. You never know. Put him back for another day."

Big Lou made them bacon rolls. Eddie said he had never tasted bacon rolls to equal them. "You get to heaven," he said, "and the bacon rolls will be like this. You ask the Pope, and he'll confirm."

Out on the canal bank, Eddie said that he thought that he saw a movement in the water that could be a large pike. Or it could be a rat, he said. Bob wondered whether ferrets could swim. Eddie told him they could. "They can do most things they need to do," he said.

It was a warm day, and the sky was wide and empty. To the south, the land sloped up towards the Pentland Hills. The air was mostly still, but there was just enough wind to move the top branches of the trees in their full summer foliage. A plane, an elegant white tube of metal, dropped down towards the airport a few miles away. Bob saw the sun glint off the aircraft windows. There was no sound.

Eddie said, "I think there might have been a fish going for my bait. I felt something."

Bob looked at the float in the water. "No," he said. "I think that was just the wind on the float."

"True," said Eddie. "But still, you never know, do you?"

You don't, thought Bob. You don't.

# 57

## *Kindness*

The Fall of Galactica MacFee was how Miss Campbell described it to her friend Jennifer, the physical education teacher in the school's primary division. That was the term she used as the two of them looked out over the playground from the staff common room, a welcome mid-morning cup of tea in hand.

"That's her over there," said Miss Campbell, pointing to the bench where Galactica was seated with another girl from her class, clearly detached from the various groups of children engaged in the activities of seven- and eight-year-olds at play. "Actually, I feel rather sorry for her. She's a right little number, but I feel a certain sympathy."

Jennifer surveyed the scene. "I haven't come across her yet," she said. "I've had plenty of experience of Olive, though, and the girl who follows her round like a shadow."

"Pansy. Yes, Olive was the queen bee, and Galactica turned up and ran circles round her." She paused. "It was quite impressive, in a way. But that's what happens, isn't it? Hubris leads to Nemesis, or is it the other way round?"

Jennifer took a sip of tea, and smiled. "Don't ask me. I'm the physical education teacher, remember. So, what now?"

"Well, the gods have stepped in, it seems," said Miss Campbell. "Galactica has been overthrown – rather quickly, perhaps – but her humiliation is to be short-lived, apparently. Had there not been a development, I would probably have had to step in and do something, but the *status quo ante* is being restored . . ."

Outside, the other girl on the bench suddenly stood up, having been beckoned by a friend. Galactica, now on her own, looked down at the ground in a studied show of insouciance. She might have sat there for some time, had it not been for the arrival of a small boy, who, having hesitated for a few moments, sat down beside her. This was Bertie.

"Are you all right, Galactica?" he asked.

Galactica took a moment to respond. "Oh, Bertie, it's you. Of course I'm all right."

Bertie considered this answer. "You look a bit unhappy. I don't think you should be unhappy, Galactica."

Galactica sucked in her cheeks. "Actually, I'm not unhappy, Bertie. I'm going to a different school, you see. I was thinking about that."

"Why are you leaving, Galactica?"

"It's because my mummy has decided that it would be easier for me to go to a school on the other side of town. There's a school near Ann Street, where we live. It's called Flora Stevenson's, and my mummy can walk with me to go there in the mornings. That's why."

Bertie nodded. "That will be easier," he said. "My granny brings me on the 23 bus. Sometimes it takes quite a long time if there's a hold-up in the traffic."

There was a brief silence, and then Bertie said, "I hope that you like your new school, Galactica. I hope that you'll be happy there." He looked at her. People like Galactica MacFee can't help it, he thought. Nobody can help it, really, and we should tell ourselves that before we are nasty about them. And if they couldn't help it, then perhaps we should be kind to them. Perhaps we should be kinder to *everyone*, whatever they were like – then they'd be kind back to us, and there would be less unhappiness.

"I'll be really sorry when you go, Galactica," he said.

She fixed him with a surprised stare. "Will you, Bertie?

Will you miss me?"

Bertie nodded. He hoped that she would not notice his crossed fingers. Just to be safe, he sat on his left hand. If you crossed your fingers you could say things that were not true – everyone knew that, although there were some people, Tofu being an example, who never bothered to cross their fingers at all. But there was nothing anybody could do about Tofu – once again, that was something that everybody knew.

"I'll miss you, Galactica. Definitely."

"And Ranald Braveheart Macpherson?" asked Galactica. "Will he miss me too, Bertie?"

Bertie glanced across the playground to the spot where Ranald was lurking, watching this encounter, trying, largely in vain, to make himself inconspicuous.

"Yes," said Bertie. "Ranald Braveheart Macpherson will miss you terribly, Galactica."

Galactica became more cheerful. "Will you come to play at my house?" asked Galactica. "Do you know where Ann Street is, Bertie? Will you come there?"

Bertie hesitated. "Sometimes," he said. "I'm very busy, you see, Galactica."

Galactica seemed satisfied with that answer.

Then Bertie said, "I'm so sorry that our engagement's going to be off – now that you're going. But there we are. We have to accept these things. That's what my granny says."

"I suppose so," said Galactica.

Bertie felt an immense surge of relief. And the pleasure he felt was doubled when Galactica reached into a bag at her feet and extracted a bar of chocolate. This she handed to Bertie. "I'd like you to have this, Bertie," she said. "You've been so kind. You can have this to remember me by. Like a photograph in a silver frame. Like that."

Bertie accepted the chocolate and thanked her politely.

"You should have a piece now," said Galactica.

Bertie unwrapped the bar of chocolate and broke off a piece. As he popped this into his mouth, Ranald Braveheart Macpherson appeared at his side. "Is that chocolate, Bertie?" he asked.

Bertie gave his friend a large piece.

Now Tofu arrived. "You've got some chocolate, Bertie? Remember, you owe me some."

Bertie did not remember, but he did not argue with Tofu, who broke off an entire row of pieces and stuffed them into his mouth before helping himself to a further three pieces. Then came Olive and Pansy, who ignored Galactica, but who quickly accepted the chocolate offered to them. Then Moss and Socrates Dunbar, who took the final pieces before handing the empty silver wrapper back to Bertie.

From their window, the two teachers watched this in silence. Their tea was turning cold, but they were rapt.

"I'm not quite sure what we've witnessed," said Jennifer, "but I suspect that it's something quite significant."

Miss Campbell agreed. "We've just seen something done by a little boy who, quite frankly, gives us all reason to carry on."

"Oh yes?"

"Yes."

They put down their cups and turned away. There was a time when the audience of the play should get up and leave the theatre, on rare occasions in complete silence, reflecting on what they had witnessed. Applause is not always necessary, because sometimes it can just be felt, and is all the more profound, more affecting, for that.

# 58

## *The Earliest Scottish Poem*

"So," said Bruce breezily. "Here we are, then. Review time."

He was seated in Big Lou's café, along with Ben, Catriona and Matthew. Matthew had been the last to join them, having been engaged in conversation outside with a passing neighbour who wanted to discuss some matter of concern to local traders. He had eventually managed to detach himself and join the others over coffee.

Matthew looked at Ben, who was taking a sheaf of papers out of a briefcase. He thought that Ben looked a bit serious, as did Catriona, who was sitting back in her seat, watching her husband. Matthew's eye was drawn to Catriona's blue-rimmed spectacles. Would she look less glum if the frames were red? What was it about blue that suggested melancholy?

"We may as well get straight on with it," said Ben. "I've made a copy for each of you." He handed a sheet of paper to the others.

"Is this the survey you talked about?" asked Matthew.

"Yes," said Ben. "This is what we got a firm of marketing consultants to do. And they charged five thousand pounds."

"These people can be expensive," said Matthew. "They charged my dad fifteen thousand for a bit of work once. He said he'd take them to court."

He looked down at the sheet before him, noticing the words in bold type at the bottom: *extremely limited*.

"Not good?" asked Bruce.

Ben sighed. "The bottom line is that they say there are too many attractions as it is. Something like a Pictish centre would struggle to get its market share. And part of their survey – they asked two hundred people – shows that only 3 per cent of people have any idea who the Picts were." He pointed to a column of figures. "And less than .03 per cent said that they would even consider going to spend a weekend at a Pictish Experience Centre."

Bruce's face fell. "They don't know what they'll be missing," he muttered.

Ben turned to him. "That's nice of you to say that, Bruce," he said, "but I'm afraid it means that our business model doesn't stack up."

Matthew was secretly relieved. He had been prepared to stand by his earlier offer to invest in the project, but he knew that Elspeth would be relieved when he told her it was not going to happen.

Bruce now said, "Of course, sometimes these people get it wrong, don't they?"

"I don't think they do," said Catriona. "We may want them to be wrong, but they won't be. They know their onions."

"Perhaps," said Bruce. He looked at his watch. "You said the Prof was going to come and tell us about his translation – not that it matters any longer."

"It'll be interesting," said Ben. "And when we finish doing up the house and we sell it, it might be an important feature of the property. Every cloud has a silver lining, after all."

Donald Macdonald arrived, apologising for being slightly late. "The 23 bus is usually very much on time, but the traffic on Morningside Road sometimes . . ." He looked about him. "Bad news?" he asked.

"Business glitch," said Ben. "We're all very keen to hear about your translation."

Donald cleared his throat. "Well, as I said a few days ago, this is a very, very important inscription. I can confirm, moreover, that this is, in my view, the earliest work of Scottish literature. This is the first Scottish poem. Fourth century – way before anything else we have. It's quite exceptionally important."

They listened in rapt attention.

"It is not a lengthy poem," Donald went on. "Three lines, but it is utterly authentic."

"I can't bear the suspense," said Ben.

Donald smiled. "Well, here we go." He took out a photograph of the stone and, pointing to the symbols, gave his translation. "I've rendered it into Scots to reflect the authentic voice. And it reads as follows:

> *I'm going to get smashed, the night!*
> *The bevvy's ready, all right!*
> *I'm going to get mental, the night!*"

(*Trans*: I'm going to get very drunk tonight; the drink is ready, all right; I'm going to get seriously inebriated tonight.)

Nobody said anything. Ben's eyes were wide with surprise. Matthew frowned. Catriona adjusted her blue-framed spectacles.

Eventually, Matthew broke the silence. "Are you quite sure?" he asked.

Donald nodded. "I'm afraid so," he said. "Our culture, perhaps, is not always what we would like it to be."

Ben sighed. "We can't let that get out. What will people think? They'll get a terrible impression of Pictish culture – and of Scotland." He shook his head ruefully. "I'm so ashamed."

"Remember this was a long time ago," said Donald. "This is the fourth century, after all. Things were different."

"It doesn't seem that way," said Bruce. "There's a contemporary ring to this poem. Govan, perhaps."

"There are many instances in other cultures of poems about the pleasures of wine," Donald pointed. "Some very old

Chinese poetry refers to sitting with a friend in a courtyard drinking wine. That sort of thing. And there's Roman poetry to the same effect. I seem to recall one of Horace's *Odes* making reference to his Falernian wine, of which he was rather proud. No, it's a common theme."

Ben digested this. "Yes, but . . . I don't know. Poems like that are just a bit more . . . sensitive. This is pretty . . ."

"Direct?" prompted Matthew.

"You could say that," said Bruce. "Mind you, Scotland is a fairly direct place, isn't it? Especially somewhere like Govan."

"Nobody said it came from Govan," pointed out Catriona. "It came from somewhere in Stirlingshire. Govan didn't exist then, anyway. And let's not add to unhelpful stereotypes."

"Perhaps we could donate it," said Ben. "Even give it to Govan, and put a sign on it saying *Not really from here, but still*. It could be a tourist attraction. It could become a major cultural site. UNESCO could list it. That way, some good will come out of it."

"It's your stone," said Donald. "Perhaps the right thing to do would be to pass it on to Historic Scotland. They've probably got a lot of Pictish bric-a-brac tucked away. They'll look after it. Other scholars might look at it."

"And come to a different conclusion about what it means?"

Donald shrugged. "That's perfectly possible, although I do stand by my translation."

"Oh, well," said Matthew. "I can't see it being included in future anthologies of early Scottish literature."

Ben smiled. "You know something?" he said. "I rather like it."

"It has a certain charm," agreed Donald.

Matthew looked thoughtful. "And it's not incompatible," he said, "with a whole current of Scottish literature – one that survives today, don't you think?"

They all smiled.

# 59

## And Outside, the Evening Sun

In the kitchen of her flat in 44 Scotland Street, Domenica Macdonald was sitting with her friend, Dilly Emslie, preparing canapés for the party that she and Angus were throwing that evening – a gathering that had become a fixed and important feature of that point in the Edinburgh summer. The guest list was usually the same – a few old friends, neighbours from Scotland Street and Drummond Place, and the occasional new acquaintance to whom either of the hosts wished to extend the hand of closer friendship. And the sequence of events at the party followed the same pattern each year: a glass or two of wine, canapés, a buffet dinner of pasta and salad, and then the recital of a poem by Angus, written specially for the occasion. Nobody wanted any of that to change – why change things about when you are already doing things you like to do? Angus asked. And, unsurprisingly, he felt that nobody had ever come up with any convincing answer to that.

It was early evening, about half an hour before the first guests would begin to arrive, and Dilly had offered to come round to help Domenica prepare, as had James Holloway, who always attended, and who had recently returned from a motorcycle trip to Finland. This had been with a group of Edinburgh bikers led by Caroline Hahn, who lived within sight of Scotland Street. They had enjoyed the privilege of riding with a regiment of Finnish motorcycle cavalry along a fifty-mile stretch of the bleak forest road bordering Russia. The road had been rough, lined on one side with barbed wire, mile upon mile of it, and surveyed by watchful towers;

the Finns had been determined, clear-eyed, knowing their history.

Now, in the comfort of Domenica's kitchen, that experience seemed a long way away, and James was listening to Dilly talking about the book she had recently read and the one she intended to read next. Domenica had read neither of these books, but was pleased that Dilly had read one and would read the other, as she would then be able to ask her about them if needs be.

Domenica moved on to art, which of course James knew a great deal about. She had been in the Open Eye Gallery, a gallery on a corner of Dundas Street, not far from Big Lou's café, and had seen a painting by Robert Maclaurin that had made an impression on her. "He's a landscape artist," Domenica said. "He's Scottish, but lives in Australia. He paints both Scottish and Australian scenes. He can do large, haunting paintings, or much smaller ones. But he gets emptiness – he really does. His paintings of places like Knoydart capture that quality of the Highlands, although he likes to put a figure in, if it seems right: somebody standing there, surrounded by the emptiness. Somehow, that accentuates our own smallness when viewed alongside nature."

James said that he thought there were two or three of Maclaurin's paintings in the National Galleries of Scotland. "But what about Adam Bruce Thomson?" he asked. "I believe there's to be an exhibition of his work coming up."

Domenica put down the knife she was using to spread pâté on small cheese-flavoured biscuits. "Now there's a painter," she said. "I think he was Scotland's answer to Bawden and Ravilious. A wonderful draughtsman."

"Of course, James Cowie could draw too," said Dilly.

"We're so lucky to be surrounded by all this art," said Domenica. "To have art to accompany us through life. Imagine what it would be like not to have that."

They were silent for a moment. Then Dilly asked, "What about downstairs? What about Irene?"

There was a momentary drop in the temperature, as if, in a police state, somebody had uttered the name of some forbidden figure.

Domenica resumed her task of spreading pâté. "Well," she began, "that story has taken a dramatic turn."

"I thought she had come back to Edinburgh," said Dilly. "I heard that a lot of people were thoroughly disappointed."

"She did – sort of," said Domenica. "She came back, met up with Stuart again, and they decided to have another go at making it work."

James looked doubtful. "Somewhat unlikely, I would have thought."

"The plan was to spend a certain number of days each week in Edinburgh, and then the rest in Aberdeen. She's still working on that PhD of hers."

Dilly rolled her eyes. "I feel so sorry for Bertie."

"Nicola," Domenica went on, "she's Stuart's mother, as you know; she's been very down about the prospect of Irene's return, but then the most extraordinary thing happened. It was enough to make one believe in a benevolent providence, Nicola said to me."

The two guests waited. At length, Domenica said, "Irene was washed out to sea – during cold-water therapy."

This brought a sharp intake of breath. "No!" said James.

"However, she was rescued by some fishermen from Peterhead," Domenica went on.

Both James and Dilly tried hard not to look disappointed. Domenica was watching them.

"And now she's moved in with the skipper."

A knife and a biscuit were dropped in succession, and in astonishment.

When he recovered sufficiently to speak, James stuttered,

"Does he realise?"

"Apparently she's a wonderful fish filleter," Domenica said. "And you never know with these affairs of the heart. You never know who's going to be taken with whom."

"But she's still doing the PhD?" asked Dilly.

"I believe so," answered Domenica. "And she's taken it upon herself to translate the works of Freud into Scots, particularly the Doric, which is the version of Scots that her new family speaks. She's making good progress, I heard. She's working on some of the case studies."

"I can't believe it," exclaimed James. "I just can't."

"Apparently Little Hans," Domenica said, "has become Wee Eck."

James smiled. "Well, there you are. You have to admire her, you know."

"She's without equal," said Dilly. "And the family down here?"

"Nicola is over the moon," said Domenica. "She'll be coming to dinner this evening. You'll see a spring in her step."

"And Bertie?"

"He's a real little Stoic, that boy," said Domenica. "He accepts whatever comes his way."

Domenica looked at her watch. "We'd better get on with our canapés. People will be here before we know where we are."

Outside, on Scotland Street, and over the whole city, the evening sun was touching the grey slate roofs, the chimneys, the treetops, with a warm and gentle gold. Above them, through the open window, they heard a seagull mew in a dispute over some scrap, or a slice of sky, perhaps, the same things over which humanity was so often, so disappointingly, given to argue.

# 60

## *Love Is There, It Just Is*

The guests at Angus and Domenica's party had seated themselves in small groups, some around the kitchen table, others perched on sofas and sofa arms, or on cushions around the hearth. There was a place for everybody to sit if they were not too fussy or too selfish – just like the world we inhabit, Angus was fond of saying. There was enough room as long as one was prepared to share.

Domenica had caught up with Dilly and James over the preparation of the canapés, when they had exchanged, and reacted to, the latest news of Irene, and her new life on the cold, fish-haunted coast of North East Scotland. Filleting fish for her new trawler-skipper partner? Translating Freud into Scots . . . There seemed to be no limit to her ability to surprise.

Now Domenica, plate of pasta in hand and a glass of white wine spritzer on the table beside her, engaged a small group of her guests in conversation. Judith McClure and Roger Collins were with her, as were Mary and Philip Contini, and Matthew and Elspeth. Matthew was asking Judith and Roger about their latest visit to Argyll, and about Roger's book on the history of Europe and Asia, which was taking some time to write. Roger had written a book about the history of the papacy, which he said had been a simple task by comparison. Philip Contini had been to Italy, and had discovered a new wine in Puglia that he thought could take the world by storm. Unfortunately, the Italian winemaker had only thirty-two cases of the previous year's vintage, had become a Buddhist, and was threatening to go off to a monastery in Thailand.

"These things happen," said Philip. "Not all that often, admittedly, but they do happen."

Matthew said that he would be rather interested in going off to a monastery in Thailand, and did Philip have the address? Elspeth gave him a sideways look. "With the triplets?" she asked. To which Matthew replied that he had seen pictures of Buddhist monasteries, and many of the monks in their saffron robes were, in fact, young boys. Perhaps Tobermory, Rognvald and Fergus might qualify for a place . . .

Domenica laughed. "It's tempting, isn't it, to get away?"

"If one wants to," said Elspeth.

Domenica thought about this. "The world of most of us has become rather large, hasn't it? When I was a girl, we could go hardly anywhere. Now almost everyone can go almost anywhere. But has that necessarily made us any happier?"

That sort of question is asked, thought Matthew, by those who have been privileged enough to be able to get away . . . Mind you, he went on to say to himself, Domenica is probably right: we have become too careless of what we are doing to the world by criss-crossing it with our planes and vehicles.

His thoughts were interrupted by James, who, on the other side of the room, struck the side of his glass with a teaspoon. He looked at Angus as he did this.

"Angus? A poem?"

A number of guests added their encouragement. "You have to," said Matthew.

Angus rose to his feet, with every appearance of reluctance. Matthew looked at Elspeth, and then at Domenica, and they both smiled at him, as members of audience will do to one another as they await a favoured moment.

"Dear friends," Angus began. "I can't say that I am unprepared for this moment: I am. I would not press my views on anybody, least of all on my old friends, as we gather on a social occasion. But tradition is tradition, and there is often a reason for it, a justification, that we, who have inherited the tradition, may not fully understand. And so the safest thing to do with any tradition is to continue to observe it until it is shown to cause harm to others or to impede defensible progress.

*Change in itself is not always a good thing,*
*Only the unthinking will take that view;*
*Familiarity, remember, is a consolation*
*That anchors and binds, makes for a sense*
*Of being somewhere and being someone.*
*Where are we, dear friends?*
*We are in a dark wood, I think,*
*The same dark wood in which an age ago*
*Dante found himself; young men die*
*In trenches, snatch what sleep they can*
*When the guns go briefly silent;*
*Our poor, damaged world reels*
*Under the intolerable burden we impose,*
*Under our rapacious appetite*
*For everything and always:*
*It reproaches us as we turn away*
*And deny the things we see."*

Angus paused, "And yet up and down the country, there are people who are doing their utmost to halt and reverse these grave threats. They act in the face of indifference and scorn and fatal rapacity. What drives them? It is not, I think, any abstract principle; it is love – love of others, love of this dear planet on which we live. It is that simple.

*And you do not need to know why love exists,*
*Why it drives us as it does; do not ask*
*Where the wind comes from when it blows:*

*It just does; do not ask why you should feel*
*The way you feel when you see the hills*
*Of this lovely country, Scotland, that is our home,*
*And when you look upon an island shore*
*And the green sea beyond, do not enquire*
*Why your heart is full of love;*
*Love requires no justification, no excuse,*
*Nor does kindness, which is at love's right hand;*
*Love is there, it simply is – that is all."*

Nobody spoke, because, Matthew thought, there was nothing to be added to what Angus had said. Except just outside the half-open flat door, on the stair, where a whispered conversation was taking place between Bertie and his friend, Ranald Braveheart Macpherson, who asked him, "Will we ever get back to Glasgow, Bertie?"

Bertie thought for a moment before answering. "No, probably not, Ranald."

Ranald looked momentarily disappointed, but then he asked, "What are they saying in there, Bertie?"

And Bertie replied, "Mr Lordie is saying something about kindness, I think. He always says something at these parties."

Ranald Braveheart Macpherson looked thoughtful. "Kindness is important, isn't it, Bertie?"

"Yes," said Bertie. "It is."

# THE 44 SCOTLAND STREET SERIES

"Will make you feel as though you live in Edinburgh....
Long live the folks on Scotland Street."
—*The Times-Picayune* (New Orleans)

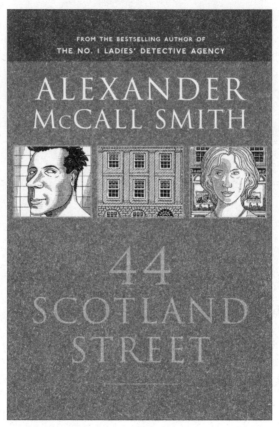

**44 Scotland Street**
—Volume 1

# THE 44 SCOTLAND STREET SERIES

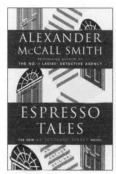

**Espresso Tales**
—Volume 2

**Love Over Scotland**
—Volume 3

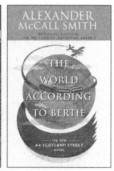

**The World
According to Bertie**
—Volume 4

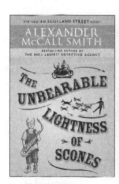

**The Unbearable
Lightness of Scones**
—Volume 5

**The Importance of
Being Seven**
—Volume 6

**Bertie Plays the Blues**
—Volume 7

# THE 44 SCOTLAND STREET SERIES

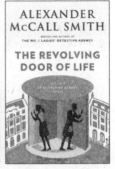

Sunshine on
Scotland Street
—Volume 8

Bertie's Guide to Life
and Mothers
—Volume 9

The Revolving Door of Life
—Volume 10

The Bertie Project
— Volume 11

A Time of Love and
Tartan—Volume 12

The Peppermint Tea
Chronicles
—Volume 13

# THE 44 SCOTLAND STREET SERIES

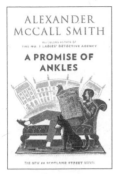

**A Promise of Ankles**
—Volume 14

**Love in the Time of Bertie**
—Volume 15

**The Enigma of Garlic**
Volume 16

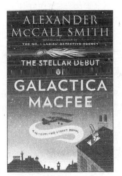

**Stellar Debut of
Galactica Macfee**
— Volume 17